C000050136

BROKEN RHODES

Kimber Silver

Silver Plains Publications

First Edition published 2022
Silver Plains Publications

Author disclaimer:
This is a work of fiction and any resemblance to any person living or dead is purely coincidental. The place names mentioned are real but have no connection with the events in this book.

Printed in U.S. by IngramSparks

Cover design by: The Book Khaleesi at www.thebookkhaleesi.com
Typeset and production by 2QT Publishing Services

A CIP catalogue record for this book is available from the Library of Congress in the U.S.

ISBN 979-8-9860836-4-3
Also available as an eBook
ISBN 979-8-9860836-3-6

For my grandma and grandpa and their motley crew of angels.

*"There are dark shadows on the earth,
but its lights are stronger in the contrast."*

Charles Dickens

CHAPTER ONE

Cold Wind

Harlow, Kansas, 2014

Sheriff Lincoln James eased the front door open, clinging to the hope that his friend had simply overslept. "Henry!" he called out, ears pricked for any signs of life. His optimism quickly waned as each subsequent shout went unanswered.

The morning sun peeked over his shoulder to light the way as he stepped farther into the house, but it did nothing to scatter the shadow that darkened this reconnaissance. "Henry, it's Lincoln James. I've come to check on ya."

Silence cut him to the quick as it breathed a tale he didn't want to hear.

CHAPTER TWO

Stranger Things

Kinsley drummed her fingers on the gold-flecked Formica counter as she waited for the dispatcher, who, according to her badge, was named Charlene. As the call wrapped up, Kinsley leaned closer to the speaker hole in the bulletproof glass enclosure, impatience stiffening her voice. "Any idea when Sheriff James might be showing up?"

"He said he'd be here." Charlene pursed her red lips. "Hold your horses."

Kinsley instantly regretted the decision to leave Kansas City at midnight so she'd arrive early in the morning. There seemed no choice but to wait for the sheriff in a lobby reminiscent of a 1960s' doctor's office. The musty smell was difficult to ignore.

The sharp click of her stiletto heels against the brittle linoleum mirrored her sour mood as she crossed to the waiting area. Two mid-century modern chairs stood against the wall; their avocado-green upholstery, emblazoned with a bold geometric pattern, was nearly worn through. She took the seat closest to the door for a quick escape if she needed one. Her gaze fell on the magazines that lay scattered across the teak end table: fishing, hunting, and four-wheel drives.

Good Lord, I am back in redneck hell, she realized.

The cinderblock wall served as an uncomfortable

headrest. Kinsley mustered hope that this sheriff would be along presently. That thought had just evaporated when the phone jingled on the other side of the glass.

"Hey, Linc," Charlene chirped into the receiver. "You're at Pearl's? Yeah, a cinnamon roll. Tell Pearl hi."

While the dispatcher was distracted, Kinsley slipped out the door. She had a new strategy: if the sheriff wouldn't come to her, she would intercept him at the diner.

When she arrived, she noted the number of cars surrounding the red-brick building that housed Pearl's. It looked like every resident in town was here. Kinsley took a deep breath and pressed on; she needed to get this meeting done.

Once inside, her misery blossomed. Her gray pencil skirt, coupled with a black-silk blouse, made her stand out among the jeans and flannel shirts of the local populace, and she wished she could disappear. The irritating buzz of whispers burrowing into her ears told her how visible she was to the diners. Kinsley sighed and scanned the room for anyone resembling a cop but saw no uniformed officer. To her chagrin, she would have to ask someone about the wayward sheriff.

As she approached the register, the waitress ceased her flirtatious conversation with a tall cowboy who was leaning against the wall, drinking coffee. The guy plucked a ringing phone from the breast pocket of his shirt while his azure eyes drifted leisurely over Kinsley from under the brim of his black Stetson.

She raised an eyebrow at his overt appraisal. *Look on, buckaroo,* she thought. *You won't be getting an eight-second ride on me.*

"Geez! I haven't seen *you* in years." The waitress drew Kinsley's focus away from the cowboy. "Don't you remember me?"

As Kinsley struggled to place the vaguely familiar face, the woman frantically waved her hands towards herself before shouting, "Sheila Clark!"

With the name, recognition fell into place. It would be impossible to forget Sheila Clark's snide comments about thrift-store clothes and second-rate haircuts. Add to that the countless rumors Sheila had perpetuated that had left Kinsley branded with a virtual scarlet letter.

"Hi, Sheila."

The blonde placed one hand on her ample hip and scanned Kinsley from head to toe. "Ol' Kinsley Rhodes back in town. Here for the funeral?"

"Yes, I am," replied Kinsley without enthusiasm. "But at the moment I'm looking for your elusive sheriff." Attempting polite conversation with this vile woman was only making the bad morning worse.

"Sure. He's…" Sheila turned toward the space recently occupied by the coffee-drinking gawker. "He was just here." A bewildered look materialized on the waitress's face as she rose on the balls of her feet to search the room. Eventually she shrugged. "He musta went to the station. Sorry."

"Thanks," Kinsley replied stiffly, and strode out of the diner. She cursed under her breath, none too pleased to learn that the Marlboro Man lookalike and the sheriff were one and the same. She climbed into her SUV and slammed the door, even more determined to track him down.

***

The screen door banged shut as Kinsley entered the sheriff's department for the second, and hopefully last, time. As she approached the divider, steam rose from the fresh cinnamon roll in front of Charlene, caressing the glass—breakfast courtesy of the cowboy, no doubt.

"Missed him. Shoulda stayed put." The smug look on Charlene's powdered face fanned the flames of exasperation burning in Kinsley's chest.

"When will Sheriff James be back?"

Charlene cut a bite-sized piece out of the treat and held it at the ready. "He said to leave your number and he'll call you. You stayin' at Henry's?"

Kinsley retrieved a business card from her wallet and slapped it down on the counter with a satisfying pop that ricocheted off the hard surfaces of the waiting area. "Yes, I'm staying at Henry's. Tell Sheriff James to get a hold of me as soon as possible."

As she stepped out the door, she inhaled a deep, cleansing breath. Her eyes came to rest on the tall cedar trees that surrounded the parking lot and lent shade to the building. Standing there, the quiet of the small Kansas town washed over her. After her fiasco of a morning, it was a welcome moment of solitude.

Back in her car, she zipped over a block and turned left on Main Street, noting the businesses that had been there since she was a kid. This town was caught in a perpetual state of stagnation. The same three thousand or so people were still living the same small-town life. They thought they ruled the universe from the confines of this one-mile square, yet their world ended at the city limits.

Reynold's liquor store was a welcome sight. Kinsley whipped into the parking lot and sat in her car, relishing the memories of trips to this mysterious store with Grandpa when she was a child. The proprietor, Clementine, had a deep, full-bodied laugh and a bouffant hairstyle reminiscent of Mae West's, which made her unforgettable. Kinsley was looking forward to seeing Mrs. Reynolds again.

As the door swished shut behind her, the pretty bottles invited her touch and a familiar sandalwood-scent lulled her into a sense of well-being. Strangely, though, the shop didn't seem as endless as it had when she was little. A quiet male voice interrupted her journey toward the coolers. "Kinsley?"

When she turned to find her friend standing there, she smiled. "Dusty, I didn't know you still worked here."

The man nodded enthusiastically. "Grandma owns it, so it's more of a family obligation, but yes, I'm here part-time. I'm sure sorry to hear about Henry. Are you going to be here for a while?" He moved in for a brief awkward hug that was more air than arms.

Kinsley twisted the lanyard on her keys as she considered his question. "I'm going to get out as quickly as I can, but I'm sure I'll be here for a week. We should go for dinner if you have time."

"Sure! Man, it's good to see you."

She opened her purse to retrieve a business card. "I just got a new phone number. You can call me if you want."

"Awesome." Dusty read the card before looking up. He had inherited his grandmother's infectious happiness, and Kinsley was instantly at ease with him again.

"How is your grandma? I was thinking of her."

They fell into step while he filled Kinsley in on where his life had gone since high school, which was pretty much nowhere. Talking to Dusty brought back good memories with a serving of awful around the edge; it plunged her back into a past that she would have preferred not to dredge up.

As they approached the register, side-stepping a precariously stacked pyramid of empty cartons, it occurred to Kinsley that she had the contents of an entire life to pack up. The ugly reminder of her current circumstances sliced through her like a Bowie knife. "Could I take some boxes?" she asked, struggling to recover her composure.

"Please take some," Dusty volunteered. "You can pull your car up to the door. I'll help you. There isn't much business at ten in the morning."

It wasn't fifteen minutes before several customers showed up, causing the two of them to joke about how wrong Dusty's earlier statement had been. Liquor was evidently a popular choice before noon.

After one last trip, Kinsley said her goodbyes. "I'll talk to you soon." Balancing the last of the empty boxes, she stepped out into the late-morning sun. She felt a warmth inside her that hadn't been there in a very long time.

With the last carton stacked in her vehicle, a remembered line from one of Dusty's favorite songs about being lonely out in space made Kinsley grin. The song played in her head until a sinister laugh, one she had hoped never to hear again, made the blood crystallize in her veins.

Brian Johnson stood five feet away from her with a leering look on his face that made her skin crawl. The sound of his voice still haunted her nightmares. "Back for another round, Rhodes?" His malevolent grin reflected the evil she knew he was capable of inflicting.

Kinsley closed the hatch and moved quickly to the driver's door. The second she was in, she checked twice to make sure the doors were locked. Johnson didn't hang around and, after watching him saunter towards the store, she dropped the car into gear.

It was a short drive to her destination. The fear that had boiled in Kinsley's guts only moments before was suddenly replaced with nostalgia as she gazed at the small white house where she'd been raised. Seeing her childhood home again took Kinsley back to the day when Grandpa, in his usual flamboyant fashion, had explained to her that the rows of humble dwellings were built for gas-company employees in the early 1930s, after it was discovered that the town of Harlow sat right in the center of an extensive natural-gas field.

A thunderbolt of pain daggered her chest as she remembered that Grandpa wouldn't be at the door to hug her this time. He was her 'one', the only person she knew who would love her no matter what. A hollow, bone-breaking ache radiated out from her heart and enveloped her.

***

Lincoln enjoyed the warm breeze that was blowing in through the open window of his pickup as he drove out to the country. The temperatures were unusually balmy for May, and they didn't seem likely to change until

September rolled around.

The police radio crackled to life a moment before Charlene's voice came over the speaker. "Linc, you there?"

He retrieved the handset. "Yep."

"City left her card and a dent in the counter where she slammed it down." The amusement was evident in the dispatcher's voice.

"Ten-four."

Lincoln hung the radio microphone back on the hook as he pondered the oddness of his morning. An unexpected call about a broken-down semi-truck on the roadway with no flares on board had prompted him to leave the diner in a hurry. He had dropped off Charlene's cinnamon roll on the way. When she had asked if Kinsley Rhodes had caught him at Pearl's, Lincoln's confusion had led Charlene to provide a full description.

A smile tugged at the corner of his mouth as he recalled the way she had marched across the diner, shoulders back, not a hint of timid. His usual preference leaned toward the Marilyn Monroe type, but Miss Rhodes' long dark hair, paired with a slim, athletic build, looked good on her. Her eyes sold the look: gray with a hint of blue, the color of slate, and every bit as hard. Kinsley Rhodes was not at all what he had pictured.

To be fair, she hadn't been due in until the evening, and getting the truck situation under control took priority since it was presently blocking one lane of a main two-lane road. Once that was dealt with, he'd planned to interview Jack Levine; only then could he get back to town early to meet with Miss Rhodes. With no help until tonight, the plan was to meet her at Henry's around seven o'clock. The fact that she had arrived early and, according to Charlene, was more than a bit perturbed, wasn't ideal.

Lincoln felt that he owed it to Henry to be cordial to Kinsley. Her grandfather had become a good friend over the years; he and the sheriff had spent nearly every evening during the warm months with a six-pack of Pabst Blue Ribbon between them as they swapped stories of their navy days. Although decades separated them in age, they had bonded over similar experiences.

Ever the consummate storyteller, Henry had recounted how he had met his wife, Rose, at a USO dance while he was stationed in San Diego. "Linc," Henry would say in his mid-west twang, "if ya ever get the chance to love a good woman, that's when you'll know there's a heaven because somethin' so wonderful could only be sent from above."

Lincoln doubted he'd ever experience that kind of love. At thirty-six, and after eighteen years of being single, the 'one' didn't exist for him.

Though Kinsley had come back to see Henry from time to time, her car in the driveway was the only evidence of her visit. Henry would warn him before her arrival, "She's not social, so I'll see ya when she goes home." Lincoln caught his meaning and stayed away.

Henry had loved Kinsley more than life itself. He'd spoken of her often, pride spilling out of him. "My girl is as tough as nails, but don't let that fool ya. Her heart is as soft as velvet." Sadness crept into the end of every story. Lincoln knew only too well how someone could be missed the way Henry missed his granddaughter.

While Lincoln openly shared stories of his son, Thomas, the old man spoke of his own son just once. "Darrell was a good boy, but his mom dyin' hurt him deeply. I just couldn't reach him after that." Recalling the regret in Henry's voice, Lincoln hoped he would never have to live through the loss of a child as Henry had with the death of his only son. That kind of pain must be near impossible to overcome.

Henry Rhodes was a stand-up guy who didn't deserve what had happened to him. Lincoln's desire to catch the murderer and find justice for his friend burned hot.

CHAPTER THREE

The Beginning Of The End

For the past few days, Kinsley had flatly refused to think about Grandpa's death. Her ability to shut away painful things had been honed to a fine point through the years, but being back home forced her to confront the reality that he was gone. With a heavy heart, she exited her vehicle and slogged through a mire of grief to the front porch.

The weighty wooden door screeched open, releasing a stale scent of pipe tobacco and Old Spice that stirred memories of such intensity her knees nearly buckled. Kinsley took a deep breath; for a fraction of a second, she could believe that Grandpa was waiting inside.

She stepped farther into his home, surveying the piles of papers that had multiplied since her previous visit. As she ran a hand over the back of a sagging brown-leather couch, she had to concede that the fight to keep this house tidy had been a losing battle.

A flash of silver from the end table caught her eye, prompting her to pick up a framed photograph of her eighth-grade graduation celebration. Kinsley traced the old man's proud smile with the tip of her finger as his ghostly presence swirled around the room. She fought off the urge to cry as she returned the photograph to the table and disturbed a thick layer of dirt. Brushing dust from her skirt, she cut the memory short and distracted herself with thoughts of what to do next.

The click-clack of her designer pumps on the hardwood floors echoed off the walls as she approached her former bedroom. She gave the door a tentative push, and it creaked open to reveal a shrine to the horror that was her youth.

Band posters for Clear Blue still adorned the charcoal-colored walls, and a black satin bedspread shone softly in the dim light that struggled through sheer ebony curtains stretched across a window at the far side of the room. The scent of Love's Baby Soft perfume still hung in the air. It was plain to see that this was where the housekeeper Kinsley had hired focused most of her attention because, unlike the living room, there wasn't a speck of dust.

She placed her palm on the slippery bedspread and her past rushed in as she soaked up this familiar space. A hollow laugh bubbled up and quickly dissolved into tears. She dabbed at her eyes with the back of her hands to try and quell the rising tide of feelings. Dealing with emotions was not her strong suit, so she pushed through and turned her attention to an old dresser.

The bottom drawer protested but eventually gave way with an indignant squawk. She ran her fingertips over a threadbare concert T-shirt that lay beside a faded pair of Levi's that were perfect for housework. She slipped into them without an ounce of trouble. The fact that they still fit granted her a moment of smug satisfaction before she pulled the souvenir top over her head. With her feet ensconced in black cowboy boots, she took a lingering look at herself in the full-length mirror. A girl from a decade earlier stared back—a weak, bullied teenager. That girl no longer existed. Kinsley looked herself in the eye. "Time to get with it."

As she returned to the main part of the house, she felt that a robust bout of cleaning was just the cathartic release she needed. Kinsley retrieved a beer from a six-pack she'd left by the front door beside her purse and a few boxes from the liquor store. She opened it and took a drag from the longneck bottle.

She filled empty boxes with sheets of paper until they overflowed, and within two hours the stacks had been neatly corralled. The furniture, and a threadbare area rug with its faded black south-west design, were once again the focal points. Kinsley surveyed the tattered scene before her and, for the briefest of moments, wished she had left it hidden from view.

The dining room proved to be no different. "Good Lord," she sighed as she faced an untidy mountain of paper. Kinsley flipped quickly through the sheets on top of one pile; they appeared to be mostly fertilizer bills and elevator statements, which she transferred into the remaining boxes.

Finally, the wooden table came into view, stirring up memories of many meals eaten there with Grandpa. The most joyous were the holiday dinners they shared with friends, as well as anyone in town who had no place to go. They jokingly called these the 'gatherings of the misfits,' because everyone was welcome.

As Kinsley leaned against the doorframe and looked over the room, her satisfaction turned to dread. What she had accomplished today was a mere drop in a bucket;

the workload that accompanied the death of a relative was a gargantuan undertaking. At that moment, a clear image of Grandpa chuckling sprang to mind. 'Like eatin' an elephant, baby girl. One bite at a time.'

Housecleaning was not her only task. The table now allowed a place for both of her laptops. Kinsley set them up and tried not to think about the painful reason she was here.

***

Lincoln rested his forearm on the bed of his pickup while he and the trucker waited for a tow. He kept an eye out for oncoming traffic as they discussed the weather, travel, and the driver's seven children. The conversation was waning when a wrecker appeared and saved them both.

Once the situation was in hand, Lincoln headed over to the Levine farm, knowing that lunch was a good time to catch Jack at home. Mr. Levine harbored a serious addiction to a particular noon-time television soap opera and wouldn't miss it unless the sky was falling.

Jack Levine swung a squeaky screen door open when Lincoln stepped up onto the porch. His liver-spotted fingers swept along the bill of his John Deere cap. "Sheriff."

Lincoln noted a soup-stained napkin tucked into the farmer's flannel shirt. "Hey, Jack. Sorry to bother you at lunchtime. I wondered if you'd seen anyone messin' around out here or over at the Rhodes' place?"

"Naw. Nothin' is happenin' 'round here. I heard about Henry. You got a bead on a killer yet?"

"We're workin' on it. What's the word on the street?"

Lincoln buttressed himself against a porch post and waited for Jack's reply.

"My ol' lady said she heard at the grocery that Rhodes was stabbed to death by a rover, but I doubt it. Henry was a tough old son. One rover couldna done him in."

Lincoln tugged on the brim of his hat, seating it a little lower over his eyes. With an ongoing inquiry, he would have to play it close to the vest. This town wanted answers, and he'd have to figure out how to dodge them without offending anyone in the process. "Yep, Henry was a tough man."

"S'pose there'll be lotsa talk. The lady folk are nervous as cats on a hot tin roof." Jack let loose a menacing chuckle. "Sum bitch better not try nothin' out here. I'll fill 'em full of lead. I don't care if I know 'em or not. An' I bet dollars ta doughnuts we all know 'em. This murder feels close to home, Sheriff."

Lincoln made a noncommittal sound of acknowledgment as his thoughts wandered to Kinsley, who was waiting for him to get back to her. "Thanks for takin' the time to talk to me, Jack. I better let ya get on with your meal. If you see or hear anything, could ya let me know?"

"Sure 'nuff. Good luck, Linc."

Lincoln hiked back to his pickup, perturbed that the local women were already drawing unfounded conclusions about the way Henry had died. He agreed with Jack: the murder seemed personal. Beating and strangulation—that level of rage took quite a bit of effort and time. A stranger passing through town would not be likely to linger to perform such brutality. And anyway, Henry Rhodes was an easy-going fella, not known to push someone to that kind of anger.

Lincoln drove toward town so deep in thought that he almost missed seeing Brad Wilkinson fixing a fence. Running down that man to talk to him had been nearly impossible. He pulled his pickup into a shallow ditch on the side of the dirt road and hopped out. "Hey, Brad. What's goin' on?"

"Aw, them damn cows. They think my grass ain't good enough." The man grinned as he pulled a pair of pliers out of a holder at his waist.

The sheriff yanked on his buckskin leather gloves. "Here, let me hold that." He grasped the post and held it steady while Brad worked on the wire.

"How's the investigation goin', Sheriff?" The pliers slipped, prompting the older man to let out a string of expletives.

Lincoln pressed his lips together to keep from laughing at Brad's inventive use of the word 'ass.' "Workin' on it. What have you heard?"

"The wife said Kinsley got to town this mornin'." Brad jerked the wire tight, catching Lincoln unprepared. He stumbled forward, nearly impaling himself on the wood. "Damn, Sheriff, you sure are easy to move. Get a hold of that stake." The men laughed in unison as Lincoln set his feet.

"Yep, Kinsley is here," Lincoln replied easily. "By the way, did you see anything unusual last Tuesday or since?"

"Naw, we keep to ourselves out here. Henry came by a few weeks back to borrow some tools, but he returned 'em." Brad stopped working and rested against a pole as he shook his head. "Hard ta believe he's gone."

The aged farmer brushed his hands on his jeans then cleared his throat. "I know you and Henry were close. It's good you can help Kinsley. I feel for her. She babysat our grandchild for us. She was a real gentle girl." He straightened and started pulling on the wire again. "Sheriff, I'm gonna have to fire ya if you don't use some of that size you got there."

Lincoln burst out laughing as he steadied the rod. "Fixin' fence isn't exactly my field of expertise."

With nothing better to occupy their time, Brad's neighbors had stopped by to watch them work. They had plenty of advice as to what the pair were doing wrong to repair the barrier, and even began to argue among themselves. Lincoln used the opportunity to extract what information he could, but his audience knew nothing more about Henry's murder than anyone else in town.

Once the fence was secure, the sheriff returned to his pickup and headed back to town. The sun was giving way to a dusky evening sky by the time he checked in at the office. "Hey, Charlene," he said as he picked up mail from the end of her desk.

She didn't acknowledge him at first and continued to tap steadily on her computer keyboard. Without looking away from the monitor, she asked, "How'd City take the news?"

"Haven't talked to her yet," Lincoln responded.

Charlene swiveled in her seat to grace him with a dramatic eye roll. "Oh, this is gonna go well. Me and the ladies from church made some casseroles for her on account of Henry's passing. You better show up there bearing gifts, or you might get shot."

Lincoln nodded and strolled to the kitchenette. He removed a stack of dishes from the refrigerator and called back, "Doubt ol' City even knows what a gun is. She might hit me with one of those dangerous lookin' shoes, though. I think I'll survive."

When he returned, the air was tainted with his dispatcher's irritation. "Either way, please take the food," she instructed. "It's the right thing. Henry was her grandpa and a good man, no matter how she acts."

"Will do." Lincoln took the haul and headed for the door; he knew better than to defy the fiery redhead. He laid the prepared meals on the passenger seat then drove through town, thinking about his friend and his friend's granddaughter.

A tingle prickled his spine as he stepped up onto Henry's wooden porch. He closed his eyes and made a mental note to avoid using humor to alleviate any moments of tension—a habit that most of his associates found asinine rather than humorous. *Those haters wouldn't know witty if it bit them*, he mused before ringing the doorbell.

CHAPTER FOUR

Book Covers

The door chimes sounded just as Kinsley popped the top of her second chilled beer. Distracted by wondering who it might be, she headed for the front of the house and stubbed her toe on a terrier-shaped iron doorstop, causing her to spew a series of choice words. She hopped on one foot and peeked out the window to see who was there, and the revelation made her curse again. So that damn sheriff had finally decided to show up.

Kinsley glowered and swung the door open aggressively. She was about to give him a piece of her mind he wouldn't soon forget when he greeted her with a lopsided smile. "Dinners from the church ladies."

Lincoln pushed the casseroles toward her, leaving Kinsley with no choice but to receive them with open arms, the longneck bottle still dangling from her fingers. "Beer at the door? Now that is hospitality." He plucked the frosty drink from her grasp, took a long swallow, then strolled into her house as if it were his own.

Mouth agape and her arms full of dishes, Kinsley seethed with anger at his brazen familiarity.

"You cleaned the place up. I didn't even know there was furniture in here," he said, trying to be funny. "Wouldn't have guessed you were the domestic type."

Kinsley scowled as she remembered her grandfather mentioning what a nice guy the sheriff was, and how he wanted her to meet Lincoln someday. How could Grandpa have thought that this man was someone she would want to know?

Eyeing him, she noted his ridiculous grin. Despite his bravado he seemed to be sweating bullets, so she thought it prudent not to utter any of the rude responses running through her mind. Instead, she moved silently into the dining room and set the meals on the table, taking a minute to process what had happened.

Had he just shoved a load of casseroles at her and grabbed her beer, or was she being punked? Kinsley felt as if she'd been cast as an unwilling participant in a real-life version of a 1950s' television sitcom. A happy memory of watching TV with Grandpa gave her the strength to collect herself and return to the living room.

Her mood clouded again when she saw that the sheriff had made himself right at home on the couch with her beer.

Lincoln continued to drink as he perused the surroundings. "Looks like a house in here now instead of storage. You did a lot of work in a day."

Kinsley's glare never wavered as she watched him remove his Stetson and lay it on the back of the couch before running his fingers through his dark hair. She pursed her lips. How competent could this cop of a one-horse town be? She seriously doubted he had the wherewithal to solve her grandfather's murder. "What is it you want, Sheriff James?"

Lincoln looked at her, surprised. "We were supposed

to meet tonight, remember? We made the appointment over the phone for this evening. We could visit and have dinner."

Kinsley bristled. "You don't honestly expect me to make you dinner, do you?"

His eyes moved slowly over her face, then he sat up and became more serious. "No, I don't expect you to make me dinner. I brought food, remember? No cookin' needed." When she remained defensive, he changed tactics. "Convenient, right?" he asked teasingly.

His manner caused the dam holding back her frustration to give way, unleashing a tsunami of spite. "Oh, I do apologize! I forgot I'm back in good ol' boy country,' she sniped. 'Let me fetch my apron so I can wait on you hand and foot. What can I get for you, Your Highness?"

Lincoln's mouth twitched almost imperceptibly. "I could eat. Thanks for askin'. Dinner … talkin'… It'll be nice."

Kinsley remembered her upbringing and managed to hold her tongue. Dammit, Grandpa would expect her to practice some decorum, no matter how irritating the company. "Dinner will be served in the dining room shortly."

She escaped to the kitchen, itching to give the sheriff a good ass whippin'. She took a plate from the cupboard and silverware from the drawer before returning to the dining room.

Lincoln was standing in front of her computers. The program she'd been writing was visible. "What's all this for, City? You a rocket scientist?"

Taken aback by the nickname, Kinsley snapped, "Did you call me City?"

Lincoln glanced at her but said nothing.

"No. I am not a rocket scientist." She slammed the laptops shut and slid the plate in his direction. "Would His Highness like another beer?"

"My name is Lincoln, but you can call me 'Your Highness' if it pleases." His eyes twinkled, but his teasing only made her more angry.

She nailed him with a hateful look. "My name is Kinsley. Please call me that."

"Another beer would be perfect. Thank you," he said, and pulled out a chair.

Retrieving a beer from the refrigerator, Kinsley scolded herself for allowing Lincoln's oddball sense of humor to get the better of her. She returned and placed the bottle next to his plate. Lincoln watched with interest as she took the seat farthest from him. "You aren't eatin'?"

Unable to keep her eyes from rolling, she responded, "No. Is that not mannerly?"

He shrugged and reached for the three-bean salad and ham, scraping a decent-sized portion onto his plate. She watched him surreptitiously, noticing he'd chosen food that could be eaten cold. She felt a little guilty for not offering to warm dinner, though that didn't dissuade him from filling his plate twice.

Although ordinarily standoffish, Kinsley had never been as hateful to anyone as she had been to the sheriff. However, there were important things they needed to discuss, so she did her best to collect herself. Her thoughts wandered over what still needed to be done, a list that seemed to grow exponentially with each passing hour.

"Not much for dinner conversation, then?" Lincoln gave polite chat another shot.

Kinsley ignored the question. Though the sheriff had ruffled her feathers, she sensed he used humor as a shield when he was uncomfortable. Undeterred by her silence, he asked, "You grew up here?"

"You mean you haven't heard all about me by now? I know how this town works." The sarcasm in her voice surprised even her.

"Can't say anyone has said a word about you besides Henry. He thought you were pretty fantastic." His warm tone as he spoke of her grandpa made Kinsley's heart thud painfully against her ribs.

"He was my grandfather. He had to love me. Ask your girl about me. I'm sure she has some choice information she'd like to share."

"My girl?" Lincoln was obviously confused.

"Your diner doll from this morning." Kinsley picked up her beer and took a swig.

He laughed quietly and shook his head.

"What's so funny?"

"You are, City," Lincoln replied. "A little bobcat, all claws and spittin' fire. Sheila is not my girl."

He must think I'm an idiot, Kinsley thought, but remained silent.

Lincoln put down his utensils, pushed the plate aside, and contemplated his dinner companion.

"What did you need to talk to me about?" Kinsley asked, afraid she might burst into tears at any moment. When he didn't answer immediately, she pushed harder.

"Come on, out with it. I have things to do and a funeral to plan."

Lincoln's voice drifted softly across the table like he was calming a wild stallion. "As I told you over the phone, Henry was murdered. There will be an investigation, and you can't bury him until we feel we have all the information we need. It could take quite a while. I'm sorry I can't share the details of his murder right now because of the ongoin' inquiry."

Kinsley laid her head in her hands and massaged her temples as the horror of her grandfather's death bore down on her. At least being mad at Lincoln had pushed the sadness away for a while. She could function with anger, but sorrow was debilitating.

"Did Henry say anything to you about a problem?" he asked.

"We talked every day, Sheriff. What specifically do you want to know?"

"Any mention of anyone harassin' him, or someone threatenin' him?"

"No, never." Kinsley closed her eyes, trying to shut out what he was asking.

"Where were you on Tuesday?" he asked cautiously.

Her eyes flew open. Was the sheriff seriously questioning if she'd killed her grandfather? The query hung between them like a poisoned cloud. "I was working. My phone records and emails will show I was in Seattle." She dropped her head again as the pain of her loss threatened to spill into tears.

Lincoln's face softened, but the damage was done. "I'm sorry to ask you. I..." He stopped, prompting her to look up at him. "I'm sorry, Kinsley." He stood abruptly. "I better go."

He stalked into the living room, his heavy footfalls causing the floorboards to groan. Lincoln swiped his hat off the back of the couch and moved to the door as Kinsley approached. His voice was taut when he spoke. "The question about where you were … it's routine. Somethin' I have to do. Nothin' personal. I'll let you know when we have information to share with you. Thank you for dinner." He placed his hat on his head and bounded down the steps to his vehicle.

Kinsley leaned against the frame and listened to the rumble of his truck before she shut off the front-room lights and returned to the dining room.

Henry was murdered. There will be an investigation. The sheriff's words drifted through her mind as she sat in front of her laptops. She surveyed the lines of code on the screen, but any motivation to work had passed. Instead, she replayed her last conversation with Grandpa. It had been a typical exchange, without any indication that something sinister might be afoot.

Overwhelmed by pain, Kinsley lowered her head onto the cradle of her arms and sobbed grievously for the first time since her grandfather's death.

***

Lincoln pulled out of her driveway and into his own in less than a minute. As he strolled across the lawn and eased his athletic frame into a wooden rocker on the porch, his thoughts centered on the rough meeting he had just left. He'd intended to distract Kinsley from the tragedy of Henry's death, but his humor hadn't gone over very well.

He rocked back and forth as he considered the riddle of Kinsley Rhodes. From the lines of code he'd seen on her computer screens, it was a safe bet that she worked in the information technology sector. Henry had never shared what she did for a living, but Lincoln knew that Kinsley paid most of Henry's bills—much to his old friend's annoyance.

Henry had blustered many times about how his granddaughter couldn't be stopped once she'd set her mind on something, but within those words Lincoln caught the admiration the old man harbored for her.

His musings were interrupted as his deputy, Butch Pate, pulled into the driveway. "Hey. How's the county?" Lincoln greeted him as he joined the sheriff on the porch.

Butch groaned as he sank into the chair next to Lincoln's. "Scared shitless. There's been a lot more calls about 'prowly' things that aren't there. It's understandable. Murder isn't something people are accustomed to dealin' with here. You have your meet-up with Kinsley?"

"Yep, I did," Lincoln responded without elucidating.

"And how did that go?" Butch asked.

"'Bout as good as can be expected, considering I'm a bit of an ass and she's hurtin'. We got it done, and I got out of her hair."

Butch nodded approvingly. "Good. Kinsley is a nice girl. I knew her when she lived here."

Lincoln leaned forward and looked over at Henry's house. "What do we know about her? I asked her whereabouts last Tuesday—probably shoulda waited on that question, but I wasn't sure she'd ever talk to me again." He craned his neck and glimpsed Kinsley's silhouette through the drawn curtains. She was seated at the table in the dining room, and he wondered how she was bearing up. "Still, I don't think she would harm Henry or anyone else. What's your take?"

"I know Kinsley has that tough outside, but she's no killer."

Lincoln agreed; he had seen his fair share of the underbelly of humanity, and Miss Rhodes wasn't cut from that cloth.

"My kid has a doctor's appointment tomorrow. I'll be in after, as long as my ex-wife doesn't kill me." Butch stood up. The men shared a knowing chuckle as he headed to his vehicle.

"Sure thing. I got it covered," Lincoln called out to him.

Butch waved as he backed out of the drive.

Lincoln's thoughts returned to Henry's case. There were still no leads. He needed to compile a list of people to question, but Kinsley wouldn't be on it; he could see how much she had loved her grandfather.

He rose and headed for his pickup. His thoughts about the beauty who'd moved in next door had gone about as far as was proper. Headquarters would keep him distracted and out of trouble.

***

When he flicked on his office light, Lincoln's eyes went immediately to the photos of the crime scene that were spread out on the conference table. He placed his palms on the surface, leaned forward and scrutinized them. "Who killed you, my friend?" he whispered.

A rudimentary autopsy report had come in and was in a folder on his desk. Lincoln took off his hat and raked his fingers through his hair as he settled in his chair. He flipped open the folder to examine its contents. At that moment his cell phone rang. He picked it up and answered, "James."

A high-pitched giggle drilled into his ear, identifying the caller instantly. "Hey ya, Sheriff. I made some cherry pie. Do you want to come over and have a piece?"

"Hi, Sheila. I'm sorry, I can't. I'm workin'. I do thank you for the invite." Lincoln guessed that she had secured his cell phone number by way of Charlene.

"Oh, come on. It's good, and I have whipped cream." Her voice gave him a toothache when she drew out the word cream, as if that would seal the deal.

"I need to work. Maybe another time."

Sheila made one last desperate attempt. "Okay, but you don't know what you're missing."

"I'll see ya." Lincoln laid his phone and the autopsy report aside. It was obvious what she wanted, but there was something about Sheila Clark that turned him off, despite her best efforts to get him into bed. He shouldn't have let it go this far.

Damn, some cherry pie did sound good. Dessert had been among the dishes he'd delivered to Kinsley earlier. He wondered if she had some whipped cream. Lincoln smiled to himself. What in the hell was he thinking? City hated him. He leaned back and laced his fingers behind his head as images of Kinsley flashed through his mind.

That smoky voice of hers when she went acid and called him 'Your Highness.' Now that was a piece of cherry pie he'd love to have...

He shook his head to clear the unbidden thoughts. The sheriff eased out of his chair and returned to the small conference table. He studied each of the crime-scene photos carefully, but his thoughts kept returning to Kinsley Rhodes. She might have the key to what they were missing. He needed to stick with her until he found out what she knew.

CHAPTER FIVE

Coffee And Conflict

Kinsley loved early mornings when the world felt new. She padded sleepily to the kitchen to make coffee, but a search of every cabinet did not yield a single bean. The urge to throw a tantrum almost won out, but instead she trudged back to her grandfather's bedroom. She flopped onto the bed and flung her arms wide. Fuming, she stared at a crack in the ceiling and ticked through the list of the day's tasks, which now included a trip to the grocery store.

A colorful butterfly, painted directly above the bed, brought to mind a memory of painting this room with her grandfather twenty years ago. Tears burned her eyes as she recalled their conversation.

"The butterfly will be like I'm watching over you, Grandpa. Then you won't ever forget about me."

"Baby girl, I could never forget about you. You're my sunshine."

The sharp pain of his absence prompted Kinsley to sit up abruptly. Maybe a run would set her right. She started to move methodically about the house, gathering what she needed before heading out the door.

The steady thump of her shoes on the pavement was comforting as she ran through the deserted town. She passed the local burger joint, housed in the same cinderblock building it had always occupied. Seeing it stirred memories of Brown Derby ice-cream cones, and the many hours she'd spent glued to a video console in there. Now that she thought about it, her love for programming was likely to have been fostered at that time.

Kinsley turned up the music and sprinted until she felt her heart was going to burst. Finally, she slowed down and walked the last several blocks to cool down.

"Gettin' your exercise, City?"

Kinsley balled her fists and stopped on the sidewalk. Angry over the moniker, she turned to glare in the general direction of Lincoln's voice. Steam was wafting from the mug he was holding. "Let me guess. You're my neighbor?"

"Yep," he confirmed and took a drink.

Her longing for a cup of coffee and one of those cinnamon rolls she'd seen at Pearl's made her stomach gurgle loudly.

"Better feed that," Lincoln said lazily.

"I'm fine," she spat.

"Sounds like it." He took another sip, still appraising her.

There was something enticing about his gruff voice and slow country drawl. She turned to leave before something was said that couldn't be taken back. "Want a cup of coffee?" he called after her.

Drinking coffee in a den of rattlesnakes would be preferable to sharing java with Sheriff James. "No, thank you," Kinsley replied over her shoulder.

"Come on. I'm harmless."

She hesitated and turned, but the pleased look on his

face stiffened her resolve. "No, thanks." She spun on her heel and stormed back to her house.

When she turned the knob to start the shower, the ancient water-heater groaned. Grimacing, Kinsley added it to her mental list of house repairs, then refocused on more immediate tasks as she waited for the water to warm.

A supermarket run was top priority; her desire for a coffee fix had almost made her give in and drink a cup with the cretin next door. That wouldn't have been wise. That man needed to stay on his side of the property line with his smirking and nicknames, she concluded, before she moved under the weak spray to shower.

Half an hour later, Kinsley scrutinized her outfit in the full-length mirror. *Why do I care what anyone in this town thinks?* she huffed. Shopping list in hand, she stepped out into the already warm morning. As she opened her car door, a big black Chevy pulled in behind her. Blinded by the morning sun, Kinsley shaded her eyes with her hand to see who was inside.

The window lowered and Lincoln stuck out his head. "Let's get some breakfast."

His cheerful demeanor only aggravated her further. "No. Get out of my driveway!" she yelled back.

Instead of leaving, he killed the engine and got out. "You're all dressed up. Goin' someplace?"

"Yes," Kinsley replied curtly.

Lincoln waited for more information. After a few seconds of silence, he said, "You need some lessons in conversation."

"No, I don't need conversation lessons. I just don't want to talk to you."

His lopsided grin emerged. "Well, at least ya don't pull your punches. What did I do to you, City?"

"Quit calling me that." Kinsley gave him a dirty look. "You don't like me, so why won't you leave me alone?"

"I never said I didn't like you." Lincoln paused before continuing. "But I think you may have access to somethin' that could help in the investigation."

"If I run across anything, I'll email it to you or leave a note on your door. Now go away and let me finish my errands."

"Okay, suit yourself." He turned back to his vehicle.

Kinsley clambered into her Range Rover and gripped the steering wheel so tightly that her knuckles turned white. Taking a deep breath, she started the engine and drove toward the local market.

Like everything else in Harlow, the grocery store was frozen in time. As she reached into the cooler for milk, Kinsley heard her name announced at full volume, as if she'd just won a grand prize. She spun to find the source of the foghorn voice. Much to her relief, the unfamiliar man quickly introduced himself. "Jason Matthews. Do you remember me? I manage this store."

She could see it now, even though Jason had some gray hair around the temples and a paunch she was sure wasn't there when they were in high school. "It's nice to see you again," Kinsley replied, doing her best to be polite.

He gave her the top to bottom. "I heard you were here for Henry's funeral."

"I am." Not able to recall Jason ever giving her the time of day in high school, it was a mystery what he

40

wanted with her now. She began to move away.

"Hey, wait. How long are you in town?"

The urge to run beckoned as she scrambled for an appropriate answer. "I'm not sure."

"We should go out sometime. Have a beer." Jason came in with the full-court press, hemming her in by placing his hand against the refrigerated shelving.

"Thank you, but I can't." Kinsley took a step back and pressed against her cart. Slipping past him, she rolled the buggy between them as a barricade.

"Husband?" Jason asked.

Kinsley considered the quandary. She could lie, play the married card, and that would be that—but why should she have to lie? Still, being unpleasant to him seemed unnecessary. Trying to ease the rejection, she said, "I have a lot to do while I'm here."

"You can't take a break for a beer with an old friend?"

The hopeful look on his face pained her. If he only knew; there was no chance for him, nor for any man. "No, I can't, but thank you for asking."

Jason made one more mumbled attempt. "You're sure?"

The guy was just not getting it. "I appreciate the invite, Jason, but I have work to do while I'm here. You take care."

Wanting to get out of the store as fast as she could, Kinsley rushed from aisle to aisle, pulling items into her basket like a contestant on *Supermarket Sweep*.

Back in the safe confines of her car, she turned the key, and the radio blared to life with a voice she knew very well: Leon Boss.

Kinsley had tried to call him a couple of times without

any luck. When she'd checked his website, she'd found that his band was on tour, having had back-to-back shows for the past few weeks. Leon had been Grandpa's best friend. Even after he hit it big as a musician, they'd remained close. She should try again.

This time, he answered. "Kinsley, sweet princess." The man's ever-present sunshine never failed to light her up.

"How are you, superstar?"

His deep laugh was like a warm embrace. "I'm good. I'm good. Livin' the life out here in Cali. What's up, my pretty buttercup?"

Drawing a figure eight on the console, Kinsley let out a deep sigh.

"Sweet girl, what is it?"

She eased into the conversation. "I have bad news."

"What's happened?" Leon's voice was caged by fear.

"Grandpa was murdered." The news rushed out with her breath. "I'm back in Harlow for a while."

There was no hesitation from the other end of the line. "I'm coming back. I can catch a flight out of here today. Are you hanging in there?"

"You don't need to come back." She was afraid canceling shows would cause him tons of trouble, though she wanted him to come home so badly.

"Let me help you with this," he offered. "You're alone, sweetheart."

"I'm maintaining, I promise. Grandpa's death is under investigation, so everything is on hold. You couldn't do a thing but sit around and drink beer with me. You can't disappoint those adoring fans. I'll keep you in the loop on the investigation."

"Kinsley, you're more important than the tour." Leon went quiet for a moment. "I know you try to be tough, but you don't have to be. I'll be glad to come back, even if we just sit around drinking beer together."

"No, it's okay. I appreciate you offering. When you get back around this way, come see me. I'll let you know when they give me the go-ahead to bury Grandpa."

The distress in his tone was palpable. "I'm sorry about Henry. I can't believe someone would kill him. You promise you will call me?"

"I promise. Thank you, Leon. I miss you." Kinsley choked back tears.

"We'll be back in that part of the country soon and I'll be by to see you, but I'll come back anytime you want me there."

"Sounds good. Keep 'em dancin'," she said, with as much gusto as she could muster.

"I love you, sweetheart."

"I love you, too, Leon."

Kinsley rested her chin on the steering wheel. Usually, she could handle the loneliness, but today it had a steel grip on her.

***

Lincoln stopped at the doughnut shop to pick up a dozen assorted pastries before going to the office. Pearl's was out of the question after the phone conversation with Sheila the previous night. Before that call, he hadn't heard from the waitress outside of their brief morning conversations at the diner. Maybe some distance between them would deliver a message.

"Mornin'," he said as he laid the box on the end of Charlene's desk.

She looked from the doughnuts to him. "No Pearl's?"

"Nope."

A wicked grin crawled across her ruby lips, "Sheila is gonna cry big crocodile tears over that. You know you are the highlight of her day."

"She and I—not happenin'," Lincoln said firmly. "Butch is off until later tonight. I'll be in my office." He picked up a twist and the mug Charlene had filled. "Thanks for the coffee." She graced him with a wink before he headed down the hall.

The big leather office chair sighed as he settled in and considered his latest encounter with Kinsley. The woman could hand out mean like no other. Henry had painted a picture of his granddaughter as a kind girl who loved animals and spent time fishing; his idealized Kinsley and the one who had moved in next door were not the same person.

The intercom on his desk buzzed. "Linc, the Millers are here."

"Thanks, Charlene. Please send them through."

Anyone who'd had contact with Henry during his last days had been set up for interviews, beginning with the Millers. Lincoln met them at the door. "Please come in."

Jeff Miller and his wife, Cheryl, sheepishly took seats in front of the massive mahogany desk.

"Thank you both for coming," Lincoln said. "I wanted to talk to you about Henry Rhodes. Jeff, you were one of the last people to see Henry alive. Can you tell me about that day?"

Jeff's big eyes widened further as his head bobbed on his toothpick-thin neck. "I went over to Henry's house to fix the faucet in the bathroom. I did my job. Nothin' was happenin'. Henry was alive when I left, I swear." His voice broke over the last few words.

Lincoln watched them. Jeff seemed suitably upset, but Cheryl looked as if she had just eaten a persimmon that wasn't quite ripe. "Did you have a conversation with Henry?" he asked Jeff. "Did he take any phone calls while you were there? Have any visitors?"

"Just me an' Henry. The ol' man was eatin' a sandwich because it was lunch. He offered to make me one, but I didn't eat because I hate bologna." Jeff tapped his spidery fingers on his leg. "He did take a phone call. I heard him talkin' to that granddaughter of his. I heard him say he was excited she was comin' back in a couple of weeks." Miller hesitated, and his voice was quieter when he spoke again. "Then Henry said he loved and missed her."

Lincoln nodded. "Very good, Jeff, thank you. Anything else?"

Cheryl leaned forward. She lowered her voice for dramatic effect. "That granddaughter is no good. You should check her out because her parents were worthless." As she raised one eyebrow at Lincoln, her heavy blue eyeshadow arched with it. A self-satisfied expression settled on her face as if she'd just solved the murder for him with that one statement.

Jeff flapped his hands at his wife like she was a fart he was fanning away. "Cheryl, stop that! This town is a mess with people talkin' about people. That girl just lost her grandfather. She wouldn't kill him."

Cheryl frosted her husband with a look, then turned back to Lincoln. "Just sayin', Sheriff. You do what you want, but this killer on the loose needs to be taken care of. It's terrifying! We had to call out Stephenson's Hardware to get us keys made for our doors so we could lock 'em. We didn't even have keys! I can't sleep with this murderer running around. I don't want to be chopped to pieces like Henry." She faked a theatrical shiver.

"Rest assured, I'm doin' all I can to catch the murderer, Mrs. Miller. You have nothin' to fear from Miss Rhodes—and no one has been dismembered."

Lincoln watched the duo while he thought about Kinsley. She was not a bad person; challenging, yes, but not evil. Cheryl Miller needed to cram it. Suddenly, he had nothing more to say to the couple. He escorted them to the door, doing his utmost to hide his annoyance. "I appreciate you both comin' down. If you think of anything else, please don't hesitate to call."

After they'd gone, Lincoln went to the window and leaned against the frame. Lost in thought, he watched the surrounding trees swaying in the stiff south wind. He was surprised that he'd felt so angry at Cheryl Miller for saying mean things about City.

He shook his head before snagging his hat from the coat rack and heading for the door. There was a murder to solve. "I'm goin' to the elevator," he said offhandedly to Charlene.

"It'll be okay, Linc. You'll figure it out," she soothed.

The sheriff gave her a sly smile. "Gettin' soft on me?"

"Hell no! Get going, ya lazy good for nothin',"

Charlene cackled. "How was that?"

"Felt good. Keep it up." Lincoln winked before he strolled out to his pickup.

***

The grain elevators were located on the opposite side of town, which gave Lincoln the chance to mull over the information from the interview and plan the next one. As he turned into the gravel lot, he saw just the person he was looking for. He parked a short distance away, and the man who had been moving grain leaned on his shovel and looked towards him with interest.

Lincoln nodded in acknowledgment before getting out of his pickup. "Hey, Josh. Got a minute?"

"Sure, Sheriff."

"I wondered if you saw Henry in here recently?"

Josh wiped the sweat from his brow with the back of his glove. "I did. Mr. Rhodes came in to do some business last week, but the manager was out. We talked for a spell. Can you believe someone would kill him like that? I mean, imagine peelin' the skin off someone and leavin' 'em to die—"

Lincoln had already noted how inventive the stories about Henry's death were becoming, but flaying was an outrageous addition. "There was no skin removal," he said reassuringly. "What did you and Henry talk about?"

Josh rubbed his chin before answering. "Nothin' really. Just sat around shootin' the shit, like normal. He said he was gonna call my dad, 'cuz the transmission in the '69 needed work."

"Did Henry talk to anyone else while he was here?"

The worker's lip curled in disgust. "Yeah, Skelly came in."

"Was it Rich or his father, Max?"

"Rich," Josh confirmed.

"Did you hear the conversation?" Lincoln watched loathing settle in the man's eyes.

With a burst of animation, Josh replayed the scene. "Rich said, 'When are you gonna sell me that land, old man?' So, Henry said, 'When hell freezes over, ya little prick.' Then Henry left. Rich said shitty things about Mr. Rhodes after he'd gone."

Henry's gumption tickled the sheriff. "What did Rich say?"

"That Henry was white trash and a bad farmer." Josh shifted his weight uncomfortably before looking at Lincoln. "Henry might not have had money, but he was a good man."

"Yes, Henry was a very good man. Is there anything else you can think of?"

"No, sir. I hope you catch the bastard that killed him."

"Thank you for your time. If you remember somethin', please call," Lincoln responded.

They shook hands before going their separate ways. Lincoln walked back to his truck, deep in thought. All evidence pointed to the fact that Rich Skelly was a turd, but the man barely had enough drive to comb his own hair. From time to time, Henry had hinted at some discord with Max Skelly, but Lincoln had never been let in on the details; it sounded more like a general distaste for one another that went back many years.

He put a pin in the thought as his phone rang. His

ex-wife's name on the caller ID made him groan. "Hey, Jeannie."

"I need money for Thomas's tuition. Five hundred."

The tone of that woman's voice could freeze molten lava. Lincoln waited a moment before he spoke. "I'm fine, thanks for askin'."

"Do we have to do that? Are you sending the money or not?" she blustered.

It amazed him that Jeannie had never grasped the subtlety of being nice when asking for a favor, but nineteen years of this behavior had set a pattern that was unlikely to change. Lincoln opened the door of his pickup and crawled in. "Nope. Mom already paid his tuition. I sent them the money."

Her voice rose in desperation. "Okay, I need the money to pay a bill. You want your kid to eat, don't you, Lincoln?"

"Jeannie, stop. You and I both know Thomas lives at my parents' house. He's fed, has clothes, and his tuition is paid. You have a husband. Ask him for money."

"You're a bastard, Lincoln James," Jeannie snarled before the line went dead.

He laid his phone on the dash and rubbed his temples to alleviate the headache his ex-wife had caused. Her voice continued to ring in his ear. Although he and Jeannie were a source of irritation to each other, their son never wanted for anything. Seven years earlier, Lincoln had made the decision to leave Tulsa to take the job in Harlow. It had been a heart-wrenching choice to move so far away from his son, but living near his ex-wife would never have worked.

In the early days of their separation, Jeannie had

shown up at his house in the middle of the night and attacked him. She'd caused scenes in public that had nearly gotten them both arrested. Her most odious act had been keeping Thomas from him, which had left him with no choice but to take her back to family court to retain his visitation rights. He'd moved away with the hope that she could finally let go and give their son a semblance of a normal life, even if his own part would be long distance.

His parents had been a blessing. They'd kept Thomas on Lincoln's behalf for much more than the agreed fifty-fifty the court had handed down. His ex-wife wasn't much of a mother, but Lincoln wouldn't deprive Thomas of a relationship with her.

Jeannie's irrational behavior had calmed down when she'd remarried a few months after he had left Tulsa. Still, Lincoln knew that if she was worried enough to call him for money there had to be something serious going on. He needed to find out before it became a fire that only a trip to Oklahoma would put out.

Lincoln dialed his most reliable source.

"Hi, sweetheart."

Lincoln's heart warmed. "Hi, Mom. How ya doin'?"

"We're all fine. Your father is driving me crazy since his retirement. I am not the entertainment committee. He needs a hobby." His fussy father gave them both a laugh.

"Jeannie just called tellin' me she needed money for Thomas's tuition. Everything goin' okay down there?"

"I'm sorry she called you, Lincoln. Thomas is fine. Lately he's been with us all the time. I don't know what she's up to, but don't worry about him."

"Thanks, Mom. I'm sorry, I have to work, but I'll call you later."

"Sure, honey. I love you. Come see us soon. I miss you."

"I love you too, Mom. I'll come down when I can get away."

Lincoln eased the three-quarter ton onto the asphalt street. As he drove down Polk Street past the old folk's home, he waved at the residents who were out enjoying the warm sunshine. Lincoln had mastered the art of the slow drive over the years. There wasn't much to be in a hurry about around here.

He continued down the street until he spotted Bob Boyd out in his front yard. Boyd and Henry had been close friends, and there might be information to be gathered. Lincoln pulled into the circle drive and leaned out the open window. "Trouble with the mower?"

"Seems so. How's it goin', Sheriff?" Bob asked.

Lincoln joined him and they both studied the machine, as if their mere presence would magically fix it somehow. "As well as can be expected, I suppose. What's it doin'?"

Bob jerked on the starter cord a few times. "Nothin'."

Lincoln pushed his hat back and contemplated the silent mower.

"How's the murder investigation goin', Linc? Boy, that's somethin'. Got me rethinkin' all kinds of things. Mary had me call a security company for a house alarm. Can you believe it?" Bob shook his head. "A damned house alarm," he muttered under his breath.

"Yep, it's got folks upset. Had you and Henry talked

lately?"

"I saw him at Pearl's every mornin', just like normal. Breakfast on that Tuesday, nothin' out of the ordinary. I've eaten breakfast with Henry Rhodes for the better part of forty years. Hard to believe that old so-and-so is gone."

"Bob, did anyone have a problem with Henry that you can recall?" Lincoln watched his friend for any reaction.

"Max Skelly. Other than him, no. A person would have to be tryin' hard to dislike Henry."

"True." Lincoln nodded. "What was Skelly's problem with him?"

Bob raised his eyes from the lawnmower and scrutinized Lincoln. "It's old wounds. Livin' in the same small town for sixty-plus years, well, life tends to get tangled up."

"I understand that." Lincoln sensed Bob didn't want to share the reason. "Is it somethin' worth murderin' someone over?"

Boyd let out a grunt as he squatted and reached out to wiggle the spark-plug wire. "Well, I suppose that all depends on how fragile your ego is. But no, I don't think Max Skelly…" He stood and yanked on the mower cord a couple of times with no result. "Aw shit, I can tell you. Henry is gone now. Let's have a sit. Iced tea?" he asked as they crossed the lawn.

Lincoln accepted and sat down in the wicker chair in the shade of the porch. He was still finding it hard to accept that his friend had been murdered. Rose of Sharon bushes planted nearby sweetened the air, and he took a deep breath to clear his thoughts.

The tinkling of ice against glass signaled Bob's

return. He sat and dived into the story. "Henry was a good-lookin' young man, a big ol' boy—and the ladies loved him. Max's wife, Lana Skelly—Lana Donald, as was—had it bad for him." He peered out across the street with a faraway stare. "Damn, I was jealous of him. Never was much of a looker myself, and it's only gotten worse with age."

Lincoln cast an eye over the retired farmer, who was the human equivalent of a beach ball, and the two of them chuckled.

"Lana was a honey of a thing. Any man would have given anything to be with her, but she only had eyes for Henry. He had the gift of gab even then. Anyhow, he and Lana dated for a short while before Henry joined the Navy. They broke up and she hurried off to marry Max, who was from money. It was easy to see why she picked Skelly if she couldn't have her first choice. When Henry came home, he brought his Rose with him, bought the house here in town, and that's how it all shook out in the end. Though if you ask me, Lana never got over Henry."

"So, Max hated Henry because he plowed that field before him?"

Boyd smirked. "He did a little planting, I'd say. Take a look at Skelly's first son, Lonnie. If he's not Henry Rhodes' child, I'm a monkey's uncle. Lana never accused Henry publicly of being the father, but he is one big boy, not like the rest of the Skelly kids. Lonnie looks just like Henry did back in the day."

Lincoln rubbed his palms on his thighs. "Thank you, Bob. I appreciate the insight. Do you suppose Henry suspected Lonnie was his?"

"I assume so. We didn't talk about it. Skelly put his name on the boy, and there was no need to stir the pot."

They finished their tea and chewed the fat for a while before sauntering back to the broken contraption on the lawn. Lincoln squatted down, unscrewed the gas cap, and peeked into the completely dry tank. "Needs some gas," he said, before replacing the cap and standing up.

"Well, son of a bitch! Thanks, Sheriff."

"Welcome. Have a good day."

As Lincoln made his way back to the station, Boyd's information churned out a new suspect. If Lonnie Skelly knew he was Henry's son, he might have worked up enough hatred to beat Rhodes to death. An easy six-foot-two, maybe more, it was possible Lonnie could have done the job. Henry might have let him in the house to talk, never expecting to be attacked.

That ol' Henry was always a surprise.

CHAPTER SIX

A Trick Of The Light

With the grocery shopping completed, Kinsley shut herself in the house determined to clean the kitchen until it sparkled. The encounter with Jason dominated her thoughts as she pulled on rubber gloves and dumped cleanser into the sink. She concluded that he must have heard the rumors from years ago and pegged her as an easy mark.

She began to scrub work surfaces with a vigorous intensity, remembering the countless times she'd wished for the strength to stand up to her tormentors. She was a whole new animal now.

By early evening, the kitchen was as clean as it was ever likely to be. When she'd arrived yesterday, her initial plans for burying her grandfather had been sidelined with the news that the investigation would delay the funeral. Harlow was going to be her temporary home for much longer than she'd expected.

The cork from a chilled bottle of white wine came out with a satisfying pop. Kinsley's only plan was to relax and watch an old movie, but she was interrupted by the door chime's familiar rendition of *Für Elise*. When she was a child, Grandpa had told her that the song was Grandma Rose's favorite; from that day forward, she had imagined the grandma she'd never met was saying hello each time the tinny tune sounded.

Almost certain who her visitor would be, Kinsley exchanged the wine for a beer before ambling to the front of the house. She dragged open the door and held out the bottle to Lincoln. A mischievous light warmed his eyes, and she wondered how he could be so pleased to see someone who had treated him with such contempt.

"City, you *can* be trained. Good to know." He followed her as she returned to the dining room and sat down at her computers.

"What do you want?' she demanded. 'I have work to do." Kinsley hoped her tone would dissuade him from staying.

"What are you workin' on?" He leaned on the table and eyed her screens.

"None of your business."

Oblivious to her bad manners, Lincoln said, "I'm hungry."

Stupefied, Kinsley sat back and stared at him. "I'm pretty sure there's no diner sign hanging out front."

"I know you have meals you're never gonna eat," he remarked breezily.

"Are you planning to come over every night for dinner?" Her voice was laden with sarcasm.

A slight smile crept across his lips. "Well, thanks for invitin' me."

Kinsley had to know what made this guy tick. "Why won't you go away?"

Lincoln took a pull from the bottle before he answered, allowing himself a moment of reflection. "You're over here by yourself with food. I'm alone over there with no food. Why would I go away?"

"For several reasons," Kinsley snapped. "We don't like each other. I don't people. I work and that is all. Surely that's not difficult to understand."

When he continued to stand there, watching her with that annoying half-smile, Kinsley gave in and went to preheat the oven. She was hungry, though she probably wouldn't have eaten if the sheriff hadn't shown up.

Lincoln trailed her into the kitchen. "You don't people? What does that mean?"

"I have very few personal relationships. I like being on my own," she replied without looking up.

"Why?"

Kinsley pulled plates from the cabinet. "I think that's more information than I'm willing to share with someone who hates me."

"I don't hate you, City."

"Why do you insist on calling me that when you know it pisses me off?"

When his eyes crinkled with delight, she stared at him in disbelief. "Oh, my heavens. What is wrong with you?"

Lincoln's smirk widened before he answered. "Not a thing."

Kinsley leaned against the counter and let her eyes slide over him. He was very pleased with himself without being arrogant; her hostility only seemed to challenge him.

"I heard Jason asked you out." Lincoln peeled the label off his beer, trying to hide his amusement.

It galled her that folks in town still talked about her. Never once had the gossips nailed their facts, and the lies they had passed about her when she'd lived here had turned her life into a nightmare. Kinsley had cried herself to sleep so many times in the past that she'd finally run the well dry.

"I suppose people think there is something terribly wrong with me since I told him no?" Her irritation spilled out.

"The possibility was discussed at Pearl's during lunch."

She couldn't tell if he was joking and her fury erupted like a volcano. "You people talk behind people's backs about things you know nothing about! You all should mind your own doorsteps! What can I do or say to make you go away, Sheriff James?" she asked bitterly. "What do you want to know?"

Momentarily thrown, Lincoln regrouped and changed the subject. "Did you find any paperwork or letters when you were cleanin'? Anything that struck you as suspicious?"

They returned to the dining room. Lincoln carried the plates, and she brought the flatware and placed it on the table. "I put everything in these boxes." She waved her hand toward the overflowing cartons along the wall. "I didn't look at much because the house was a disaster. I had to get the rooms livable first."

"Do you mind if I take a gander? When we did the initial investigation, we didn't find anythin' obvious. There was so much paperwork layin' around, I thought that now that you have things in more of an order, there might be some clue we could dig out."

"Have at it." Kinsley sat down. A lead weight had taken up residence in her chest. For a brief moment in the kitchen she'd thought the sheriff might be different, someone she could become friends with, but it seemed he was precisely like everyone else in this town.

Lincoln hauled a box to the table and removed a few papers. "What do you do for work?"

"I own my own company."

"What does your company do?"

"Why do you ask? Everybody at Pearl's want to know?"

Lincoln didn't try to hide his amusement. "You'll never get a boyfriend being secretive like that."

She ignored his attempt to draw her in with humor and continued to work.

"Your business must pay well. That's an expensive car you drive," he continued.

There was no getting rid of him; he was like gum stuck to a shoe. "You ask a lot of questions," she grumbled and adjusted her screens.

"I'm a cop. It comes with the territory."

Kinsley's eyes narrowed. "Do I seem like a criminal?"

"Maybe." He grinned.

The timer on the oven dinged. When she returned with the food, Kinsley watched delight settle on Lincoln's face.

"May's secret chicken casserole."

"You know this by smell? I'm impressed." Kinsley sat the dish and her wine glass on the table.

"Been around for quite a few funerals," he said. She dished up a single portion before Lincoln interjected. "I'm not you. Load it up. So, besides breaking Jason's heart, what did you do today?"

Kinsley cast him a sideways glance. "You mean you didn't hear at the diner?"

"No. It seems no one saw you come out of the house after you went grocery shoppin' in your hundred-dollar jeans."

She sat back and crossed her arms. "You discussed the price of my jeans? Do you people have nothing better to do than gossip about me?"

"You don't deny they're hundred-dollar jeans?"

"They were a bit more than that," Kinsley replied haughtily. She took a bite from her own plate and savored the creamy sauce that clung to the chicken and homemade noodles. May's secret was definitely the hand-churned butter she made.

Lincoln clicked his tongue. "Do tell. I'll pass the word. I need to get that pricing straight."

"I wish you wouldn't talk about me at all." Part of her was angry at the gossip, the rest because there was only one bite of the scrumptious casserole left on her plate.

"Is that all you're going to eat?" he asked. "Here, let me get you another piece."

She put out her hand to stop him. "How much I eat is not your concern, Sheriff."

"You could use a little meat on your bones."

"Oh, like your diner doll? No, thanks," Kinsley replied brusquely.

The sheriff laughed. "Sheila is not my doll."

"Could've fooled me with all the ridiculous giggling." She took a sip of her wine, unwilling to admit she was starting to enjoy their banter. "Another beer?"

Lincoln nodded. "Thanks for askin'."

Kinsley went into the kitchen and put the plates in the sink. She was pouring herself another glass of wine when he came in with the casserole. "Your Highness will lose his macho-man club card if anyone catches you doing that woman's work," she taunted.

"No worries, City. I have enough macho to stay in the club."

"Yes, I can see that." Kinsley scanned his six-and-a-half-foot frame.

He raised an eyebrow. "You think I'm macho?"

Her burst of laughter surprised him. "Lincoln, stop teasing me." When Kinsley realized she'd used his given name for the first time, it felt too intimate. A flush crept up her neck. As he stepped forward to put down the casserole, she backed away.

Lincoln watched her take on the look of a trapped animal. He stayed where he was and gently set the dish on the counter. When he took two steps back, she visibly relaxed. He turned back to the dining room and resumed his search of the boxes of papers to give her the space she obviously needed.

Eventually she joined him and turned on some music at a low volume before sitting at her computers across the table from him.

As he read through the financials, Lincoln confirmed what he had suspected: Henry wasn't making much money. It crossed his mind that Kinsley might know things about the farm no one else could. "Have you been to the old homestead?" he asked.

She shook her head. "Not in years."

"You own it now. I can take you out there."

Kinsley worried her bottom lip while she considered his offer. "I know where it is."

"I need to take a look as part of the investigation. Since I'm goin' anyway, why don't we go together?"

Kinsley paused before responding. "No."

Even though she'd rejected his offer, Lincoln didn't want to let this moment of calm between them pass. "Can I ask you about Henry? When did you two last speak?"

Her eyes slowly rose to meet his and, in silent compliance, she closed her laptops. "On that Tuesday at lunchtime," Kinsley answered flatly.

Edging into the conversation as if traversing a minefield, Lincoln chose his words carefully. "Could you tell me what you talked about?" He was watching her closely, but she wasn't an easy woman to read.

"We talked about the crops this year, and he told me it was going to be a good harvest. Leon, his friend, had called and we talked about him. The pickup had some issues." Kinsley stopped and tapped a fingernail on the tabletop before continuing. "I was going to come home in a couple of weeks."

Lincoln saw the misery she was fighting back, but he kept quiet and let her talk.

"He said he loved me and missed me. That was it—it was like every other conversation we'd ever had. I've played it back a million times, Lincoln. Why would someone kill him?"

The desperation in her voice pulled at him. "I can't imagine, but I intend to find out. Did Henry have any enemies that you know of?"

She shook her head. Wayward strands of hair escaped from her ponytail to frame her face. "Everyone loved Grandpa—well, except the Skellys. He didn't like them and they didn't like him. I was cautioned to avoid them when I lived here. I don't know why."

Lincoln had information about Henry that Kinsley didn't seem to know, but he decided to wait before sharing his suspicion about Lonnie Skelly, her newly revealed uncle. She had enough on her plate. He assumed that the bad blood between Henry and Max Skelly was related to Henry's illegitimate son. Then again, the Skellys were horrendous human beings.

"Thank you for talkin' to me. I swear, I will find out who killed him. It's important to me, too."

Kinsley smoothed her hand over the closed lid of her laptop. "Should I be worried about staying here? They killed him in this house. I'm not going to lie. I want to be where his things are, but my grandpa died here and it's disquieting." She abruptly wiped away a tear

"You could go stay at the B&B. I hear it's nice." Lincoln knew full well that it wasn't; the owner had a clowder of cats and the place stunk to high heaven.

"Yeah. I don't think I'll do that, but I appreciate the suggestion." Kinsley waited for a moment before adding, "You can smell the place as you drive by." They both snickered.

"You know, Cit— ah, Kinsley, I'm right next door. The officers go by here all the time. I'll do my best to make sure no one hurts you."

She watched him intently. "You think it's someone he knew, don't you? Someone who lives here?"

"I'm sorry I—" Lincoln couldn't tell her anything, no matter how much he wanted to.

"I won't tell anyone. I promise."

The anguish in her voice nearly broke him but he had to do his job. Lincoln shared what he could. "The possibility that a stranger killed Henry is low on my radar."

She sat across from him, her head bowed, vulnerable and alone. Kinsley was beautiful with a side of sexy. Lincoln knew he had to go before he did something reckless. "I better get out of your way."

A cloudy look shadowed her face before she stood and walked him out.

"I'll keep you in the loop as the investigation continues. If you find anything here or think of somethin' that might help, no matter how small, please call the office."

"Sure." Kinsley looked down at her feet.

"Thank you for dinner. It was real nice."

As Lincoln stepped out into the muggy night, his thoughts centered on all that had happened that evening. Kinsley was clearly more vulnerable than the hard-nosed woman she portrayed herself to be. Had something terrible happened to her? That would explain her standoffish behavior. Several of Lincoln's interviewees had hinted at Kinsley's past, giving him the distinct impression that her time in Harlow had not been a walk in the park.

What he did know was that it made his heart pound when her eyes went soft feather gray.

From conversations with Henry, he recollected that she was about twenty-six. He was ten years older than her and had an eighteen-year-old son. Any sort of relationship between them could only be a beautiful disaster.

Lincoln trudged through the thick grass toward his driveway. He settled in his pickup, pulled out his phone, and sent a text to his son to check in before he backed out of the driveway and headed to the office.

***

As Lincoln relaxed in his desk chair reading Thomas's reply, the hollow clack of boots on linoleum in a long, even stride alerted him to his deputy's presence. "Everything goin' okay?" he asked as Butch appeared in the doorway.

"Sure, sure. Just gettin' back from a call. The Slates thought someone had stolen their arc welder, but their son Dustin borrowed it without telling them. Case closed."

Lincoln pushed the financial folder he had intended to work on to the side. Butch's eyes followed the movement as he sat down across from his boss. "What are we going to do about the budget? The three of us can't keep going nonstop as we have been. You treat me fairly, taking my shifts so I can have time with my kids, but you've not had more than a day off here and there in what? Two years?"

Lincoln rested his elbows on the arms of the chair while he thought about money. Butch wasn't wrong; they were strung thin, but there wasn't another choice except to keep going. "Aw, I'm fine. I mean, what else am I gonna do if I don't work? Not like I have a life. We have the barbeque fundraiser this summer. Maybe we can hire help after that."

"I saw you coming out of Kinsley Rhodes' house. You *could* have a life." Butch grinned when Lincoln harrumphed at the suggestion, then tapped his index finger on his thigh. "If you aren't going to give her a shot, do you mind if I do?"

Lincoln's brow pinched and he sat forward.

Butch smiled. "That's what I thought. I'll stay away from Kinsley, but you better get on that if you're going to because the wolves are at the door."

"What are you talkin' about?"

"I was at the coffee shop this morning and there is plenty of interest in Miss Rhodes. She's gorgeous. You don't have time to be cautious. If you want her, do something about it." Butch got up. "Good luck." He winked as he left the office.

Lincoln picked up a paperclip and unfolded it absently. His pal was right—Kinsley *was* gorgeous. He would love to get wrapped up with her—but the fear she'd exhibited earlier that evening worried him.

CHAPTER SEVEN

Of Pizza And Old Friends

Kinsley ran in the opposite direction through town, thereby squashing any chance of conversation with her ever-present neighbor. Drenched in sweat by the time she reached home, she stood in the shower and considered all that Lincoln had said. He doubted that a stranger had committed the murder, which meant that whoever killed Grandpa might have already been in contact with her since she'd arrived.

With the Harlow police force consisting of Lincoln, Butch Pate, and one city officer—Danny something-or-another—Kinsley decided that she should do some digging herself.

She made coffee, went into the dining room, and sat in front of her softly humming laptops. The world of programming made much more sense to her than the real world ever had, and work offered a welcome relief to the drama she'd been navigating during the past few days.

Time passed quickly as she lost herself in the ones and zeros of her coding bubble. The project was nearing completion when the doorbell disturbed her. Grumbling under her breath, she answered the summons.

The boyish effervescence that bubbled from the man who stood on her porch pulled her into his happy world. "Hi, Kins."

"Hey, Dusty." Kinsley pushed the screen door open wider to let him in. "What a lovely surprise."

"I came to take you to lunch. Let's get a pizza, like the old days." He was nearly vibrating off the stoop with excitement. "I called Gabby."

"Give me fifteen minutes to slap on a little war paint and change clothes. Do you want me to meet you there?"

"No, I'll wait for you." He scanned the house as he entered. "Looks just like it did when we were in school."

She took a quick look around. Dusty was right: the place needed a major overhaul.

"Be right back." Kinsley hurried to her bedroom. She dabbed on some makeup and slipped into her 'hundred-dollar jeans' before rejoining her guest. "Okay, my friend, let's do this."

A rush of memories overtook her as she saw his car parked at the curb. "I can't believe this vehicle is still alive—we certainly put it through its paces," Kinsley said as she advanced on the warhorse of a Toyota.

"Yeah, I've been saving for a new ride, but I can't decide what to get and this just keeps going." Dusty shrugged. "A while back, I found one of your ponytail holders stuck down in the seat."

Happiness seeped in as Kinsley thought of the good times they'd had in Dusty's beat-up car. "How did you know it was mine?"

"It's not like I have an endless stream of girls. You wore ponytails with those pompom holders you made yourself. Gabby always has hers in the bun thingy." He waved his spindly hands over the top of his head, drawing a snicker from Kinsley.

Five minutes later, Dusty's beater rattled into an empty parking lot at the restaurant and coughed once before it died.

The owner, Mr. Sassetti, had opened Mario's years ago when he was new to the area. It didn't offer the typical southwest Kansas fare of meat and potatoes, and it wasn't a chain pizza place. Kinsley was never certain if the town's upper echelon boycotted it because of Mario's New York-style pizza or his olive complexion, but the kids in town loved his food so the rich and righteous were never successful in driving him away.

Kinsley's grandpa had been friends with Mario and Lily Sassetti. The couple never failed to bring the most delicious dishes to parties, and the effusive Italian would entertain Kinsley with stories of his magical homeland: "Italy is-a heaven on earth-a, *Principessa.*"

"What are you smiling about, Kins?" Dusty asked.

"Just remembering the time we spent here." They stepped through the door and straight into the past. The red-and-white checkered tablecloths were still adorned with kitschy, jute-wrapped wine bottles that served as candle holders. Closing her eyes, Kinsley inhaled deeply. The scents of parmesan and simmering tomato sauce made her mouth water.

"*Principessa!*" Mario rushed out of the back and hugged her lightly before holding her away from him. "I'm-a so sorry about your papa, Kinsley. We will all miss him so-a much."

"Thank you, Mario." Kinsley didn't want to put a damper on their reunion so she asked, "How have you been? Where is your lovely wife?"

"We are-a good. Lily is-a at home. You must-a come to see us while you are here."

"I will do that. I would love to catch up."

Mario hugged her again before he waddled back into the kitchen, and Kinsley joined her friends. As she approached the table, Gabby stood and let out a high-pitched squeal. "Kins!"

"Gabby, it's been too long, girl." The women engaged in an awkward embrace. "How have you been?"

"As good as can be expected, considering I live in Harlow," Gabby giggled.

They all sat and Kinsley considered her friend. From the black-rimmed glasses that rested on her perfect Greek nose to the severe bun perched at the crown of her head, resembling a tidy bird's nest, nothing about the slender blonde had changed.

They had been the 'three amigos' in school. When Kinsley had run from town, she'd left them behind because it had proved impossible for her to look at Gabby and Dusty without seeing that one dreadful night reflected in their eyes.

"Gosh, Kins. I've missed you," her friend whispered as her tears started to flow.

"I've missed you too." Kinsley held out a napkin and smiled as Gabby dabbed her wet cheeks. "What have you been up to?"

"I work for the county appraiser's office. I also fill in for the treasurer part-time. Nothing exciting. How's things for you?"

"The company I started has done well. I love living in Kansas City."

"I'm sorry about your grandpa." Gabby pushed the ice around in her glass with a plastic straw. "He was a nice man."

Dusty added his condolences to the mix.

"Thanks, you guys. He was the best."

They ordered pizza and chatted happily in the empty restaurant. When the food was gone, Kinsley cleared her throat. "Hey, I'm sorry I haven't been a better friend." She peeked up at them before continuing. "After that night … at the party. Well, I shut down."

Gabby shook her head. "Kins, I'm so sorry they hurt you. I know I told you back then…" Their eyes met. "What they did took you away from all of us. Is there anything I can do to help you?"

Kinsley took her hand and silently wished she could move past what had happened to her. Right now, though, she had to snap out of her dark musings for the sake of her friends. "Thanks, you two. They didn't win. Here I am, still alive."

As Dusty dropped her at home, Kinsley felt a little lightness creep in at coming back together with these people who had been her whole world for most of her young life. Before they'd parted ways, they'd made plans to get together over the weekend to watch a movie.

Buoyed by lunch, Kinsley's fingers flew across the keyboard as she put the finishing touches to the program she'd been working on for months. The doorbell rang as she clicked send on the email invoicing the client.

Certain of who was outside the door, she headed toward it. Her mind filled with thoughts that both troubled and thrilled her; like it or not, Kinsley was anxious to see what the sheriff would say next. As she opened the door, her grip on the knob tightened when, instead of Lincoln, she was confronted with Rich Skelly's viperous sneer.

"I wanted to pay my respects for Henry." Rich had an oily charm to match his slicked-back, dirty-blond hair. A salesman's smile lay on his lips, but the goods he offered were rotten.

"Thanks, Rich." She shifted her weight from foot to foot as she waited for him to leave.

"Are you going to invite me in?" There was a tinge of annoyance in Skelly's tone.

"Nope. Thanks for coming by. See ya." Kinsley shut the door and put her back against it. Why in the hell would Rich Skelly, of all people, want to pay his respects for Grandpa? They'd hated each other, and Rich had never been a friend of hers—quite the opposite.

Rich was seven years older than Kinsley, but his ghastly girlfriend, Chelsey Riley, was her age. That woman's well of cruelty was deep, and the bulk of it had landed on Kinsley from kindergarten right up to the final horror they'd visited on her during their last day of senior year.

During their graduation ceremony, the whole town had stared at the big screen in shocked silence as the appalling nude photographs, taken less than a month earlier on the night Billy and Brian had hurt her, were put on display. Chelsey, Rich, and their friends had howled when Kinsley fled from the venue.

The police had looked into the incident but there was never any evidence as to who had replaced the childhood photos that were meant to be shown that night. Kinsley had told the authorities the names of those involved, but no one had listened to her. This town had always been run by the powerful, and 'Justice Be Damned' was their credo.

Rich Skelly was a bully, and she couldn't imagine that he had changed.

Kinsley returned to the dining room and flipped open a legal pad to a clean sheet to start a list of murder suspects. Harlow wasn't big enough to keep a killer hidden for long. Someone would make a mistake sooner or later.

CHAPTER EIGHT

A Bird In The Hand

Four a.m. found the sheriff on his porch. He'd stayed away from Kinsley for a few days because his thoughts relating to her ventured down a road that shouldn't be traveled. Lincoln took a sip of his coffee and let his mind wander over her long legs, imagining how his hands would fit around her waist.

The opening of the squeaky screen door at Henry's house ended his fantasy. As Lincoln peered through the semi-darkness, he noted that Kinsley wasn't in her usual running attire. Her light gray sweats engulfed her petite frame. Not aware she was being observed, she meandered across the street, coffee cup in hand, and wove in among the playground equipment at the back of the church, touching each piece. Her slumped shoulders and drooping head were not her usual no-nonsense way of carrying herself.

When she sat on a swing, he couldn't contain his curiosity about her out-of-character behavior.

Kinsley was humming a sad song as Lincoln approached her. Not wanting to frighten her, he came around in front of the swing set. Her eyes met his and the humming stopped, but he saw a flicker of something tender before the wall came up to shut him out. "Are you stalking me, sir?" There was a gentleness to her tone that had not been there before.

"I came to see if ya needed a push?"

A laugh popped out before she could stop it. "No, I don't need a push."

"Come on, let me push you," Lincoln urged playfully. His hand brushed her back as he crossed behind her and grasped the chains that held the swing.

Kinsley jumped out of the seat. "Don't ever touch me again!" Her shrill tone fractured the calm. She broke into a run toward Henry's and slammed the solid door shut behind her, the sound resonating off the surrounding houses.

Lincoln was shaken by her unexpected outburst; his touch had not been intentional. After this second display of fear, he was certain of one thing: Kinsley had lived through some type of trauma.

When he stepped up on Henry's porch, the boards creaked, giving away his presence.

"Go away, please." Her words drifted from behind the closed door.

"Kinsley, I'm sorry. I didn't mean to touch you. I brought your coffee cup. I'll leave it here." He placed the cup beside the door then beat a hasty retreat to his own house, his nerves a-jangle.

As he flipped on the shower and paced the floor while the water warmed, he wondered if the person who'd hurt her could be after her now. Once inside the shower, he placed his palms against the tiled wall and relaxed into the hot water. Pieces of the Kinsley puzzle were starting to click into place. Maybe she was keeping everyone—including him—at a distance as a means of self-preservation. Lincoln could relate to that because he'd been doing the same thing. The horrors his ex-wife had put him through made him leery of getting too close to anyone.

As he dressed, he thought about the additional case that had just landed in his lap. He needed more information about what had happened to Kinsley if he was going to help her.

He placed the usual call to Charlene for her breakfast order as he started his pickup. Before he had the chance to speak, she asked, "Hey, Linc. Pearl's today?"

"Okay," he grumbled. "What can I get ya?"

"Biscuits and gravy, please. Thanks."

Lincoln had to park a block away because Pearl's was packed. He ducked in through the back door and stood by the order window until Jean, the cook, looked up from the griddle. "Hey, Sheriff. What can I do for ya?"

Lincoln ordered then poured himself some coffee, doing his best not to glance in Sheila's direction. He was on a mission: to get the food and leave before she waylaid him. Less than two minutes had passed when, out of the corner of his eye, he caught a blonde streak hurtling toward him like a torpedo.

"Lincoln James, are you avoiding me?" Sheila purred.

He searched for a quick-witted rejoinder and couldn't find one. Better to stick to simple. "No, ma'am. Just gettin' breakfast, then I'm headed out. Full day."

Sheila swatted at him with an order pad. "I haven't seen you in a few days. Where have you been?" She moved closer, resting the curve of her hip against his thigh.

It would be impossible to come up with something

that would shoo her away without making her mad; pissing off women seemed to be his superpower lately. In the end, he closed his mouth and said nothing. It was his best play.

Jean smacked the bell on the counter with the spatula, making both Lincoln and his stalker jump. "Order up, Sheila. Quit messin' around with the sheriff an' get to work."

Lincoln breathed out as the waitress scampered away, then he caught the laughter in the cook's eyes. "Saved by the bell, eh, Sheriff? Here, take Charlene her breakfast."

"Thanks, Jean … for everything."

As he returned to his pickup, Lincoln gnawed on the possibility that he'd have to tell Sheila outright that they weren't happening. That was going to stir up a whole lot of trouble he'd like to avoid. He had let her flirt and, although it was never returned with much interest, he hadn't discouraged it. That was on him.

Minutes later, he stopped in front of Charlene's desk and presented the Styrofoam container. "Here ya go. I hope those are damn good biscuits and gravy. 'Bout got me into trouble."

Charlene couldn't hold in her laughter. "What happened, Linc? Sheila all over you? It's what you get for not giving her a little taste of sheriff every day."

"No. That's… Just no."

Charlene arched her perfectly drawn eyebrow. "Have your eye on a dark-haired beauty instead?"

His thoughts about Kinsley must not be as well-hidden as he'd hoped. "Damn, but you all are a bunch of cluckin' hens." The events in the park that morning still nagged at him. "Where would the files be from, say, eight years ago?"

"Anything that old would be in the basement. Why?"

"I need to do a little research. I'll be downstairs." Lincoln walked through the office, turned on the light at the top of the stairs, and descended into the dimly lit room that used to house the jail cells.

As he looked through the rows of boxes, he reflected on his conversations with Henry. From what the old man had said, Kinsley hadn't done much of anything but work since she'd moved away. It had worried Henry because having no life outside of a job was odd for someone as young as his granddaughter.

The dankness of the cellar assaulted his senses as he looked at the ends of the boxes until the years he was searching for came into view. The sheriff placed a box on a rickety card table and flipped open the lid, dust hit him in the face and stole his breath. Once the dirt settled, his fingers quickly stair-stepped through the files and abruptly paused on a tab with Kinsley's name. He removed the water-stained file and let his eyes roam over a hand-scrawled label.

A sliver of dread snaked its way through his guts as he opened the folder. Inside was a single note on a yellowed piece of paper. Lincoln raised the sheet closer to the bare bulb at the center of the room. The report outlined a sketchy complaint that stated Kinsley had been roughed up at a party. Underage drinking. No officer's name was attached to the report, and there was no indication of who had 'roughed her up.'

He let his hand drop to hang by his side. Something

had happened, but being pushed around at a party didn't seem to fit the way she acted. There had to be more to the story, or this incident was not what had driven her to hide away from the world.

***

Kinsley sat with her back against the door and her knees pulled up under her chin as her heart beat a staccato rhythm. What had happened this morning was a ridiculous reaction to the sheriff touching her back, but the fight or flight response was deeply ingrained. Years of keeping the painful truth locked away had poisoned her soul.

When she heard Lincoln's pickup rumble to life, Kinsley moved to the dining-room windows and watched him back slowly out of his driveway. He must be wondering what had happened, and she didn't want him to think he had done something wrong. A note would have to do for now.

After writing the only thing that came to mind, Kinsley ran over to Lincoln's house and stuck the message to his door. Because her social life had been a ridiculous calamity for so long, she didn't know what was normal anymore.

It bothered her that he hadn't come round for the past few days. Had he heard something in town that had turned him away from her? Since his visits had stopped, a newfound loneliness had crept in. She feared her reaction that morning might cement his absence.

Frustrated, Kinsley raked her fingers through her hair. It wasn't easy to admit that she liked being around

Lincoln, but there was a long, broken road between her and the outside world that she wasn't sure she could walk for anyone—not even him.

Dwelling on what had happened eight years ago wouldn't do any good. Instead, she turned to the mind-numbing task of sorting out Grandpa's paperwork. Hours later, most of the documents lay in categories.

A manila folder with her name written in Grandpa's distinctive handwriting had haunted her peripheral vision all morning. It was time to cowgirl up and see what was inside.

Kinsley dumped the contents onto the table and watched as pictures of her, along with school achievements, slid across the tabletop. Gathering the papers into a messy pile, she began to read through the letters she'd written to her grandfather over the years, along with the birthday cards she'd made because they couldn't afford to buy them. He'd kept the lot.

Memories played like a home-movie reel as Kinsley sank into the past. Summertime had been hands-down the best time of the year because she would go to the farm with Grandpa every day. Kinsley loved riding on the tractor. The old man would stop when he'd spy a killdeer nest in the field and move it out of harm's way. They would squat together to look at the blue, speckled eggs while he cautioned her, "Baby girl, don't touch 'em. The mama won't take care of 'em if ya do."

After work each evening, they'd pick a prime piece of real estate at the edge of the stocked tail-water pit and fish until dark. With lively eyes, Grandpa would recount stories of his childhood, his descriptions so colorful that

Kinsley felt as if she'd been there.

A closed envelope lay at the bottom of the pile. Kinsley removed the carefully folded paper. As she read, unshed tears almost blinded her.

Baby girl,

I'm no spring chicken, and I worry about you. Don't forget Leon loves you, too. You ain't alone. If you ever need help, trust Linc. The sheriff's a real good man. You're the light in my life.

Kinsley pressed the words to her breast and held tightly to her grandfather's memory.

As her grief eased, she began to analyze the note's meaning. Did Grandpa think something was going to happen to him? He knew she would never trust a stranger, and she assumed that was why he had included Lincoln in the message. No matter what it took, finding out who murdered her grandfather was paramount. If she had been killed, her grandfather wouldn't have stopped until he found those responsible and made them pay.

The rest of the morning and early afternoon sped by as Kinsley searched the piles of papers for any clue into the murder. She sat back and raised her eyes to the large painting on the wall depicting cowboys expertly rounding up cattle, and her thoughts returned to the sheriff. His police skills would allow him to see what she might miss, but how could she ask him to come over after what had happened between them? Should she invite him for dinner and suggest that they work together? Kinsley shook her head. The effort it took to let people in made her realize just how screwed up she was.

Even though patience was not her strong suit, she

resolved to wait in the hope that Lincoln would show up again.

***

Lincoln had spent the better part of his day helping Jackson Birney round up his damn wayward herd, and his cell phone had been a constant buzz in his pocket since he'd rolled out of bed. Between calls, he'd questioned farmers who owned land around Henry's place as well as people who lived near him in town. Not one of them had seen anything that could be considered suspicious.

Finally, his desire for a shower and something to eat spurred him home. As he made his way toward his house, he rolled over the details of the murder again. Rhodes had been severely beaten then strangled, and the crime had been more violent than most. There wasn't a speck of damage to the doors or windows, and it was unlikely someone had broken in since Henry wasn't known to lock his doors. Nothing was destroyed in the house, which led Lincoln to believe that Henry had had no time to fight back.

Although he was in his early sixties, Henry had been a robust man, six foot four and two hundred and seventy pounds. For the most part his work was manual labor, which kept him fit. Without the element of surprise, taking Henry down would have required some serious effort. An unexpected attack by someone he knew was far more believable.

Lincoln thought back about the timeline. The night before that tragic morning, he'd been in Ulysses helping the police chief question a suspect. When he'd returned home around midnight, Henry's house had been dark, but Rhodes was an early to bed and early to rise kind of man, so that was not unusual.

The following morning, Lincoln had sat on his porch waiting for his neighbor to fire up his old pickup and give his one-finger wave as he backed out of the driveway. That man could drive slower than anyone on earth. When there was no movement next door by sunrise, Lincoln went back into his house, dressed for the day, and crossed the lawn to check on Henry.

He'd knocked, waited, knocked again—no answer. The memory of how his heart had hammered as he'd moved to the back door and rapped on the glass was still intense. Then his professional instincts had kicked in and he'd called dispatch.

Charlene had answered on the first ring. "Hey, Linc. Bring me a cinnamon roll, please."

"I'm not at Pearl's. Henry Rhodes didn't leave for the farm this mornin'. I've tried both doors with no response. I'm goin' in to do a welfare check."

"Should I send the city unit?" she'd asked, sensing the gravity of the situation.

"Yes." Lincoln hung up and slipped on the latex gloves he kept in the holder on his belt. As he carefully turned the knob and swung it open, the door issued an ominous growl. He'd called Henry's name before entering, but there was no reply.

Lincoln had never been inside the house before, and he wasn't prepared for the unkempt state of the space as he eased his way through the entry into the living room. The morning sun filtered through filmy curtains and lit the room with an eerie glow. He called out again.

The familiar rumble of the city unit alerted him to his backup's arrival moments before Danny Singleton jogged up on the porch and stepped just inside the door behind him. "What's up, Sheriff?"

"Henry didn't come out this mornin'," Lincoln stated. "I have a bad feelin' about this."

The two men picked their way around piles of paper that covered every available surface. Lincoln swung open a louvered café door, and they entered an adjoining room. As they rounded the corner, Lincoln spotted Henry lying halfway between the kitchen and the connecting hallway.

"Call an ambulance, Danny!" he snapped as he dropped to his knees beside his friend. Though Henry was as cold as a stone, he checked for signs of life, hoping against hope that there would be some flicker left. Then he leaned back on his heels and wrestled with the pain of seeing his comrade's battered face.

Lincoln had been in law enforcement for more than a decade and, before that, the military. He'd seen plenty of death in his time. Even so, it hadn't prepared him for the way he felt.

He gathered himself. He had a job to do—mourning would have to wait. Although the scene was fixed in his mind, Lincoln gave Danny orders to take pictures of everything. A trail of blood had outlined Henry's progress around the island toward the hall. The city officer, still new to law enforcement, had gone pale and his eyes were as big as saucers.

"This is a crime scene, Danny. Be careful not to touch anything," Lincoln instructed.

Danny nodded, but Lincoln could see that he couldn't handle what they had stumbled into, so he sent him out front to wait for the rest of the crew to arrive.

The officers collected anything they believed could be evidence. The disorganized state of the house made it impossible to tell if anything had been stolen, but the fact that Henry's billfold lay on the kitchen counter with cash inside was a good indication that robbery wasn't the motive.

However, nothing went unnoticed in this town. Lincoln was confident someone had seen something, but no one was fessing up so far.

***

As he guided his pickup into the driveway at his house, Lincoln's mind wandered to Kinsley. Should he go over, maybe ask her out to dinner? The idea gained a little steam before reality squashed it. She probably wouldn't go, he decided as he killed the engine. What had happened that morning bothered him deeply.

As he stepped onto his porch and scanned Henry's property, something fluttered at the edge of his vision, prompting him to turn his attention toward the screen door. He removed a small note from the glass:

Lincoln—

Thank you for the apology. I'm sorry I freaked out. Please don't think I'm a psycho.

—City

A grin broke across his face. Kinsley had called herself City, even though she had insisted that she hated the nickname.

CHAPTER NINE

The Truce

The doorbell sounded, shattering the silence and startling Kinsley. She admonished herself for being so edgy as she hastened to the door. At the sight of Lincoln on her porch, the stress was instantly replaced with relief. "Coming by for dinner?" she teased. With a flourish of her hand, she invited him into the house.

Lincoln removed his boots and left them on the porch. "Thanks, don't mind if I do." He followed her into the living room.

She eyed his stocking feet. "Getting comfortable, Sheriff?"

"My boots are covered in cow shit."

"Very mannerly of you not to track shit through my home. Thank you." She couldn't hide her amusement. "Please, have a seat. I'll be right back. I'm going to turn on the oven."

As she moved around the kitchen, Kinsley replayed the conversation she had planned. She hoped he'd be amenable to her proposal.

When she returned to the living room with a beer, Lincoln accepted it with a sincere thank you. "What have you been up to today?" he asked.

"Your little birds aren't very effective." Kinsley's response was only half sarcastic. She still disliked that people gossiped about her.

"It seems you never leave your house."

His statement brought home how trapped she had allowed herself to become. Kinsley nodded before answering. "It's best I don't." She stole a quick look at him. "Hey, I wondered—" The preheat timer went off, cutting in on her rehearsed speech. "Just a sec."

Placing the enchiladas in the oven, she took a meditative breath and grabbed a beer for herself before returning to the living room. Lincoln raised his eyes as she entered. "What did you wonder?"

Kinsley sat, took a deep breath, and began. "I went over paperwork looking for anything that could help your investigation. I don't know what I'm looking for, but nothing jumped out at me." She hesitated before continuing. "I wondered if we could maybe call a truce and work together? I need to find Grandpa's killer. Grandpa gave up his whole life to raise me, and I have to help him now. I can't do that without you."

Sincerity softened Lincoln's features. "No truce needs to be called. I don't harbor any animosity toward you, and I'm sorry we got off on the wrong foot. I want to find the person who did this to Henry, too."

Kinsley feared her poor social skills would put this alliance on shaky ground. "I'm not good with people. I'll try not to antagonize you, but no guarantees that my … ah … *strong* personality won't slip out. It's what I know."

Lincoln cast her a playful look as he offered his own proviso. "And I'll try not to be a macho good ol' boy. But, as you said, no promises."

"I have one request—" Kinsley's nerves were about to

get the better of her.

"Okay, shoot."

She wished the next sentence didn't have to be uttered. "I'm not great with being touched, as you have witnessed."

"Got ya." He gave a slight nod. "I'll do my best not to touch you unexpectedly."

The breath she'd been holding left her in a rush. "Thank you." Then she realized what he'd said: what did he mean by *unexpectedly*?

"You're welcome." Lincoln picked at the label on his beer bottle. "I wouldn't hurt you." His deep-blue gaze held hers for a moment before she looked away.

Kinsley measured his words carefully but her trust wasn't easily won. In an attempt to escape the subject, she jumped up and moved into the dining room. "I put a lot of the paperwork in order." She placed a cardboard box on the table and motioned for him to look inside.

Lincoln joined her. "Impressive. This should make things easier." He bent over the files to get a closer peek just as the buzzer on the stove went off.

"I'll go get dinner," Kinsley said.

"I'll help," he offered, following her into the kitchen.

Kinsley removed the pan from the oven and stepped away to gather plates and flatware. Lincoln donned oven mitts, raised the dish, and inhaled deeply. "Mmm, Gurtey's enchiladas."

Her laughter trickled out unfettered as they moved back into the dining room. "You are amazing with that nose of yours."

"It only works with food." Lincoln placed the dish on

the ceramic hot pad and took his usual seat at the head of the table.

Kinsley watched him for a moment. "How many do you want?" she asked as she held a serving spoon over the casserole.

"Three should be a good start," he said with a wink.

Kinsley chuckled. "Careful, Sheriff, you'll pop the button on those jeans."

Lincoln rubbed his hand over his flat stomach. "Hasn't happened yet."

As she watched him rub his belly, a tingling ache spread through her. Kinsley busied herself with dishing up food and tried to ignore it. "Okay, but you might have to start running with me if you keep this up."

He sat back and gave her a never-in-a-million-years smile. "You're like lightnin'. Tryin' to keep up with you would kill me."

Amused, she shook her head and sat next to him.

The first bite of the flour-wrapped bit of heaven had her lost in food paradise, and her ringing cell phone was an unwelcome interruption. Glancing at the caller ID, she looked at Lincoln apologetically. "I have to take this. It's work." She withdrew to the bedroom to talk to the aggrieved new clients who were concerned that their project wouldn't be completed on time. Kinsley was well aware that they were wholly dependent on her program to get the next phase of their company rolled out and did her best to ease their fears.

Once she'd calmed them down and concluded the conversation to their satisfaction, a proud moment came over her, followed by a crushing depression. This was one of the most significant accounts she had landed, and the person she most wanted to share her good news with had been stolen away. Now there was simply no one to tell.

Kinsley composed herself and returned to the dining room. Lincoln was finishing what she suspected was a second helping. "Sorry, new clients. I had to talk them off the ledge."

"What kind of work do you do?" he asked.

She remained silent as she sat and took another draw from her beer.

"I promise, I won't tell a single person," Lincoln assured her.

Kinsley considered how much to share. Grandpa's letter had stated that Lincoln was trustworthy, but she couldn't be sure. In the end suspicion won out and she gave a minimal response. "It's specialized computer work. I'm a consultant."

He seemed satisfied with her answer as he continued to eat. She sat back and watched him. "How long have you been in Harlow?" she asked.

Lincoln settled in his chair. "I came to town seven years ago, when I took a deputy job. The sheriff position opened up a few months later. I ran unopposed and won—it seems no one wanted the job but silly ol' me." His smile spoke volumes about his love for his job. "Been here ever since."

"Where are you from originally?"

"Tulsa, Oklahoma, but I've lived in a lot of places between there and here."

Exhausted by the effort of this interaction, Kinsley smiled weakly.

"Why did you pick Kansas City instead of stayin' here?" he leaned in with interest. "Seems like you can work from anywhere."

Kinsley's answer was abrupt. "It's far from Harlow."

Lincoln allowed her words to sink in. "Why do you hate it here? What happened?"

Kinsley fidgeted with the silverware as she considered her response. Revealing her real reason for leaving was not on the agenda tonight or any night. "Square peg, round hole," she muttered.

"Sheila said you were shy in high school. Maybe people don't know you well enough."

Kinsley's anger flared and took him by surprise. "Sheila was part of the problem. She was a horrid, mean girl who did nothing but make fun of me. That bitch can go fly a kite!"

Lincoln leaned back in his chair, both eyebrows raised. "Whoa there, baby girl."

Mist clouded Kinsley's vision as she whispered, "What did you call me?"

"Baby girl?" His eyes never left her as she struggled to control the unexpected blast of sentiment.

"That's what Grandpa used to call me," she murmured, blinking away tears.

"Kinsley, I didn't mean to upset you. May I touch your hand?" She nodded almost indiscernibly, and he laid his hand on hers. After a short time, he drew back. "Are you all right?"

Kinsley folded her hands in her lap. The brief contact hadn't been as unpleasant as she'd expected. "I'm fine. It's just strange to feel another person's touch."

"You don't let people touch you? Ever?"

"I keep my physical interaction brief." Kinsley immediately wished she could take back her words. Panic set in as she thought about how this information spilling out in Harlow would cause havoc. "Please don't tell anyone. They already think I'm a freak."

"Your secret is safe with me. Why don't you let anyone touch you?"

"I don't want to talk about it," she said.

Lincoln went silent as he realized he'd stumbled into forbidden territory. He helped her stack plates and then followed her into the kitchen carrying the remains of the enchiladas.

"I'm having a shot of whiskey. Do you want one?" she asked, suddenly feeling the need for liquid courage.

"Sure."

She heard the unspoken question in his voice. As she turned to the cupboard for glasses, Kinsley wondered what it would take to be a normal human being. She didn't want to be a half-alive person anymore.

"I'm sorry if I've said or done somethin' that made you need to drink," Lincoln said.

"No, it's… It's hard for me. I am trying."

"We're fine. You don't have to turn it around in one night. How do you run your own business if you feel this way?"

"It's mostly remote work. Telephone, email, video conference. Not some big, manly-smelling cowboy, irritating the crap outta me in person." The fragrance of bergamot, with a touch of patchouli, scented the space between them. If wonderful were an aroma, Kinsley mused, it would be the essence of Lincoln James.

His warm laugh eased the tension. "Interestin' description of me."

Kinsley noticed how his blue eyes stood out against his tan skin. Hair the color of dark chocolate touched the collar of his shirt. Then she blanched with the realization that she was staring at him like some lovesick teenager. "How about another beer instead of whiskey?"

"Sounds good," he replied, retrieving two cold bottles from the refrigerator.

They returned to the dining room and started looking through files. Lincoln worked through the container that she had put on the table earlier. Kinsley dragged another box over, placed it across from him, and sat down. "What am I looking for if it's not an obvious threat?" she asked.

He considered her question. "You knew Henry better than anyone. If somethin' seems outta place, we should look at it."

Kinsley reached for the letter from Grandpa that she'd found earlier and pushed it toward him. Lincoln studied the three lines before meeting her gaze. He gave her a slight nod, set the letter to one side, and they went to work.

The first file she pulled out contained seed and fertilizer bills, and it struck her how expensive it was to farm. Still, there didn't seem to be anything unusual. She pulled another. "Do you like music or quiet?" *Please like music,* she implored wordlessly.

"I could take some music." Lincoln hooked his elbow over the back of the chair and watched her.

Kinsley stepped to the 1950s' console stereo. "We'll

channel a little Grandpa tonight. Vintage stuff." She slipped an album from its sleeve and blew the dust away, slid it over the spindle, then placed the needle lightly on the shiny black surface.

"No one has a turntable anymore. I like the crackly sound of vinyl," he remarked.

"Yeah, me too. Grandpa would listen to these for hours. Of course, I didn't appreciate the music when I was a nutty teen. I do now."

They turned back to the task at hand. Kinsley pulled a file that had given her pause earlier. "I thought this was a little odd. It's an unsolicited offer to buy the land, and the attorney is local." She laid it on the table. "Anyone who owns land out here constantly receives offers for the mineral rights, but this is for the land *and* minerals. It doesn't mention who wants to buy it."

Lincoln took a closer look at the file. "It could be a lead. We'll keep it on the list of things to look into."

While he studied some paperwork, Kinsley surreptitiously explored his profile. "Do you have a girl—?" The words escaped before she could stop them.

His eyes roamed over her face. "Not in a long time." Unable to hide a smirk, he returned to his task. "Too much damn trouble."

Kinsley scoffed at his remark as she got up to flip over the record. "Do you have to work tomorrow?"

"I won't go into the station unless there is an emergency. As sheriff, I'm always on call."

"I'm going to have another beer. Do you want one?" she asked.

Lincoln put his hands behind his head. "You're

about—what, a buck five soakin' wet?"

With his arms up like that, his shirt stretched across his chest… Kinsley concentrated on his face so that she didn't embarrass herself. "Maybe."

He scanned the empty beer bottles lined up on the table and cocked an eyebrow. "How are you not passed out by now?"

Kinsley thumbed the side of her nose, gangster style. "Tougher than I look. Is that a yes or no, cowboy?"

"Okay, since you're twistin' my arm."

Kinsley rolled her eyes. "Oh shit, now it's going to be all over town that I'm getting the sheriff drunk and taking advantage of him."

Lincoln laughed. "Can I use your facilities?"

She pointed toward the hallway. "Be my guest."

"Thanks." He continued to chuckle as he left the room.

The song playing on the stereo inspired Kinsley to sing along. When Lincoln returned, he joined in at the top of his lungs—way off-key. She couldn't help but be entertained by his clowning. "A singing sheriff?"

Lincoln waved his hands over his torso. "So many layers here, City."

"I have no doubt," she said. He danced around the table with an invisible partner in tow. "You're crazy, Lincoln."

"Been a long time since I had a good buzz." He dipped his imaginary partner.

Kinsley watched him move. Part of her wanted more than anything to stand up and dance with him, but she quickly dismissed the thought and pulled out another file.

"So, is it safe to assume you don't have a boyfriend?" Lincoln asked as he joined her at the table.

Kinsley nodded, then added, with her usual dry humor. "Males like touching, from what I hear." She returned her focus to the file in front of her, reading through each of the attorney's bills carefully. None of them was itemized. "Here's something odd." She pushed the file toward him. "Grandpa never told me about a lawyer. I helped financially because the farm didn't make much money. Why would he need an attorney? We didn't keep secrets from each other."

Lincoln scanned the paperwork. "It could be nothin', but it is odd if Henry didn't tell you about this."

Kinsley thought about what had happened to her just before graduation. Was the lawyer somehow connected with that?

"Kinsley, what is it?" Lincoln watched her carefully.

"Nothing. Can we find out what Grandpa saw him for?"

He hesitated before moving the file to the follow-up area. "We'll look into it."

The next sleeve held bills for storing grain in the local elevator, which sparked thoughts about the crops that were still standing in the fields. "Do you want to go out to the farm with me tomorrow?" she asked.

He didn't skip a beat. "Sure."

Relief accompanied his acceptance. "What time could you go?"

"We could have breakfast then go after."

Breakfast with Lincoln at Pearl's sounded like the worst idea ever. "The tongues will be wagging."

He reached out to touch her arm, then abruptly pulled back his hand. "Yes, they will."

Kinsley caught his correction and appreciated his effort. "You don't need to get mixed up with me publicly. I can cook breakfast, then no one will know." She knew how this town talked. To have their county official involved with someone they thought of as rubbish would cause Lincoln nothing but trouble.

His tone was surprisingly sober. "I'm not afraid of 'em, Kinsley."

"I'm not the sort of person Harlownians would like their sheriff to be associated with," she explained.

Lincoln's eyes softened. "I don't give a rat's ass what anyone in this town thinks. If I want to eat with you, what's anyone gonna do about it?"

Kinsley suddenly had a vivid image of his hand on her cheek, and it nearly made her sigh. "I'm trying to protect you, you hard-headed man. If I remember correctly, the sheriff is an elected position."

Lincoln made a sound like a horse blubbering its lips in response to her statement. It caught her by surprise and she laughed. "Please, just come over here. It will be nicer."

"Fine," he finally relented. "Talk about hard-headed."

"You have no idea."

Lincoln cleared his throat before replying. "I have some idea." Finishing his beer, he leaned back in his chair. "I need to be gettin' home, little lady. Keepin' me up all night long and gettin' me drunk is gonna get me fired."

Kinsley couldn't wipe the smile off her face as they wandered to the door. Lincoln dropped his Stetson onto his head with a flourish, but it landed a bit askew. He settled it with his thumb and index finger on the brim and gave her a bow. "Thanks for tonight. It was nice."

A flush crept over her cheeks as she pictured one of those big movie-type kisses. "You're welcome. Thank you for not making fun of my crazy."

"Nothin' crazy about you." He started to say something else but stopped. Instead, he asked, "Eight tomorrow good?"

"Good."

Kinsley shut the door behind him. Lincoln wasn't the macho jerk he'd first appeared to be. Was his change in behavior merely a pretense to gain her cooperation? If playing along could help solve Grandpa's murder, then so be it.

As she thought about his easy-going manner, Kinsley concluded that Sheriff James needed to knock off that charming crap.

***

Lincoln stopped to remove his sullied boots before going into his house. Not touching Kinsley was going to be a constant battle, since holding her pretty face and kissing her was foremost on his mind at the moment. A statement to that fact had nearly rushed out just before he had left her house. With a struggle, he pulled his thoughts away.

The paperwork had yielded some interesting leads. It was the second time Henry's property had come up during the investigation. Hopefully, the lawyer who represented someone interested in purchasing the land would have some helpful information.

Lincoln had had Butch ask around town about Lonnie Skelly. His deputy said the man had an alibi for the time of Henry's death: Lonnie was at the bar until closing on the night in question, and then he'd gone home with Teresa Lang. He hadn't left her house until the following day. Plenty of witnesses had eyes on Lonnie until at least 2 a.m.

Teresa had happily given a play-by-play of their activities after she and Lonnie had left the club, and even provided a time-stamped video as evidence. People never ceased to amaze him. His deputy could watch the video; that was one party the sheriff didn't want to attend. It wasn't looking like Lonnie was the doer of more than Teresa.

As Lincoln stripped and slid between the sheets, his thoughts returned to Kinsley. There were times when the unhappiness in her eyes broke his heart. He wished she would let him help with whatever haunted her, because when she smiled her eyes softened to the color of a heavy dawn fog and it twisted him in knots.

The alcohol buzz settled in, pushing Lincoln's thoughts toward her long legs wrapped around his. He expelled a heavy breath. It was highly doubtful that she would ever be that comfortable with him.

CHAPTER TEN

Love Is Made Of Moon Pies

"Do you know what we're looking for at the farm?" Kinsley asked as she flipped eggs in a pan.

Lincoln poured them both coffee and sat at the bar. "Ya know, I'm not exactly sure. I'll know when I see it."

That wasn't the answer she'd been expecting, but it piqued her interest. "Is this some police intuition thing?"

"Yep," he grinned.

Kinsley wondered if she should tell him about the incident. Guilt over keeping it from him was beginning to bother her, but so far Lincoln hadn't given any indication that he knew what had happened. She wanted that to continue.

"Kinsley, are you all right?"

In the throes of this dilemma, she could only nod.

"You can tell me anything. I promise I won't share it with anyone."

She laid the plates on the countertop. "I think I just need more coffee. Did you know my grandpa very well?"

"We were neighbors in a small town. We shared a beer on the porch pretty regularly. I helped him get that old pickup of his runnin' from time to time."

"Thank you." It eased the hurt to know that Grandpa had spent time with Lincoln. Imagining them together made her smile. They both thought they were charming and hilarious—'thought' being the operative word. Still, it might have been a hoot to watch them try to outdo one another.

"You're welcome," he said. "I enjoyed Henry's stories."

Her face lit up. "Grandpa could tell a good story, right?"

"Spinnin' yarns," they said at the same time, surprised by their synchronization.

"Did he ever make you ice cream?" Kinsley asked.

"The best homemade ice cream I've ever eaten."

"I miss him."

"I know you do. I'm sorry for your loss," Lincoln replied sincerely.

Kinsley studied this mystifying man seated in her kitchen.

"What is it?" he asked.

"Thanks for being nice to me, Lincoln."

A pained expression flitted across his face before he spoke, "You're welcome."

***

They loaded up in Lincoln's pickup and headed to the farm. Kinsley slid on her sunglasses and put an arm on the window frame as a warm gust of wind ruffled her ponytail. The sense that she was more relaxed around him pleased him to no end, but thanking him for being nice had almost shattered his resolve not to touch her. He wanted to hug her tight and make the broken pieces fit back together.

Lincoln turned on the radio for distraction, and Kinsley tapped her foot to the crooner's voice coming from the speakers. When he took a left off the blacktop onto the dirt road that led to Henry's farm, he noted a change in her. "What are you all smiles about?"

"Grandpa taught me to drive when I was eight. As soon as we turned off the main road, he would let me drive all the way to the farm." She hesitated, enjoying the memory. "I probably shouldn't be telling the law that, but what are you gonna do about it now, right?"

Lincoln grinned. "Are ya sayin' ya wanna drive my truck?"

Kinsley sniffed and shook her head. "You're a mess, Sheriff."

Lincoln slowed as they turned into the property and brought his pickup to a halt by the barn. As he opened the door and hopped out, Kinsley sat perfectly still, staring through the windshield. He leaned back into the pickup. "Somethin' I can help with?"

"I haven't been here in a long time. The best times of my life were spent at the farm with Grandpa." She got out and walked to the horse tank, dragging her fingers along its rough concrete edge. Her gaze moved across the fields as she raised a hand to shield her eyes. "Lot of activity out here. It looks like survey equipment to me." She indicated the line of machinery on the road to the south.

Lincoln turned to his pickup for a pair of binoculars and studied the goings-on in silence. Finally, he lowered the field glasses. "Did you find any correspondence about drillin' or test wells?"

She shook her head.

"Interestin'."

Kinsley produced a ring of keys and went to unlock

the barn. The enormous double doors swung wide, and Lincoln helped secure them with bungee cords. When they were fastened, she let him in on the plan. "I thought it might be a good idea to back that equipment up here and put the tractor in the barn."

Lincoln tapped the badge that hung on his belt. "I'm a cop, not a farmer."

"Thankfully, I used to be a bit of a farmer. I'll give you a ride." Kinsley hauled herself onto the corrugated metal platform to unlock the tractor door, bringing her magnificent rear to eye level, which stirred Lincoln's desire. "Come on," she urged, oblivious to the raunchy direction Lincoln's thoughts had taken.

Once he'd climbed in with her, she gave him the once over. "Probably a good thing you are a lawman and not a farmhand. You barely fit."

Kinsley took a deep breath and closed her eyes. A memory of cinematic clarity played through her mind. She was an eight-year-old girl, too small to see over the dashboard of the vehicle, but Grandpa would always find a way. That gentle man would tell her how much he needed her help as he brushed a calloused palm over her braided hair, then he'd position a thick Sears catalog on her seat and flump her squarely on top of it. "Baby girl, ya just let it idle straight down the row. I'll whoop when I need ya ta stop. Just slide on down and hit that middle pedal for me."

She'd been so excited to help. When they were done, he would sit on the dropped tailgate of the farm truck and hold her in his lap, "Kinsley, you're the best girl ever, do ya know that? Thank ya for helpin' me. I woulda never got it done without ya." Grandpa had always made her feel like she could tackle anything.

"What's on your mind?" The soft tone of Lincoln's voice disturbed her thoughts.

"It smells like I remember—diesel with a hint of Old Spice and pipe tobacco." Kinsley fired up the tractor. Looking back over her shoulder, she engaged the hydraulics and folded up the equipment. She pulled up on a lever and the plow lifted off the ground. Her eyes met Lincoln's. "So I'm city, huh?" she hollered over the roar of the engine.

With the tractor in gear, she turned it wide and skirted around the barn. When Kinsley had the plow in place, she opened the tractor door. "We have to unhook it. Come on, City."

He smiled at her turning the nickname around on him. They detached the gear and parked the John Deere inside. Kinsley's eyes sparkled as she looked up at Lincoln. "How was that?"

"It was pretty fantastic."

"I agree." She clapped her hands together one time for emphasis. "I'm really glad I didn't take out your manly Chevy. I wasn't convinced I was going to miss it."

Lincoln liked this version of Kinsley with the life in her eyes. He suspected this was who she would have been if something hadn't happened to her. Being at the farm revealed a whole other woman.

They walked together along the dirt road at the end of a stand of nearly ripe wheat that was waving gently in the hot southern wind. Lincoln studied her as she looked at the crops. In the bright sunlight, her hair reminded him of a raven's wing laying against her creamy skin.

"I need to get someone lined up to harvest this. I can't let it rot in the field," she said thoughtfully.

Henry's crops had been discussed at Pearl's by the other farmers. "The locals are ready to help you," Lincoln said.

Before she could respond, his phone rang. Lincoln retrieved it from his shirt pocket and answered. Charlene's tone was curter than usual. "Linc, can you go out to Gordon's? They're having some kind of domestic disturbance. It's not clear exactly what's going on."

"I can—" he glanced at his companion "—but I have a civilian with me."

"You do?" Charlene's curiosity peaked.

"I'm out at the Rhodes farm with Kinsley," Lincoln said reluctantly.

The tension eased as Charlene clucked her tongue. "Well, well, well."

Lincoln needed to shut her down; he didn't want this scuttlebutt all over town in record time. "We're checkin' out things as part of the investigation."

"Uh-huh. I saw the woman. I'll just bet you are checking out *things*. You dog."

Lincoln's voice took on a stern tone. "It's not like that. Don't go spreadin' that all over town, you understand me?"

"Okay, I won't. No need to get bent," Charlene huffed.

"I'll radio you." He ended the call. He was going to have to talk to Charlene about her gossiping. He noticed Kinsley's worried expression and tried to ease her anxiety.

"We have a call, Deputy Rhodes."

Kinsley looked at him cautiously. "I can go with you?"

Lincoln reassured her it was fine as long as she stayed in the pickup. They slid into his vehicle, and he removed the mic from the side of the radio to relay his status. "Ten-eight."

"Ten-four," Charlene responded.

"Hey, I heard what you said to Charlene about us being together. Thank you for that," Kinsley said.

Lincoln winked.

"What's the sitch, Cap'n?" She was beaming as she waited for his answer, and the look on her face nearly took his breath away. All the pain she usually carried had faded away.

"Domestic disturbance."

Lincoln pulled onto the dirt road. He glanced over at his passenger, and it felt like someone had hit him in the gut with a baseball bat. Kinsley Rhodes was quite possibly the most spectacular woman alive. The revelation was good, yet so very bad.

Ten minutes later, he brought his vehicle to a halt in the driveway of a farmstead. The evergreen trees that lined the perimeter of the yard had grown out of control, setting the stage for a paint-peeled, two-story house that was probably grand in its day but had fallen into disrepair. He radioed their location before addressing Kinsley. "You stay here. I don't know what's goin' on."

As he scanned the property, he pulled his gun belt out of the back seat. Tapping the black box bolted to the dashboard he said, "Radio if the shit hits the fan."

"Be careful," she whispered.

Lincoln issued a reassuring nod. "Always."

Kinsley sent out a silent plea: *Please don't let the shit hit the fan.* The sheriff wore the responsibility and danger of his job lightly, but the fact remained that he could be killed or hurt every time a call came in.

He rang the doorbell and announced himself. The door flung open, banging against the cladding as a man stumbled out, lurched forward and came to a weaving standstill in the grass just off the sidewalk that led to the house. Wasted drunk, he wore only dingy boxers and was swaying side to side like a sailor on a pitching ship.

A woman meandered through the door sporting a terry-cloth bathrobe that had seen better days. It seemed she was equally in her cups. It wasn't even noon, and both of these fools were three sheets to the wind.

The radio squawked, and Lincoln's voice came over, "Ten-twenty-four. Ten-seven."

Charlene responded, "Ten-four."

The couple waved and went back into the house as the sheriff returned to his vehicle and hopped in. Kinsley watched him intently, waiting to hear what was going on.

Lincoln cleared his throat and solemnly conveyed his findings. "All is well. The husband ate the last moon pie. It seems the wife wanted it."

Kinsley pursed her lips as she tried not to break up. "I can see how the police got called in. Serious shit, moon pies." Laughter burst out of them both at the ridiculous situation.

As he pulled out onto the dirt road Lincoln asked, "Would you go to lunch with me? I promise I won't let 'em get you."

The thought of a public appearance made her tense. "People won't like it, and you have to work here."

His voice softened. "You aren't the villain you've made yourself out to be. I don't think it will be as bad as you imagine."

Kinsley took a teasing swipe at his arm. "You doubt my villainy, Lincoln James? For shame." Then she sobered. "I'm no longer the shy, wilting flower I was back in the day," she warned him. "One mean comment, and someone gets knocked out."

Lincoln glanced over at her. "Don't make me arrest you, please."

"No promises."

"Give 'em a chance?" he requested.

Kinsley acquiesced. If she wanted a different life, she had to make different choices. Maybe it wouldn't be as bad as she'd anticipated. She struck up a new conversation. "What are the 'ten' things you say on the radio? I assume it's code or something so nosy people don't know everything?"

"It's a quick way to say what's happening, and yes, it's to keep folks out of our business a little. Since the internet, anyone can find out what the codes mean. But ten-eight means I'm in service, ten-seven means I'm out of service."

"What is ten-twenty-four?"

"The assignment is completed. I can give you a list if you want to study up. You're provin' to be a pretty fantastic deputy, Miss Rhodes," he teased.

She rolled her eyes but couldn't hide her smile.

***

Lincoln brought his pickup to a stop outside the diner and phoned Charlene. "We're at Pearl's for lunch. You want anything?"

"Sure, a BLT and fries. Thanks, Linc."

He ended the call and turned to Kinsley. "Are you ready?"

She looked warily at the building before climbing out of the pickup. Sheila had the hots for Lincoln, and she was about to see them lunching together; that would go down like a lead balloon. The sheriff hadn't thought this through.

The diner fell as silent as a graveyard when the door slammed shut behind them. Lincoln tensed but plastered on a smile and strode toward a table. Hostile eyes stabbed at them and the whispers began. As Lincoln was her only haven at that moment, Kinsley fixed her eyes on him in an attempt to shut out everything else.

A waitress stopped at their table, snapped her gum loudly, and said, "Hi, Kinsley."

Though she recognized the woman, Kinsley didn't let on, hoping that she would go away or, even better, burst into flames. The server continued, unaware as she'd always been. "Debbie ... Debbie Langley, remember? Hey, we probably shouldn't have done what we did to ya back in the day. That's history, right? No harm, no foul." Her inappropriate braying laugh proved her total lack of remorse.

That would have been the end of the matter had Debbie not added to her thinly veiled insult with a less-than-playful thump to her former target's shoulder.

Kinsley's hands slowly curled into fists. *Don't punch*

her. Don't punch her. The mantra echoed in her head as she willed herself to stay in her seat. Only Lincoln, sitting across from her, kept her from satisfying the impulse.

The torments she'd received from Debbie and her crew came to mind. They had locked Kinsley in a closet at school for an entire day; thankfully, her grandfather had come looking for her when she hadn't come home. Another time, they'd kidnapped and blindfolded her, bound her wrists, and forced her into the trunk of a car. Then they'd dumped Kinsley in the middle of nowhere, leaving her to make her way back to town in the dark. But worse than the physical assaults were the sickening lies they, and others, had spread about her.

As if on cue, Sheila stomped up to the table. She wasn't giggling today as she glared at Lincoln. "Her, then?"

Lincoln glanced at Kinsley, then at the new arrival. "Sheila, leave it."

The curvy blonde's face twisted into the mean girl from high school, and her narrowed eyes landed on Kinsley. "Looks like what they said about you in school was right on." Then she whispered, "Whore," under her breath.

With a smile that said she'd finally arrived at her golden moment, Kinsley let fly the words that she had waited years to deliver, "I win! How do ya like me now?" An exaggerated wink added fuel to an already raging fire.

Lincoln stood and held out his hand to her. "We'll eat someplace else," he snarled. He led her through the rapt audience of diners and out the door.

As she stepped into the bright sunshine, Kinsley felt a sense of victory but as she crawled into Lincoln's pickup her joy faded, replaced with the realization of what she'd just said. Sheila and Debbie had laid on the pressure, and the blister Harlow had rubbed raw finally burst.

"You're one cool customer, Kins," Lincoln said admiringly.

A dry chuckle rattled in her throat. "Not really."

"Yes, really. They deserved that and more."

"My comment wasn't exactly without malice," Kinsley confessed, embarrassed.

He grinned. "That was a pretty smooth response to their spiteful behavior. Seriously, I've never seen these people act like this." He put the truck in gear and pulled into the street. "I'm truly sorry. I can see that growin' up here was hard."

His soothing voice calmed her. "Thank you, Lincoln."

He pulled up in front of the local Tex-Mex place a block from the diner. "We better get Charlene fed, or there will be trouble."

Kinsley opened her door. "Well, let's get with it, Sheriff. If we fall down on the job, we'll be let go."

***

Charlene buzzed them in when they arrived at the office with lunch. Kinsley handed her the box. "Thank you, Ci— Kinsley."

"You're welcome. After this morning, I think your sheriff is more city than I am." She posed a fake thoughtful face before delivering her next line. "Maybe that should be *his* new nickname."

Kinsley's humor wasn't lost on Lincoln. "I don't think so," he replied.

Charlene piped up, "I heard you let Sheila and Debbie have it at the diner."

"I actually didn't let them have it. Lincoln wouldn't let me. Amazing how fast word gets out around here."

Lincoln was also astonished by the speed of gossip but proud of Kinsley's pluck. "Come on, fighter. We can eat in my office." He led her down the hall and opened the door, taking a quick look to make sure all the investigation information on his desk was covered.

She looked at him quizzically. "Making sure your girly mags are put away?"

"God, no." Lincoln couldn't hide his amusement. "Come on in."

Kinsley surveyed the room. "Very manly," she said. "I can feel the testosterone rushing into my pores."

"Why, thank you. I try." He pulled out a chair at the small conference table for her, which she shyly accepted.

Kinsley picked up a fried tortilla strip and waved it around in a circle. "Before the whole 'who ate the moon pie' sitch," she smiled, "I was hoping we could contact that survey company we saw working down the road. There could be something to them being close to Grandpa's land."

Lincoln considered what she'd said. "You probably shouldn't sell his land until we find out."

"I have no intention of selling. Grandpa loved that land, and it's all I have left of my family now." Kinsley paused. "After you told me about the murder, I made plans to stay as long as necessary. My business is virtual. I can work from Harlow." She pushed away the box with half the food left uneaten.

"Is that all you're eatin'?"

Kinsley raised an eyebrow. "You need to get over this food obsession."

He raised his hands in mock surrender. "I only wanted to know if I can have the rest."

"Careful, cowboy." She reached over and poked his abdomen. "Holy cats! Your stomach is as hard as a rock. Do you work out?"

"I'll never tell," he replied lightly.

He was leaning toward her food box as the intercom went off. "Linc, Ted Smith is having some trouble with those Butcher boys out at his place. Can you go?" Charlene cleared her throat as she waited.

He stood, crossed the space to his desk, and pressed the button on the intercom to answer. "Will do." Lincoln turned to Kinsley. "Sorry."

"It's okay. I want to visit the library next door. I appreciate you taking me to the farm." Kinsley stood. "I'm sure I'll see you again. I do still have food at my house."

"Takin' you to the farm was a pleasure. How will you get home?" Lincoln had hoped she would go with him; he wasn't ready for their time to end.

"Sheriff, I run all over this town every morning. I think I can manage to walk a few blocks home. Thanks for caring." As they walked into the front office, she said, "It was nice to see you, Charlene. Keep this guy in line, if you can."

Lincoln recognized the impish look that meant Charlene was plotting. "Oh, I'll keep him in line. Someone has to. Come see us again."

From the doorway, he watched Kinsley jog through the parking lot until she was out of sight. She had been someone entirely new today—the woman Henry had described to him.

Lincoln's relationship history was a series of catastrophes, and he wasn't about to hurt Kinsley; she'd been through enough in this town. His first priority would be to protect her. And he knew that, although she'd said she could run her business from Harlow, she would go back to Kansas City when the investigation was over.

"She's a lovely woman. Maybe you should do something about that smile Miss Rhodes put on your face, Linc," Charlene mused.

He shook his head at her, but he couldn't hide his delight.

CHAPTER ELEVEN

In The Genes

Kinsley grasped the brushed-metal handle and pulled open the glass door. The intoxicating smell of books greeted her as she stepped inside the entrance to the county library. The library had always been her refuge; it was as if nothing could harm her inside this brick house of dreams.

Heddy Martin had been the head librarian when Kinsley was a little girl. A quiet, small-framed woman, she fit the profile of a spinster librarian from her head to her toes; she could have stepped out of a 1950s' Sears and Roebuck catalog. Kinsley had loved spending time around her solid silence.

"May I help you?" The stern voice belonged to a dour-faced woman who stood on the other side of an oak platform desk. This new librarian was no Heddy Martin.

"Yes, I'd like to look at back issues of the newspaper, please."

"Certainly." The woman's beady eyes peered over the top of her wireframe glasses. "You *do* know how to use a microfiche machine?"

"I do."

A vision of curt efficiency in her orthopedic shoes, the librarian led Kinsley to the furthest room at the back of the library. She gave a firm warning to put everything away before disappearing between the stacks, leaving a vapor trail of eau de menthol in her wake.

Kinsley sat on a canary-yellow fiberglass chair; the same seating had been there since she could remember. With the flick of a switch, the old microfiche machine roared to life and, after a few flickers, the screen glowed. She loaded film and delved into the copies of the local news.

Kinsley stopped at her grandparents' wedding announcement and stared at the photo of the beautiful couple, him in his Navy uniform and her in a stylish dress. The print only fueled her determination to find her grandfather's killer.

She took a pen from her bag and started noting anything that caught her eye. Each edition of the weekly publication consisted of only three pages, so scanning through them proved quicker than she'd expected.

Much later, seated in a soft-leather reading chair, Kinsley closed the hard copy of the latest issue that was spread across her lap. The last ten years hadn't been transferred to film. She leaned back and rubbed her eyes, trying to process the overload of information she'd taken in about the town.

In addition to serving as commissioner for the past eight years, it appeared that Max Skelly had his hand in every pie: farming, politics, a large hay operation, and cattle. The creep owned it all. As people fell on hard times, Skelly was there to help them out by buying their land.

Kinsley conducted a last scan of the room before setting out to walk home. As she reached her front porch, ribbons of smoky clouds decorated a tangerine sky—a perfect scene to round off a very good day.

Confident that Lincoln would come over for dinner, Kinsley wanted to thank him for taking her to the farm. Her specialty, 'pasta à la Kins,' should fit the bill. Everything was cooking when the door chime announced his arrival.

Her stomach did somersaults as she moved to the entrance. When she opened the door, she took in Lincoln's dark-wash jeans and what looked like a new pearl-snap shirt. He had gone to a little extra effort tonight. She whistled. "Sheriff, you are looking snazzy."

He gave her that half-smile—the one that used to piss her off. "Those the hundred-dollar jeans?" he teased.

Kinsley turned her back to show him the fancy pockets. "Yes, sir, these are the infamous jeans."

A sound akin to a wolf growling came from his direction. As she glanced over her shoulder, she saw the guilty look on his face. She frowned as she faced him. "What's that look for? Don't you like them?"

"Yes, they're very nice," Lincoln returned a little too quickly.

"Thank you—I think." Kinsley led him toward the kitchen as she recited the menu.

"Sounds good. Smells good, too."

Curious to know more about him, she asked, "Where is your family?"

"My mom and dad, Connie and Dale, are in Tulsa. I have a brother, Grant, in California. One of my sisters, Reagan, is in Texas. My baby sister, Kennedy—last I heard from her, she was stationed in Japan."

Kinsley arched an eyebrow. "Lincoln, Grant, Reagan, and Kennedy. What happened with Kennedy? Run out of Republican names?"

Lincoln smiled. "Don't mention her name to my dad. He's still mad at my mom about Kennedy's name. He's a dyed-in-the-wool Republican."

Since they lived in a red state, Kinsley was hardly surprised about his father's political affiliations. "What branch of the military is your sister in?"

"Navy. Kennedy is crazy, like me. The other two are calm, more like our mom."

"You don't seem wild to me. In fact, you're pretty laid back."

A mischievous sparkle hit his eyes. "I didn't use to be. I've calmed down considerably."

"What about your brother in California?"

"Grant is in Los Angeles. I haven't seen him in a very long time. He never leaves the West Coast." Regret tinged his voice.

"Did you used to be close?"

"We were, but Grant hates the Midwest. He and our dad don't exactly get along."

"I see." She plated the food and placed it on the bar. "Need a beer?"

"Sure, thanks."

When she turned holding two longnecks, Kinsley saw Lincoln gazing at the food, but he didn't move to eat. "It's not poison, I promise."

His eyes swung from the food to her. "Looks good."

"Thanks. I try." She blushed at the compliment as she sat beside him.

Lincoln took a bite, closed his eyes, and let out a low satisfied rumble from deep in his chest. "Holy shit, Kins. That is freakin' fantastic."

Kinsley smiled. "I'm glad you like it."

"Like it? I love it. Did you make the pasta?" She nodded. "Wow." He held out his hand, palm up.

Kinsley considered his silent invitation for an instant before placing her hand in his. He brought their intertwined flesh to his mouth and kissed her fingers. Electric currents traced paths down every nerve to the pit of her stomach. "You like it that much, huh?"

"Even more than that."

Another crimson flush swept up her neck. "Lincoln, really, it's just food."

"No, it's heaven," he replied.

"Guess I found the way to your heart, big man."

"I guess you did." His eyes wandered over her face, lingering on her lips.

Kinsley looked away. "We should eat before it gets cold."

Reluctantly he released her hand and picked up his fork. Their light conversation during dinner banked the fire between them, allowing her to relax. Lincoln stirred up the most exquisite sensations that both terrified and intrigued her in equal measure.

***

He made a point to leave plenty of space between them as they moved into the living room. Kinsley turned on the radio, and they settled on the sofa. "Never a Mrs. Lincoln, then?"

"I was married a long time ago. I have a son," he confessed.

"You have a boy? Here in town?" Kinsley was caught off guard. "What's his name?"

"Aren't you suddenly the curious one?" he teased.

"Sorry, I'm being too nosy."

"I like it, Kins. It's just unusual for you." He smiled reassuringly. "My son's name is Thomas. He's eighteen and lives in Tulsa with my parents."

"Eighteen? You can't have an eighteen-year-old boy, Lincoln. You're so young."

"Thank you, but I do. My high-school sweetheart. It's a long story, and one I don't want to bore you with, but Thomas is great. I hope he comes up soon. I haven't seen him in a while."

A good song came on the radio, prompting Lincoln to stand and hold out his hand, "Would you dance with me?" Kinsley looked up at him. "I'll be careful."

Her eyes stayed on his as she stood and stepped into the circle of his arms.

"I'm going to put my hand on your waist." His touch barely grazed her shirt. He held out his other hand, palm up, and let her move at her own pace. "Let's waltz."

Lincoln took a step forward and they danced slowly around Henry's living room. He moved with the caution of a man defusing a live bomb. When their eyes met, it took every ounce of his willpower to keep from kissing her.

"This is nice, Lincoln, thanks," she whispered.

"Thank *you* for dancin' with me."

Kinsley flashed him a crooked grin. "You are a sneaky charmer."

Lincoln's voice grew a little deeper. "Hardly charmin'." But as he tightened his fingers around her waist to hold her more securely, she went stiff as a board. "Kinsley, how's it goin'?"

She shot him a questioning look.

"You're frownin', and your hand is shakin'."

Kinsley stepped away from him. "I'm sorry. I'm being ridiculous. Thank you for trying to help me." She snagged her beer from the end table and chugged what was left in the bottle.

"It's okay. A little at a time. I'm a patient man."

She turned toward him, frowning. "What are you being patient about?"

Lincoln hesitated. "Nothin' in particular. I'm just generally an easygoin' guy." He had told himself a dozen times that Kinsley was off-limits, yet here he was having a dance with her. "I better get some sleep or work tomorrow is gonna be rough."

"I had fun, Lincoln. Thanks for today," Kinsley said, as she followed him to the door.

He dropped his hat in place and tipped it to her. "Me too. Maybe I'll see you tomorrow?"

"Yep."

Tickled at her use of his favorite word, he said, "Uh-oh, I'm rubbin' off on ya."

"Seems so." She patted his arm as he stepped onto the porch. "Sweet dreams, Sheriff."

Lincoln gave her a hundred-watt smile. "Sweet dreams, City."

Kinsley grinned and shook her head as she headed back into her house.

As Lincoln slipped between the sheets, what Butch had said about the wolves at the door crept into his thoughts. When that stunning woman had looked up at him during their dance, his heart had felt like it would burst from his chest. Those wolves had better back the hell off; Kinsley Rhodes was not on the menu.

CHAPTER TWELVE

The Purge

The investigation into Henry's murder was at a standstill; nevertheless, Lincoln followed every clue, no matter how small. Desperate to come up with something, he started to re-interview people.

Hazel Bishop had invited him over for coffee. Her house was positioned catty-cornered from Henry's, and that, coupled with her busybody ways, made her top of the list for knowing what was happening in Harlow. Despite her advanced years, she was still sharp enough not to miss a thing. As he pulled into her driveway, Lincoln saw the curtains twitch. Before he had a chance to ring the doorbell, Hazel was peering up at him through the screen.

"Good morning, Sheriff James. Nice to see you." The tiny woman with her Barbara Bush hairstyle pushed open the door with a shaky hand. "Please come in, and we'll have a piece of cake with our coffee."

"Thank you, Mrs. Bishop." Lincoln followed her into a perfectly decorated pastel space where every piece of upholstered furniture was preserved with clear plastic, the like of which he hadn't seen since his grandmother had passed away. The memory of the sweat-fests produced by sitting on those covers during hot Oklahoma summers took him back to his childhood.

"Come into the dining room, Sheriff," she beckoned.

He watched as Hazel gingerly placed china plates and silver forks on linen placemats, then removed a crystal cover from a cake in the center of the table. "I hope you like lemon Bundt cake."

"That sounds good. Thank you."

She motioned for him to sit and poured coffee into matching china cups that were reminiscent of a child's tea set. Lincoln's finger wouldn't fit through the handle, which forced him to hold the cup with the tips of his fingers to take a sip.

"What have you been occupying your time with lately, Sheriff James?" Hazel asked.

"I'm still investigatin' Henry Rhodes' murder. I know we spoke the day we found him, but I thought you might have remembered somethin' or heard talk since then."

Hazel put her hand to her chest. "It's just terrible. You know, we haven't had a murder here in over twenty years." She laid a piece of cake on his plate.

Lincoln picked up a fork that must have come from the same miniature set. In a scene reminiscent of *Gulliver in Lilliput*, he struggled to fit into Mrs. Bishop's tiny world as he waited for her to speak.

"Well, let me see. I saw the dark-haired girl over there. She runs around early in the morning nearly naked." She leaned closer. "But these girls nowadays are a little freer with their favors than we were back in my day."

Lincoln chewed thoughtfully until his amusement abated. "Kinsley is Henry's granddaughter. She's stayin' there."

Hazel graced him with her sweet old lady smile as if

he were an idiot and she needed to humor him. "Yes, I remember when she lived here." She paused reflectively. "If her father, Darrell, were alive, I would suggest that he had killed poor Henry. A bad seed, that one."

Lincoln revisited the questions they'd asked her on day one. "Did you remember seeing anyone visiting Henry that day?"

"The plumber was there at lunch, then Henry left and didn't come home until dark." Lincoln waited patiently while she ate her cake. Then she added firmly, "It was the aliens."

Lincoln had just taken a drink, and he swallowed hard to keep from spewing coffee all over her starched tablecloth. "You think aliens killed Henry Rhodes?"

"Definitely. Mable Evans said they took Henry's penis. Who would want a penis except for aliens?"

Lincoln put his hand over his mouth and feigned thought to cover his amusement. "Mrs. Bishop, I thank you for the cake and coffee. I really should be goin'. I appreciate your insight. Please don't be worried. I'm workin' to catch the killer."

Mrs. Bishop patted his arm when they reached the front door. "I'm not worried, Sheriff. I don't have a penis," she said, her saccharine smile firmly in place.

Once he was safely ensconced in his vehicle, he howled with laughter. Aliens? All righty then. That, plus hearing eighty-year-old Hazel Bishop say penis several times, was almost more than he could handle.

As he headed out, thinking about aliens and penises, his ringing cell phone halted his train of thought. "Hey, Charlene. What's goin' on?"

"Hi, Linc. You asked me to look into complaints about parties from around eight years ago. I honestly thought you'd gone nuts, but I found something. Gabby Chambers and Dusty Reynolds filed complaints against two local boys. Witness statements to an assault."

"Who was assaulted?" He was sure he already knew the answer.

"Kinsley Rhodes."

Lincoln flipped a U-turn and headed back toward the office. "I just finished with Mrs. Bishop. I'll stop by on my way out of town."

***

In need of tax documents related to her grandfather's land, Kinsley crossed the deserted lobby of the county courthouse. The open space surrounded by glass walls intensified the sound of her boots against black terrazzo flooring.

"Kinsley Rhodes! Well, I'll be damned."

Late afternoon sunlight glanced off the polished floor, momentarily blinding her. She shielded her eyes to identify the speaker, and her good spirits faded at the sight of Max Skelly.

The commissioner wasn't as oily as his son, Rich, but she suspected his expensive suit was only window dressing. Grandpa always said you couldn't make a silk purse out of a sow's ear. The salacious look in Max's eyes after an extended scan of her body left her feeling violated.

"Hello," she said and tried to move on, only to have him step into her path. "Is there something you need?" she challenged.

"Is that any way to speak to an elder? Why, I'd have thought Henry would have taught you some manners." His appraisal of her chest made her skin crawl.

"Mr. Skelly, I have an appointment." Kinsley had no intention of showing this serpent any respect—elder or not.

"It's Commissioner Skelly, Missy. Where are you off to in such a hurry?"

"*Commissioner* Skelly, if there isn't anything you need, please allow me to be on my way."

She tried to step around him, but Max grabbed her upper arm in a bruising grip. Without hesitation, she swept his ankle, causing him to lose balance. In an effort to regain his footing, he released her arm. Before he could right himself, Kinsley placed her hands firmly on his chest and shoved, sending him crashing to the floor.

She hit the doors at full speed and darted across a stretch of grass before barreling into the sheriff's department at the rear of the courthouse. Panting, she came to a stop at the bulletproof glass.

Charlene looked up in alarm and immediately released the lock to let her into the office. "What's wrong, Kinsley?"

"Th… The … com—" Kinsley took a deep breath.

Commissioner Skelly flung open the outside door. It banged against the wall as he limped into the lobby.

"Please call Lincoln," Kinsley pleaded. "That man assaulted me."

Charlene's eyes flashed from Kinsley to Max.

"That little slut broke my ankle. I want to file charges," Skelly croaked.

Kinsley pulled up the sleeve of her T-shirt and revealed a clear handprint on her upper arm. "It was self-defense. I'm filing charges against the commissioner for battery. I think if you pull the camera footage, you will see exactly who did the attacking."

Suddenly, Max raised his hands. His snake-oil salesman leer settled into place. "Now, I think we are overreacting. I was simply trying to have a friendly conversation, and little Miss Rhodes got the wrong idea. It's all just a silly misunderstanding. We should calm down. Right, Miss Rhodes?"

"Hell no, it isn't a misunderstanding. You grabbed me and refused to let go until I defended myself. I intend to put that on record, *Mr.* Skelly. I'm not afraid of you. You'd best get that straight right now."

Charlene had a huge smile on her face as she spoke into the phone. "Linc, you'd better get back to town. We have a situation at the station."

Kinsley went home after filling out paperwork to file a complaint and a request for a restraining order against Max Skelly. The worm pleaded, and blustered about her past, even threatened to run her out of town on a rail, but she never gave an inch. After Max's wife picked him up to take him home, Lincoln and Charlene told her how proud they were.

Later, as she sat on her porch swing, she wondered if she'd done the right thing. It was obvious from Max's leer that his intentions were not snow white—but what kind of a hornet's nest had she stirred up?

***

Lincoln pulled into his driveway, sat in his truck, and watched Kinsley swing. She'd impressed him today; if she was afraid of Skelly, she hadn't shown it as she calmly filled out forms. On the other hand, the commissioner had lost his cool. Lincoln was forced to keep him in the lobby and warn him that he would be arrested if his tirade continued.

He grabbed a pizza and six-pack from the passenger seat before strolling across to Kinsley's porch. "I come bearing food and drink."

She made room for him next to her. "You're as handy as a pocket on a shirt, Lincoln."

Opening the lid, he offered her a piece of the pie. She selected a slice, took a bite, and smiled proudly at him.

"I'm pleased you stood your ground," he said.

"That creep didn't give me much choice. You should've seen the way he was looking at me." A shiver ran through her. "I won't let him hurt me, if I can help it."

Lincoln thought about the complaints Charlene had found this morning. If Dusty and Gabby's accounts were accurate, Kinsley had been hurt very badly. What had she lived with all these years?

The accusations the commissioner had hurled at her today about being a woman of low virtue were more than Lincoln could stomach. If he were to venture a guess, none of what Max Skelly thought he knew was true. Kinsley was shut off from people, and solitary confinement wasn't the action of someone who gave herself freely, as the commissioner had alleged.

Lincoln had stopped by Reynold's liquor store earlier and talked to Dusty. The reports weren't filled out completely and he wanted more information, but Dusty respectfully declined to discuss the incident. He said that the story wasn't his to tell, and suggested Lincoln should talk to Kinsley about what had happened.

Of the two boys mentioned in the complaints, one had left town and the other, Brian Johnson, was a good friend of Rich Skelly.

"What's with the weird face, Linc?" Kinsley brushed her shoulder playfully against his. "Something on your mind?"

"You know you can tell me anything. You can't shock me."

Kinsley watched him for a moment before gulping the last drop of wine in her glass. "Are you talking about what the commissioner said today?" She looked down and shook her head. "He's wrong." She stood up. "I'm going to turn in. Thanks for bringing over pizza. It's been a big day, and I'm tired."

"Hey, I didn't mean to upset you. I was only offerin' to lend an ear if you need one. I'm a pretty good listener." He tried to pull her out of that dark place she'd retreated to once more. "We're friends now, aren't we?"

Kinsley nodded. "Goodnight, Sheriff. Thank you for helping me today and for being my friend." Her fleeting glance revealed that troubled look he'd seen so often.

CHAPTER THIRTEEN

Turning The Page

The commissioner's rant at the sheriff's office about Kinsley's past had been terrible, but when he'd called her a 'party favor', it reminded her that the nickname had been given to her by his son years ago, and she'd struggled to control her rage.

As Kinsley crawled into bed, well-worn springs added their two cents before she settled in the middle. She should have just told Lincoln what had happened at the party. After the desire she'd seen in his eyes a couple of times, there was a flicker of hope that they might become more than friends. Convinced her past would be a barrier to a relationship, she grudgingly decided to speak to him. He needed to know the truth.

She rolled onto her side, picked up her phone from the bedside table, called him and started talking before he could even say hello. "Lincoln, I do have something to tell you. I've been worried it could have something to do with my grandpa's murder, but I couldn't bring myself to talk about it. I've never told anyone, so I'll get through it the best I can, okay?"

Lincoln's voice over the line was soothing. "Do you want me to come over?"

"Please just listen. Then you can do with it what you wish."

"I'm listenin'," he said, and went still while he waited for her to begin.

"A month before I graduated from high school, I was invited to a party given by the head cheerleader, Gale Lee. I assumed there'd be drinking and whatnot. I wasn't a drinker back then—but I was super unpopular, so it was a shock to get invited. They had always kept me on the outside, and I thought maybe they'd finally let me in. Grandpa didn't want me to go, but I begged until he agreed."

Kinsley paused. An agonizing silence filled the space while she remembered her grandpa trying to talk her out of going. Why hadn't she listened to him? If she had, her life might have been vastly different.

Lincoln was so quiet that Kinsley wasn't sure he was even there. "Are you still with me?" she asked.

"Yes, I'm here," he reassured her softly.

Kinsley strangled the urge to cry. "I ... I went to the party. One guy was very nice to me. I was seventeen, but I'd never had a guy look twice at me. He was on the football team, good looking, and I was flattered. I was also the stupidest girl on the planet." The story spilled out of her like a vile infection from an untreated wound. "Billy Long—that's his name. I was unwise to the human capacity for evil until th-that night." She hesitated, too choked to continue.

"Kinsley, you don't have to tell me," Lincoln offered.

"I h-have to." Kinsley stumbled to regain control. "What if it has something to do with Grandpa?"

"Okay. I'm here. Whatever you need, I'm here."

"Billy asked if I wanted to take a walk. I wasn't

completely clueless, and I thought he might want to kiss me, so I went with him. They had a hired-hand house on the property. He… I went in with him. He held me down. I said no… I-I tried to get away. He ripped my clothes and…"

"I get it."

Lincoln's simple statement belied the rage she could hear building behind his words. "No, you don't. You don't get it. Billy couldn't… It wouldn't … work. He couldn't perform. He was so angry…" Kinsley stared, unseeing, at the ceiling as she revisited the memory. "So angry, and he blamed me. He beat me just short of unconscious. He did other things... It was…"

She took a deep breath. "Billy called his friend Brian. They held me down and took pictures. My friends burst in before Brian could—before he…" Kinsley couldn't say the word. "Dusty and Gabby got me away. But the pictures, those horrific images, were shared all over school while Billy and Brian lied. They said I had sex with both of them, and that I liked it rough." She broke down.

"My God, Kinsley. I'm so sorry." Lincoln's heart ached for her. The revelation was more horrific than he'd imagined. He understood now why she was livid about them talking about her at Pearl's, and why she kept everything about herself a secret.

"None of it was true, but people are monsters. Those rumors were passed around, and the stories grew out of control. When Grandpa saw me that night, he lost it. I don't know what he did—he never said, and I never asked. I didn't see Billy Long again." Kinsley let go the deluge of tears that she'd held back for years.

Lincoln was sure angels wept with her. "Can I come over, please?"

"I'm sorry, Lincoln."

The devastation in her voice reinforced his decision. He pulled on his boots and ran across their adjoining lawns. "I'm at your door. Please let me in. You don't have anything to be sorry for."

Kinsley opened the door and rushed into his arms. He held her while she clung to him. "No one should have to carry this burden alone. I'm here for you. You know that, right?" He brushed her tears away with his thumb, and they moved to her couch

"You went to the police?" Lincoln knew she had, but he didn't want her to think he'd been looking into her personal life.

"Grandpa did. The police said I should be more careful who I hung out with. The sheriff at that time was corrupt, only interested in who had power and money—the whole force was without a moral compass." Kinsley wiped her face on the sleeve of her T-shirt. "At the next election, Grandpa and his friends made sure that man and his cronies were no longer the law in Harlow."

That bit of information solved the mystery as to why there hadn't been a permanent sheriff seven years ago when Lincoln had come to town.

He remembered the single piece of paper in Kinsley's police file. Those worthless pieces of shit had done nothing; they'd called a beating and sexual assault roughing up. A volatile cocktail of rage and despair roared through him, though he did his best to control it. He would deal with that when he'd comforted Kinsley. "Can I hold you?" he asked gently.

She curled up to his side while he wrapped her in his arms. "Do you hate me now?" Her words were muffled against his shirt.

"I could never hate you." Lincoln stroked her hair. "I'm furious that those boys hurt you, that the cops failed you, and that you went through such a nightmare."

"No one has touched me since that night. Men make me uncomfortable. I can't stand it."

He opened his arms to release her, but she pulled him back. "I know I'm damaged, Lincoln. I had to tell you in case Grandpa's death has something to do with what happened to me." She peered up at him through wet lashes, and it drove the jagged blade of her pain deeper inside him.

"Thank you for tellin' me." Lincoln laid his cheek on top of her head. "You're safe with me, Kinsley."

CHAPTER FOURTEEN

Pulling At Strings

They'd talked for hours and, by the time he left, he had even managed to make her laugh. Lincoln's suggestion that she seek counseling led her to fight back hard. In the end, he let it go. Kinsley liked that about him; his feathers rarely got ruffled. Maybe it was time for her to talk to a professional; keeping it locked inside had done her no favors.

She ran her hands over the skin of her stomach, closed her eyes and imagined for a moment that they were Lincoln's hands. Then she bounced out of bed to start her day.

Guilt niggled at her when she saw the sleepy look on her neighbor's face as she came down the sidewalk toward his house. "Good morning, Sheriff." His goofy smile eased her conscience a little as she stole one last glance before taking off.

"Be here when you get back," he called after her as she sprinted away.

It was the first time in years that Kinsley could remember being truly happy. All the terror of that night, and the years of keeping it hidden away, had festered inside her. Once she'd let go, it spewed out like a shaken can of pop, easing the pressure, allowing her soul to finally catch a breath.

Kinsley waved to Lincoln as she finished her run. "What kind of greetin' is that?" he hollered.

"I'm sweaty," she protested.

"I'm not afraid of sweat."

"I'm sure I'm stinky," Kinsley argued.

His warm smile and the offer of a cup of coffee convinced her to join him. "You asked for it," she said as she sat in a rocker next to his. "What major crime are you off to solve today?"

"I have to cover the late shift for a few nights. My deputy needs some time off."

"So why in the world are you awake now?" Kinsley asked.

Lincoln took a sip of coffee. "I'd miss my morning runner. I do have to go to work for a while. Can I see you for lunch?"

"Of course. I'd be disappointed if you didn't come by. Thank you for the coffee, Sheriff … and thank you for last night."

Lincoln's smile made her insides clench. "Have a good mornin', Kins."

***

He'd finally managed to arrange an interview with Diana Locke, who lived directly behind Henry. Previously the woman either hadn't been around or was intentionally avoiding him, but she had agreed to come in early as long as no one found out. Lincoln had the willies about being alone in the office with her, so he'd insisted a deputy be present. She'd agreed to let Butch join them.

The streets were virtually empty at six in the morning,

and it would be more than an hour before Charlene came in. As he pulled into the lot, he was relieved to see Butch was already in the office, along with Diana. As he entered, her watery-blue gaze landed on him briefly before darting away.

"Good-mornin', Ms. Locke. Thank you for comin' in." Lincoln noticed she was gripping the coffee mug she was holding so tight that her fingers were pink around the edges. She nodded as she tucked a piece of stringy blonde hair behind her ear, but she didn't meet his look. "Let's go get your statement."

Diana sank uneasily into a club chair in front of his desk.

"Please don't be anxious," he said reassuringly. "I'd just like to know if you saw anything suspicious goin' on at Henry Rhodes' house on the night he was killed."

Her eyes flicked from Butch to Lincoln. "I work third shift at the beef plant in Liberal. I'm home at odd hours and up sometimes when other people aren't. Even when I'm off work, I can't sleep at night anymore." She paused. "Sheriff, what if the killer tries to kill me because I talked to you?"

"Ms. Locke, no one will know you were here. Do you know who killed Henry?"

Diana shook her head. "I was taking my trash out that night. I'd just lifted the lid of that huge damn bin, and I heard Henry's storm door bang shut. It must have been eleven or eleven-thirty. He was never up at that time, so I was startled. I saw a big man running—well, not running… Walking away fast. He had a limp."

"Who was it?" Lincoln pressed.

"Our alley is black as tar. If there hadn't been a full moon, I might not have seen him as well as I did. He was far away from me and moving south. Big, and definitely a man."

"By big, what do you mean? Can you give me details?"

She worried her lip. "The guy looked to be more than six foot tall. Broad shoulders, not thin, not fat. Big, ya know, like you are." She eyeballed Lincoln suspiciously.

"I can assure you it wasn't me. I was in Ulysses with the Chief of Police at that time. I'll be glad to let you talk to him," he offered.

"No, no. I'm sure you're fine. But yeah, from what I could see the man was built a lot like you. As I said, it was dark and he was moving fast, despite the limp."

Butch jumped in. "You didn't see anyone else?"

"Fuck!" Her features twisted into a grimace. "You think it might be more than one person?"

Taken aback by her spiking fear, Lincoln recovered quickly. "We need to explore all possibilities."

Diana chewed the inside of her cheek before answering. "I only saw one guy. The door slammed, and he split down our alley."

"Did you see where he went after he left the alley? Did you see him get into a vehicle?"

Her tension backed off a notch. "No, I went back to my house. I left for Amarillo to visit my sister right after that."

Lincoln found it suspicious that she'd kept the information to herself. "Is there a reason that you didn't call in the activity?"

"Ain't my business, Sheriff. I don't bother people, and

they don't bother me. No one gets killed here. I couldn't have known that guy was up to no good. Sure, I thought it was strange, but as I said, it's not my concern. Sometimes people have visitors late at night that they don't want people in this town to know about."

Lincoln understood. Diana Locke was a smart cookie for a newcomer, and she had provided the most valuable information so far in this investigation.

"When I got back from Texas, it was the first I heard about Henry's murder. I'm not eager to get involved—I moved here a few years ago to start over. I want to stay out of people's way."

"Is there anything else you can remember?"

She started to shake her head, then stopped. "Yeah, that fuckin' Skelly was over there right after lunch on that day."

"Rich? Or his father, Max?"

"I don't know their names. He drives a fancy red car." Diana mumbled something else.

"What was that?" Lincoln leaned forward.

"I said, that's some garbage right there." Her steady look moved from Butch to Lincoln as if to gauge which side of the Skelly clan they were on. "Money or not, that man is a creepy piece of shit."

"Has Rich Skelly done somethin' to you?"

"No, but I have an ex that has the same look. Cruel eyes. Skelly's a woman beater, I'd bet on it."

"If Rich or anyone approaches you or threatens you, don't hesitate to let us know. We don't put up with that kind of behavior here, Ms. Locke. I assure you we will take care of any problem," Lincoln stated.

The faintest hint of a smile crossed her lips as she

nodded. They all stood and walked to the front. "Thanks, Sheriff. You and ol' Butch here are good men. I wish you luck in catching whoever did this."

"Thank you, Ms. Locke. We appreciate you comin' down so early."

"Oh shit, Sheriff, call me Diana. I guess my secret's out, and the law knows I'm here now." She graced Butch with what could only be interpreted as a suggestive glance.

The two men refilled their coffee cups and returned to Lincoln's office. As he reclined in his chair and studied the water-stained ceiling tiles, he asked, "Who do we know that is built like me?"

Butch pursed his lips. "Hell, the county is full of big ol' farm boys. None as big as you, but close. From a distance, in the dark, it's hard to tell. She said he was limping. I can go to the hospital, see who might have come in for a foot or leg injury lately."

"Good call, Butch. I think it's time I talked to Rich Skelly. His name has come up several times durin' this investigation."

The deputy eyed his boss with disbelief. "Linc, the commissioner isn't going to like that. He already hates you. Questioning his son in a murder investigation isn't going to improve relations."

"It doesn't matter what the commissioner likes. If his son is involved, all the money and power in the world shouldn't stop justice from being done. Max Skelly doesn't intimidate me."

Butch sipped his coffee. "I know you're right, and you know I got your back, but the world is rarely fair. Money and power usually win."

"That's why there are guys like us to make sure we even the score, right?" Lincoln's half-cocked smile pulled a laugh from his deputy and eased the tension that had been building.

"I suppose." The deputy stared at a spot on the wall before looking at Lincoln. "Do you think we should run a background on Diana? She said some kinda sketchy things."

Lincoln gave a curt nod. "I agree she did. I suspect she's hidin' from the wife-beatin' ex she mentioned and that is all there is to it, but we should know." A squawk from the entry door being opened alerted them to their dispatcher's arrival. "Best I go get Charlene breakfast at Pearl's. I'm sure Rich is there. He always is."

"Hey, thanks for covering a few nights for me again," Butch stated with a tinge of guilt.

"You need uninterrupted time with your family. I'm glad to do it."

"Miss Rhodes will cry sleeping all alone." Butch's eyes crinkled at the corners.

Lincoln shook his head. "She'll be fine."

"Yeah, I heard you're stayin' separate. Better nail that down before someone else does."

"Things are fine with Kinsley and me. You gossipy hens need to leave it," he replied good-naturedly.

They sauntered into the outer office, where Charlene greeted them with her customary sarcasm. "Boy, you two are early birds."

"I'm gettin' breakfast. Place your orders here." Lincoln pantomimed making a list while they laughed at his clowning.

As he neared Pearl's he spied Rich Skelly heading for his red Beemer, which was parked prominently in front. Lincoln parked and hurriedly left his vehicle. "Hey, Rich, I wondered if you could come over to headquarters to answer some questions about Henry Rhodes for me?"

Rich regarded him coolly, and Lincoln could see this wasn't going to go smoothly. "I'm not coming in. Ask what you need right here."

Lincoln knew the twerp intentionally tried to infuriate people, but he wouldn't let him gain the upper hand. "Did you see Henry the day of his death?"

"I'm going to go out on a limb here and say you know I did." An arrogant sneer settled into place. "I was there at lunch."

"And what was your business that day?"

"That's above your pay grade, James," Rich said, and spat on the ground at Lincoln's feet.

"Hidin' somethin'?"

"No, I am not. Henry Rhodes was alive when I got there and when I left. What I talked about with him was personal and none of your concern. Am I under arrest?" His smug look never slipped.

"You aren't under arrest. Thank you for your time, Rich."

Skelly yelled a final dig at Lincoln's back. "Maybe you should be working on the case instead of driving it home with Miss Rhodes every night."

Without missing a step, Lincoln threw back a clipped reply, "You have a nice day."

Once inside Pearl's, he scanned around and made a mental note of men about his size. That was one thing

Rich had going for him: he was much smaller than the man Diana had described. Lincoln's best guess was that Rich couldn't be more than five foot ten.

But Skelly's name had come up more than once, so something was going on; however, solid proof needed to be found before even a hint of an accusation could be made. A person with financial means like Rich Skelly could slip the noose before it tightened if all the pieces were not in place.

Slow and steady, Linc, he told himself.

CHAPTER FIFTEEN

Politics And Lies

Lincoln slipped his phone from his pocket to check the time. It was almost noon, and he'd been held captive in a mind-numbing council meeting for hours while Commissioner Skelly droned on about his many achievements. His final order of business was tax revenues; they had unfortunately fallen short again, and that would call for belt-tightening. Lincoln shook his head. Law-enforcement budgets couldn't get any tighter.

His eyes wandered over the gathering, stopping when he reached a blonde sporting a severe bun. The woman frowned before pushing her glasses back into place as she regarded the commissioner. Her pinched brow didn't seem to corroborate what Skelly was saying.

After they were released, Lincoln caught up with her as she scurried toward the treasurer's office. "Hey. Gabby, is it?"

The slip of a woman stopped and pivoted slowly toward Lincoln. "Gabby Chambers." She shuffled a laptop, papers, and a notebook under one arm before stiffly sticking out her hand to shake.

"Sheriff Lincoln James. Sorry I haven't introduced myself before now. You're a friend of Kinsley's?"

"I am." A secret smile flitted across her lips; it made him curious about what Miss Rhodes had shared with this woman.

"I wondered if we could talk off the record? I promise it's just between us," he assured her as she peered around nervously.

Gabby swallowed hard. "I—"

Commissioner Skelly slithered up to the pair. "Miss Chambers, shouldn't you be back at work by now?"

"Yes, sir. On my way." Gabby took off like a shot, leaving Lincoln alone with Max.

"I didn't know you and Miss Chambers were acquainted, Sheriff James."

"We both work for the county. I know her." Lincoln started to walk away.

Max placed a manicured hand against the sheriff's chest. "We need to talk. Let's go to my office."

This meeting smelled like trouble but, in the interest of keeping the peace such as it was, Lincoln followed. Max closed his office door, and they both sat. Skelly studied Lincoln for a while in what could only be viewed as an intimidation tactic.

"For the past few years," he said, "we've had to cut back because of revenue downturns. I know what a strain that is on those of you who are left. I saw the estimate for repairs to Butch's vehicle. We can't afford it."

A muscle in Lincoln's jaw worked as he held on to his composure. "He has to have transportation."

"Maybe we should consider letting him go. The way things are looking, it won't be long anyway," Max suggested.

"No. We can't keep calls covered the way it is. I can't do it by myself."

Skelly looked down to hide his grin. "Well, the

sheriff's election is coming up next year. Perhaps it's time you gave up your position to someone who can do the job."

"We're done here." Lincoln stood abruptly. "I know you don't like me, but I do my job. Your election is comin' up, too."

He stalked across the lawn to headquarters and went straight to his office. Lincoln was determined to keep Butch and Charlene—they were a team—but he needed to find a way to pay their salaries. His only hope was that the upcoming fundraising barbeque would raise enough money for them to get by until elections. They just needed someone who could beat Skelly.

Lincoln opened his budget ledger and looked through bills. He had been paying for his own gas to help. His deputy had to have a unit. He picked up the estimate and read through it. Eight grand—it might as well be a million.

A soft knock ended his contemplation of the monetary crisis. "Come in," he called out and sat back in his chair. When the door opened, Kinsley was standing there with a covered plate balanced on her hand. "What a surprise! Please, come in. What did you bring me?"

"Charlene said you were tied up here, so I thought I'd deliver lunch to you both." She offered the dish as Lincoln approached. "I made fried chicken. I think you said you like it?"

"I love fried chicken. Thank you."

Kinsley relaxed at his approval, but she sensed his unease. "What's wrong?"

"Nothin'. I'm okay. You'll stay while I eat?"

She nodded and settled into a chair across from him. "You don't look like everything is okay. What is it?"

"Aw, just the commissioner. He's gonna cut budgets again and won't pay to get Butch's vehicle fixed after he hit a deer. Same ol' shit."

Kinsley frowned but said nothing.

Lincoln attacked the food like a ravenous bear. "Mmm, perfect. Yes, this is what I needed."

"I'm sorry that Skelly is an asshat. I hope he loses the next election." She played with a notepad on the table.

"That makes two of us."

"Maybe something will break loose. Never can tell."

"Let's hope, or this is gonna be a town without law enforcement." Lincoln placed his napkin on a now-empty plate. "Thank you for lunch. That was very kind."

"You're welcome. I'd best get home."

He followed her out. Charlene thanked her for lunch and handed back her plate.

"You two keep them bad dudes in line," Kinsley joked before departing.

Lincoln waited until she'd driven away before asking, "How is the barbeque comin'? We need money, or we are goin' under."

Charlene retrieved a folder she'd been keeping the event information in and flipped it open. "More cars this year than ever before. It should be a pretty big ta-doo. Kinsley has been helping. She called some of her friends up in Northern Kansas to put the word out, and volunteered to bake pies to sell. She's working on a website to advertise for us."

Lincoln smiled and started to respond when the front

door opened. Charlene threw him a surprised look as Gabby Chambers entered.

"Not a word to anyone you saw her in here," Lincoln instructed. The dispatcher nodded open-mouthed as he went to let Gabby past the secured door.

The young woman was skittish as she glanced at Charlene. "Don't worry. She didn't see a thing. Come on back." Lincoln smiled in an attempt to ease her anxiety.

As they sat down, she shook her head. "I know what you're after. You want to know if the commissioner is lying about revenues." Gabby raised her eyes and met his boldly. "This is one of the wealthiest counties in Kansas, Sheriff James. Tax money coming in every year from gas royalties alone is astronomical. However, there's a hole somewhere. Commissioner Skelly is slick, but it's him. I'd bet on it."

"I don't have any proof because he has help getting it done before it's recorded in the county books." She continued, "Over the last several years, I've noticed that revenues on specific plots of land have dropped significantly from year to year. It's almost as if tax statements that were sent out were not the ones filed. I've gone over the books with a fine-tooth comb, and I can't find an imbalance, but I know there is one. I can feel it in my bones."

Gabby shifted uneasily. "I was there when Dale Langley lost it in the treasurer's office. They said Mr. Langley didn't pay his taxes for several years. He swears he did, but there was no proof because he'd paid in cash and all the receipts mysteriously disappeared. I know his taxes were paid, but I couldn't help him. Then Skelly ends up with Langley's land when the poor man couldn't secure a bank loan to pay back what he supposedly owed. What a coincidence, right? Skelly is president of the bank board, too. He's a crook, Sheriff. Someone has to stop him. I'm sorry I've been too scared to say anything before. I wasn't sure who was on his payroll and who wasn't."

"I appreciate you comin' in. I plan to stop him," Lincoln said. "I don't know how, but I will."

Gabby's hands curled into fists. "He's an evil person. I hate him."

"You and me both, Gabby. You and me both."

CHAPTER SIXTEEN

Fishing For The Truth

The decision to skip her morning run so that she could work preyed on her mind as Kinsley checked her email to ensure there weren't any project emergencies while she waited for her friends to arrive. Being back in Harlow for an extended time had stirred up distractions, and she was going to have to hire help. Falling behind was not an option after all she had put into building her company. She quickly typed up an email to her lawyer, Bill Schneider, asking him to set aside some time to talk later in the day.

Dusty and Gabby hollered as they walked in. "Girl, you work too much," Dusty drawled as they joined her in the dining room.

"I can't be away too long. I assign projects to my team, and I've got to keep things moving along." Kinsley shut down her computer. "Ready?"

"Ready as I'm gonna get," Gabby said. "Where are we going?"

"The cottonwood by Grandpa's land." The remote location was Kinsley's favorite place to relax.

As they left the house, they were met by TJ Smith who had just stepped up onto the porch. Kinsley hadn't seen him in years. His father, Ted, farmed land close to her grandfather's and was an old family friend. Since she'd been back, Ted had called and offered to help with a few farming tasks.

"Hey, TJ. We're going fishing. Do you want to come?" Kinsley asked.

TJ shook his head. "Naw, just droppin' off bills from Dad." He held out some papers. As soon as Kinsley took them, he stalked back to his father's Dodge and drove away.

"He always seems so lonely." Gabby voiced what they were all feeling. "It's too bad."

They piled into Grandpa's '69 Chevy pickup, and Kinsley drove them out into the country. They parked in the shade of a massive cottonwood tree alongside a small stream. Dusty helped Gabby out of the cab. "Nice spot, Kins, but isn't this private land? Should we be here?"

"I have permission. Grandpa used to bring me here arrowhead hunting."

As they strolled along the edge of the river, Dusty stopped and pushed around the dirt with the toe of his boot. He bent down, picked up a perfect black arrowhead, and held it up proudly. After a chivalrous bow, he placed the find in Gabby's open palm. Kinsley watched the two of them; it was hard to believe they had never dated. It seemed their mutual attraction was obvious to everybody but them.

"Good eyes, Dusty, but watch yourself. I'm an excellent hunter." Kinsley sat her tackle box on the ground. "Let's fish."

Gabby spread out a blanket, and they all picked a spot to sit. "Hey, Kins, I want to talk to you about your grandpa. Would that be all right with you?" she asked.

Kinsley nodded, and her friend shared the information she had given to Lincoln. "I've been thinking since then. You don't suppose Skelly would kill your grandpa, do you?"

"I've considered it, yes. Do you know something?"

"I know Skelly is buying up land like it's goin' out of style, though I don't know why, other than to own the whole world. Also, I can't prove it, but I think he's forced some sales by unscrupulous means. Something is going on in this town." They fell into a contemplative silence before Gabby spoke again. "Be careful, Kins."

"I will. You and Dusty, too. The Skellys are nothing but trouble."

No sooner were the words out of her mouth than a pickup rolled in, kicking up a cloud of dust. The three stood and watched Rich Skelly struggle from his vehicle. His standard self-confident swagger was soaked in booze, which made his stride seem almost cartoonish.

"Speak of the devil, and he shall appear," Gabby murmured.

Rich's eyes raked Kinsley, just as his father's had recently. "This ain't your land, Rhodes. Better get goin' before ya get shot." He raised the hem of his plaid shirt to reveal the butt of a gun pressed against his hairy beer belly.

Dusty stepped in front of the women.

"Reynolds, don't play the hero. You'll end up dead," their tormentor brayed. His brother, Harry, emerged to his left. Together they took up a threatening stance.

"We have permission to be here, Rich. It isn't your land, so you'd best go on now. We aren't causing any trouble," Kinsley said as she stepped up beside Dusty.

"You're nothing but trouble, whore. Why don't you go back where ya came from? No one wants your kind 'round here."

Fury flashed to life, and Kinsley took another step toward the brothers. "You'd best be careful, Rich, before you bite off more than you can chew." The cold steel of her own weapon strapped to her ankle was reassuring.

Rich reached for her but, before he could gain a hold, Kinsley caught a blur out of the corner of her eye as Dusty's fist connected with Skelly's mouth. "Leave her alone, Skelly!" he shouted.

Harry grabbed Dusty and held him as Rich lit into him. The girls flew at the attackers like crazed banshees, forcing them to drop their hold on Dusty to defend themselves. Then Rich and Harry backed away as a second pickup came sliding to a stop.

A sizeable, dark-haired man jumped out and approached with his hands raised in submission. "Come on, Rich. Let's leave them alone," he ordered.

"The son of a bitch hit me, Lonnie," Rich whined and pressed his hand to his mouth, holding up blood-covered fingers as evidence.

Lonnie shoved Rich roughly toward his pickup. "And you no doubt asked for it. Let's go."

"We aren't through, Rhodes," Rich yelled over his shoulder as he was pushed toward his ride. Lonnie nodded an acknowledgment to Kinsley as he walked around the front of his pickup and got in.

"I know the blond, short, fat one was Harry, Rich's brother. Who was the other guy?" Kinsley asked.

Gabby whispered, "Rich's oldest brother, Lonnie."

Kinsley nodded slowly. "He doesn't look anything like Rich or Harry. I guess I've never seen him." Even so, Lonnie seemed strangely familiar. "Well, that was a hell of a mess, right?"

Her companions' nervous titter became full-on laughter. "It certainly was," Dusty huffed, still trying to catch his breath. He patted the women's arms. "Holy shit, you two are wicked. I love it."

They went back to Kinsley's to clean up Dusty. Before her friends left, they made plans to give their picnic another try soon.

This situation was officially out of hand. It was time to call in help. Kinsley took a seat at the dining-room table and began to scroll through the contacts on her phone.

CHAPTER SEVENTEEN

Father's Sons

Lincoln stood in his kitchen drinking coffee and thinking about Skelly and the scuffle Kinsley had told him about last night after dinner. Imagining her letting loose on Rich and Harry amused him, but it was also concerning. He'd asked her to promise not to go out into the county alone again. Kinsley was resistant at first, but eventually agreed.

The sheriff picked up his keys and headed for the office. He'd barely stepped inside headquarters when Charlene raised both her eyebrows higher than he'd ever seen them as she tilted her head toward the waiting area. Lincoln followed her prompt to the last person on earth he expected to see.

"Son, what are you doing here?"

Thomas fidgeted with a strap on the backpack that hung from one shoulder as he stepped closer to his father. "Can I stay with you, please?"

Lincoln couldn't quell his happiness at seeing his boy, but this request made the unexpected visit worrying. He wrapped an arm around Thomas's shoulders, Charlene buzzed them in, and they headed to his office.

"Have a seat and tell me what's goin' on. Does your grandmother know where you are?"

Thomas shook his head, his eyes glued to the floor.

"We better call her before she alerts the National Guard." Lincoln picked up his phone and called his mother.

"Lincoln, thank the Lord! We can't find Thomas." Her panic resonated over the line. "I went to wake him about thirty minutes ago, and he wasn't there. His pickup is gone."

"That's why I'm callin'. Thomas is with me, Mom. Let me talk to him. I'll call you back."

"That rotten poop! You tell him he scared the living daylights out of me, and I'm going to swat his bottom." Connie breathed a deep sigh of relief. "Tell him I love him, too."

He had to laugh at his firecracker of a mother. "I'll tell him. Talk to you in a bit."

Lincoln laid down his phone and considered his son, who was sitting there like a deflated balloon. He'd never seen him like this before. Gently he said, "I assume this is serious since you drove five hours without tellin' anyone and scared your grandparents to death."

Thomas glanced at his dad and chewed on his bottom lip before he spoke. "I went to visit Mom. She says I can't see you anymore, that you cut her off and won't help us." He hesitated, then finished shakily, "She said you don't want to be my dad."

Lincoln's ex-wife could be cruel, but he didn't expect her to shred her own son to the core. He came around his desk and leaned against the edge as he considered his disheartened child. "Thomas, please look at me." The young man immediately obeyed; the devastation in his eyes made Lincoln's heart ache. "I will always be your dad, no matter what happens. It's true that I can't help your mom anymore. She's gonna have to help herself, but that has nothin' to do with you and me. I'm sorry she said that to you."

Thomas jumped up from his seat and threw his arms around Lincoln, hugging him tightly. When he let go, his eyes were bright. "Then I can move here and live with you? I want… Well, there are some things I need to talk to you about."

"Linc, we have a call." Charlene interrupted over the intercom.

"Okay, be right out." Lincoln tapped his fingers against the desk as he thought about what to do. "Tell ya what, we can discuss this later so don't worry about it. Since you're here, you can help Charlene. We're in the middle of plannin' a big barbeque, and she could use your assistance." Lincoln pulled his wallet out and handed over some money. "Go get breakfast for you both and do whatever she tells you, without hesitation, until I get back. Deal?"

Thomas beamed. "Deal."

"Now, there is nothin' else goin' on that I need to know about? You aren't in trouble with the law or somethin' like that, right?"

"Gawd, no. I just want…" Thomas hesitated. "Mom has gone crazy. We need to talk."

"Okay, we'll talk. You keep yourself out of trouble. Charlene is meaner than I am by a mile."

Thomas grabbed his dad in one last bear hug before they went back out front. "I love you, Dad."

"I love you too, son."

Lincoln left Thomas in Charlene's care, chuckling as he walked out to his pickup. With a long list in hand and a twinkle in her eye, his dispatcher was going to run that boy ragged. His next task was to call his mom. It was barely eight o'clock, and his day had already been a circus.

He dialed his mother's number as he drove to his assignment. Connie wasted no time on greetings. "What is going on with Thomas? Why would he do something like this?"

"He's gonna stay here at least for today and tonight. I need to talk to him. I suspect this arises from me refusin' to give Jeannie money. She told Thomas I cut them off and didn't want to be his father. He was understandably upset, but we got that worked out. I'll find out what else later. I have to go to work, so I left him with Charlene for the day."

"Lord, why does Jeannie have to try to hold on to you like this? I'm glad you cut her loose. Poor Thomas. Maybe it would be better if he was there with you."

"I don't know why Jeannie won't let go, but I'm not givin' her a choice. I've supported her crazy for eighteen years—hell, longer. I'm done. I have to go, but I'll call you later."

"Okay, honey. I love you."

"Love you too, Mom."

It had never crossed Lincoln's mind that his son would show up unexpectedly. Having Thomas with him would be wonderful, but there were more opportunities for him in Tulsa. They had been able to get him into a good trade school, and a facility of equal caliber didn't exist in a town as small as Harlow. Although Lincoln hated the thought of sending his son away, he had to make the right choice for his well-being. Thomas needed to go back to Oklahoma and finish school.

***

Kinsley's stomach rumbled as the third conference call of the day ended. The clock above the mantle showed half-past noon. She got up, wandered into the kitchen and absently plucked a few moon grapes from a fruit bowl on the counter.

Her deliberation about what to make for lunch was suddenly interrupted by a light rapping on the back door. A peek around the corner revealed a flaxen-haired young man standing on the porch. His deep tan and sunny smile rounded out a California beach-guy vibe. "I'm Thomas James," he shouted through the glass. "Lincoln is my dad."

Kinsley rushed to unlock the handle. "Thomas. Great to finally meet you. Please come in." She stepped aside and scanned the brown paper sacks he was carrying.

"Charlene said to bring this pie-making stuff to you. Where do you want it?"

"On the kitchen counter, please. I'm surprised to see you. Lincoln didn't say you were coming."

The youth sat his packages down and rested a hip against the cabinet. "Yeah, he didn't know. I kinda' surprised him." Thomas sported a rascally look that brought about a snicker from Kinsley.

"Well, either way, I'm sure he's happy you're here." She started to unpack bags, and he pitched in to help.

"How is HVAC school going?"

"It's going." His pessimistic tone spoke volumes.

"You don't like school?" she asked.

"I love school. I don't like air conditioning."

Kinsley chuckled.

"I mean, I like air conditioning as a general rule, but I don't want to work on it," Thomas added, smiling.

"I was just going to have lunch. Do you want to stay?" He hesitated long enough that Kinsley thought she shouldn't have asked. "You don't need to feel like you have to say yes. I understand if you have other things to get back to."

"I'd love to stay, but I'm on thin ice with my dad. I don't want to piss him off."

"I'll take the hit. Tell Lincoln I made you eat with me." She winked and pulled out sandwich makings for them both. They took their plates and moved into the dining room.

Thomas stopped at her open laptops, ogling her screens. "What's all this for?"

"I'm a programmer. I was working."

He whipped his head up as enthusiasm filled his coffee-colored eyes. "Omigod! Be right back." He set down his plate, sprinted out the front door, and was back in a flash with a backpack. He took a chair beside her and pulled out a laptop. "Seriously, I can't believe you know code. Dad didn't say he knew a programmer."

"To be fair, he doesn't know what I do," she said as they focused on his screen.

"I've been working on this game for a while, but I'm stuck. Do you think you could help me, please? I mean if you have a little time. Maybe tell me where I went wrong?"

Her smile deepened. "Let's eat, and then I'll take a look."

Kinsley gave Thomas her undivided attention as he shared his love of coding. He lit up like a Christmas tree as he spilled out his plans for developing his game. She could see this was where his passion lived, and air conditioning repair was getting in the way.

They finished eating and pushed aside their plates. "I have to warn you. I don't do gaming code. I'll help as much as I can, but no promises." She didn't want to disappoint him; she was impressed that the young man had done this with no background, schooling, or help. "Thomas, this is very good. Why aren't you going to school for programming?"

His eyes slid to her and back to his screen, but he said nothing.

"You obviously have a gift. Is there some reason you didn't want to make a career of it?"

Thomas continued to type for a while before he answered. "My mom's soon-to-be ex-husband is an HVAC tech, so they decided I would be too. None of them understand this like we do. They think I can't get work, so I was outvoted. I don't want to disappoint Dad and my grandparents." The desolation on his face touched her.

"Why don't you talk to your dad? If you tell him how you feel, maybe you can get him to understand."

He tapped the keys a few more times, then smiled so wide she could see every tooth in his mouth. "*You* could convince him. You make a living doing this." He shot Kinsley a puppy-dog face that made her giggle.

"Lincoln and I are just friends. I don't know that he would listen to me about matters that concern his son's future."

"Charlene said—" Thomas stopped abruptly and turned his attention to his laptop.

"You can't just start something like that and not finish. What did Charlene say?"

"I shouldn't." He did his best to hide another grin.

"You better," Kinsley teased.

Thomas peeked over at her. "Charlene said my dad likes you."

"As I said, we're friends. Of course, we like each other."

"Not that kind of like. He like-*likes* you. She said Dad has quit going to Pearl's because some people were mean to you, and he spends all his time with you. She told me he stands around staring into space. Are you dating him in secret?"

Kinsley tried to ignore how her heart warmed at this new information. "No, Thomas, we aren't dating. I think Charlene is stirring up something that isn't there."

Thomas gave her a look that said he didn't believe her just as the door chimes rang. "If it's Dad, please say you'll help me talk to him?"

Kinsley patted his shoulder as she got up. "I'll do what I can."

***

Lincoln stood on Kinsley's front porch as mad as a hornet. When he'd gone to pick up Thomas, Charlene reported that she had sent him to Kinsley's around lunchtime and hadn't seen him since. He was annoyed that his boy hadn't reported back to Charlene after he'd left specific instructions to behave.

Kinsley swung the front door open and gave him a big smile. "Did you come to see your son?"

"Thomas is still here? Has he been here all day?" Lincoln grumbled, though seeing Kinsley happy softened his anger.

"Not all day, since lunch. We've been working on his game. Do you know that he has a gift for programing?"

"Oh Lord, he's been buggin' you with that crazy game thing? I'm sorry, Kinsley. I'll get him out of your hair." Lincoln started into her house, but she put a hand on his arm.

"Lincoln, you have a wonderful son. I'm a programmer. You knew that, right? Thomas and I have a lot in common."

"I guess I didn't know exactly what you do." Warmth curled in his stomach as he looked at her. "My kid has some silly ideas, though."

"I hope you'll listen to him. He's brilliant. I've made a good living doing a similar type of work."

"Are you two making out or what?" Thomas hollered.

They laughed awkwardly and Lincoln followed Kinsley into the dining room. He laid a hand on his son's shoulder. "Kins and I are friends, son, and you are a mess. We better get out of here because you've kept her tied up all afternoon."

"It was no imposition at all," Kinsley objected. "I've enjoyed Thomas being here. Do you both want to stay for dinner? We can order a pizza and chat."

The younger James nodded enthusiastically. Lincoln hesitated, then said, "Looks like I've been overruled. Harlow doesn't have delivery. We'll have to go get it."

Thomas jumped up. "I'll go and be back in a little bit. You two relax."

Kinsley pulled some money out of her pocket and pressed it into Thomas's hand. "Tell Mario hello."

As the boy headed out the door, Kinsley turned to his father. "Do you want a beer, Linc?"

"Sure." Lincoln trailed her into the kitchen. Kinsley waved off the money he offered her to pay for dinner, but he insisted and laid cash on the counter. Then he leaned against a cabinet and watched her. "Why do I feel like you are about to talk me into somethin'?"

Kinsley shot him a grin before leading him through to the living room. She turned the music on low and planted herself on the couch. Lincoln took a seat beside her. "Thomas is a great kid with a talent for coding not many people have. He hates HVAC work, but he'll do whatever pleases you. Let him be happy, Lincoln, even if you can't understand. I'm telling you, a good living can be made doing what I do."

"Not here, it can't." The sheriff wiped at the condensation on his bottle.

"If I can make a living here, so can he. What I do know is that he'll never be content working at something that's been chosen for him. There is a possibility he'll have to move away for certain opportunities—who knows?" She laid her hand on his. "But promise you'll keep an open mind?"

"You're special, Kinsley Rhodes." Lincoln let his eyes roam over her face. "I want to kiss you."

"Why don't you?"

He didn't need a second invitation; for weeks he'd thought of little else. Lincoln cupped her jaw and brushed her silky skin with his thumb, enjoying the electricity building between them. Before he could make his move, Kinsley planted her mouth on his with such enthusiasm that she knocked them both back against the sofa cushions, leaving Lincoln torn between her velvet lips and keeping his beer upright.

When they came up for air, he whistled. "Whoa there, tiger."

"I was afraid you'd change your mind." Kinsley propped herself against his chest and watched him.

Lincoln placed his beer on an end table. He pushed back her hair and caressed her cheek. "I'm not changin' my mind." His full lips brushed softly across hers as he wrapped his fingers in her hair and brought their mouths together. When he broke the kiss, he delighted in her parted lips and flushed face.

"You're really good at that," Kinsley said dreamily. "Let's do it some more."

Lincoln was only too happy to comply.

CHAPTER EIGHTEEN

Turn, Turn, Turn

Spring had turned to summer and, as Kinsley drove through town, she reflected on the past couple of months and how dramatically her life had changed. Grandpa's body had been released, and his cremation had taken place. The order of service for his memorial had been finalized, meaning her time in Harlow would soon be coming to an end.

In between their work and other responsibilities, Kinsley and Charlene had almost everything primed for the sheriff department's benefit. The park was in readiness for a day of festivities: a car show, food, entertainment, and games for the kids. Afterwards, there would be a dance at the VFW hall across the street from the park. Dusty, Gabby, and Thomas had pitched in, and it was shaping up to be one almighty shindig.

Thomas and Kinsley had become fast friends, and he came over every day to work on his game. When it was decided that Thomas would be staying in Harlow, he and Lincoln took a quick trip to Tulsa to fetch his belongings. Kinsley used what pull she had in the IT community to get Thomas into the programming curriculum at a community college in a nearby town. The young man's magnetic personality had landed him a part-time job at Mario's Pizza Parlor. Everything was coming together nicely in her little corner of Kansas.

Kinsley and Lincoln spent nearly all their free time together, but they weren't officially 'an item.' She secretly feared his reluctance had something to do with her being damaged goods, but she didn't want to break the magic they were enjoying by asking him.

Kinsley pulled her vehicle into an empty spot at the sheriff's office, picked up Charlene's lunch and went inside. A midday catch-up with the dispatcher had become a regular routine.

"Hey, Kins. Thanks for lunch." Charlene unsnapped the lid and peeked inside. "What yummy thing did you bring me today?"

"Oh, just a little stir-fry. Thomas said he was actually going to die if I didn't make him some." She rolled her eyes, but her smile said she enjoyed the boy's company. "How are things today? Anything I can do?"

Charlene held out an invoice. "Strangest thing. We got a bill from the butcher for the barbeque this weekend, and it's been paid."

After she scanned the document, Kinsley replied, "Maybe someone caught a generous bug?"

"That's about five grand worth of generous," Charlene said, while shuffling through paperwork. "Oh hey, I got calls from several car clubs up in northeast Kansas. They're coming down, and they've already paid their entry fees. It's gonna be the biggest fundraiser ever."

"Nice. You guys need the money." Kinsley's phone rang. She glanced at her caller ID and smiled broadly. "This might be good news." She moved into the hallway to take the call in private. "Hi, Leon."

"Hi, princess. I got your voicemail about Henry's service on Friday. If we show up there, it's going to turn into the Leon Boss show. It shouldn't be about me, it should be about Henry. What do you want me to do?"

"You know better than I do how that famous thing works. It's sweet of you not wanting to turn Grandpa's service into a spectacle. I know you loved him." Kinsley hesitated; she disliked requesting favors. "I did have another reason for calling. Please say no if… Well, I know you're a superstar now, so…"

"Out with it, Kinsley Dawn," Leon teased.

"I wondered if you were going to be close to home this weekend. We need donations for the sheriff's office. We're having a dance on Saturday night. If you could stop by, it would be huge." Kinsley held her breath as she waited for him to answer.

Leon's warm laugh put her at ease. "Kinsley, I could never say no to you. We'll be in Amarillo on Friday, and we'll come up Saturday afternoon. It will be perfect. I can pay my respects for Henry that way."

"Leon, you are the best! Let me know how much, and we'll get you paid."

"Tell ya what, we normally charge twelve grand for a small show, but I'll match whatever donations you can raise, and we'll play the whole dang dance. That'll be all right with you?"

Her squeal bounced off the cinderblock walls. "I can never thank you enough. I'll let you present the donation when you play."

His deep, throaty laugh preceded his reply. "Sure, that would be fine. See you in a few days, sweetheart."

"See you, Leon. Thank you so much!" Kinsley ran back down the hall to the dispatch desk.

Bewilderment stopped Charlene mid-bite. "What the hell, Kins?"

"I got Leon Boss to come play Saturday night."

The dispatcher dropped her fork and stood up. Her voice rose several octaves. "What? He's a superstar!"

"I know, right?" Kinsley beamed.

"Holy moly! How did you do that?"

"I know Leon. I have to get the word out." Kinsley started to leave, then turned around. "I'll get my dish tomorrow. I have to run. Exciting!"

Kinsley hurried home to share the good news with Thomas, who was in his usual place at her table. She'd put him in charge of a website she'd created for the barbeque, and she watched as he made changes. Together they called local radio stations and newspapers to let them know that Leon Boss would be performing in Harlow.

Kinsley smiled with satisfaction, knowing that she had found just the thing to make this barbeque epic. Her delight turned to dread when she glanced out the front windows and saw Rich Skelly pull into the driveway.

"Kins, what's going on?" Thomas asked as he tailed her to the front of the house.

"This guy is trouble," she whispered over her shoulder. "Stay behind me." She flipped the lock on the storm door into place and called through the barrier, "What do you want?"

Rich immediately dropped his salesman act and sneered at her as he stopped at the door. "You don't have any manners."

"No, I don't. Get off my porch, dick," Kinsley hissed. Silently she dared him to try to come into the house.

Skelly's beady eyes cut to Thomas then back. "You think this skinny kid is going to protect you?"

"You are trespassing. Get off my property, or I'll have you charged."

"By who? No one is going to arrest Rich Skelly." He placed a hand on the doorframe and leaned in.

"Wanna try me?"

A police cruiser pulled up to the curb in front of her house, and Danny Singleton clambered out.

"There is your ride, Skelly," Kinsley said.

"Bitch!" Rich barked, his spittle landing on the glass between them.

Kinsley felt Thomas try to push past her. She extended her arm to stop him and shook her head. Her eyes never left Rich. "You bet I am."

Skelly's voice raised a pitch. "I want to buy Henry's land from you."

"Nope. Go away. You have five seconds," Kinsley warned.

"His land is too small to farm successfully, and some corporation has bought up everything around it. Come on," he begged, "sell it to me before that mysterious conglomerate buys it."

"You're out of time, Skelly," she announced.

Rich stumbled and ran off her porch. In his hurry to escape, he nearly knocked down Danny. The cop's stare followed him to his car. "You okay, Kins? Thomas sent me a text."

"I'm good, Danny. Thanks for coming. Skelly is a

problem."

The officer watched the red BMW speed down the street. "Looked like Rich was running away."

"Yep. Not as dumb as he looks."

"I heard Leon Boss is going to be here for the barbeque."

"It's going to be a hell of a show." She reveled again in the win.

"Sure is. See you two later." The policeman tugged the bill of his hat lightly and nodded goodbye.

"Bye, Danny. Thanks again." Kinsley closed the interior door and patted Thomas's shoulder. "Thanks for calling in backup." His unwavering stare prompted her to ask, "Did you need something?"

"Has that guy hurt you?"

"Not physically, but the possibility remains."

Thomas followed her back to their makeshift office and they resumed work. Kinsley's phone rang a few minutes later. "Hi, Lincoln."

"Skelly is gone, right?"

"Yep, he didn't like the prospect of going to jail. Go figure." Kinsley tried to ease his concern. "Thomas is fine. Don't worry."

"I was worried about both of you," Lincoln replied. "What did he want?"

Kinsley thought about the conversation. Skelly had seemed desperate. His father owned hundreds of acres; why would one measly section matter? "He wants to buy Grandpa's land."

There was a brief hesitation before the sheriff spoke. "Hm. Peculiar."

"Yes, it is," she agreed.

Lincoln jumped to her other news. "Hey, you amazing woman. I can't believe you got Leon Boss to come Saturday."

It pleased her that he was impressed. "I did. Exciting, right?"

"How'd you pull that off?"

"Leon is an old friend. His band has a gig down in Amarillo on Friday night, so it worked out for him to drive up for the barbeque." She couldn't contain her elation. "I'm thrilled he's coming. I haven't seen him in a while. You'll like Leon. He's a fun guy."

"You're the best. I'd better go, but I'll be over for dinner."

"See you then," Kinsley said before ending the call. She stroked her thumb across his name on the screen of her phone before it vanished.

***

Lincoln slid his pickup into park while he thought about Rich's offer to Kinsley. He looked up at the sign on the building in front of him: Brooks and Brooks Law Offices. It vexed him that he couldn't figure out what was so unique about Henry's piece of land. He picked up the file that contained the offers they'd found and headed inside.

A sharply dressed paralegal took his name before she seductively swayed down a hall, only to return a few minutes later to announce, "Mr. Brooks will see you, Sheriff James." The sharp citrus scent of her perfume preceded him to the last door, where she left him with a promising wink.

As Lincoln entered, a rotund man who occupied most of the space behind an enormous glass desk pointed toward a chair, while continuing to rail against whoever was on the other end of the phone. Gavin Brooks looked like he would be a cold-blooded adversary. This situation had Skelly written all over it.

The receiver rattled against its base when the lawyer ended his call. "Sheriff James, what can I do for you?"

Lincoln cut right to the chase. "Mr. Brooks, I have letters from you to a man in Harlow that I'd like a little information about." He handed over the file.

Gavin flipped it open and quickly scanned the contents. When he didn't raise his eyes, Lincoln's suspicion went on high alert.

"Henry Rhodes turned down all offers. That's all I can tell you." The lawyer's scowl slowly morphed into a deep belly laugh that made the objects on his desk rattle. "That man was a corker. I have never met such a direct person in my life. He physically removed me from his porch."

"He's been murdered, Mr. Brooks. I need to know where this offer came from, and why it was made. What is it about the Rhodes farm that would interest someone enough to hire you to try and buy it?"

"All I can say is that land is a valuable thing, Sheriff. Even if I knew why—and I don't—you know that I can't share that information. I am sorry about Mr. Rhodes, but you're barking up the wrong tree here."

Lincoln could see he was wasting his time. "Thank you for seein' me, Mr. Brooks."

"Certainly, Sheriff. I wish you luck with your investigation."

Gavin Brooks might be a tough lawyer, but he was a lousy liar. Lincoln was certain that the man knew the reason for the offer. He was just as sure that Max Skelly had paid the lawyer a sum large enough that he might be willing to go to jail to keep the secret.

***

Kinsley worked through tickets and made a call to a new programmer she'd hired, justifying the expense by telling herself that her company was too busy. The truth, however, was that she wanted to spend more time with Lincoln, Thomas, and her friends.

Thomas left for Mario's at five, leaving Kinsley on her own to start dinner. Lincoln hollered from the front door just as she flipped chicken fried steaks to finish cooking. "Kins, I'm here."

"Kitchen," she called back, then stopped a bag of flour from tipping over onto the counter.

The sheriff came around the corner and smiled. He moved up behind her and kissed her cheek before checking out what was in the pan.

"Mmm, you smell good." Kinsley leaned back against him.

He brushed his jaw against her temple. "Like what?"

"Hay, outside, and you." She turned around and rose on the balls of her feet to kiss him.

"You taste good," he said before he moved to get out the plates. "What was the deal with Skelly earlier?"

Kinsley washed and dried her hands before she dished up the food. "That was a surpri—" The doorbell stopped her. She put the plate she was holding on the counter and turned off the burner. "I'll get it."

It had been a day for unexpected visitors, and Ted Smith rounded out the assembly. Kinsley hadn't seen him since she'd been home, though she'd spoken with him over the phone a couple of times about tasks around the homestead. "Hi, Ted. We were sitting down to eat. Do you want to join us?"

"Sure, if you don't mind. That would be great."

Kinsley noted his deeply lined skin, tan from years of working outside, and his fringe of gray hair. Life had taken its toll on Mr. Smith. As they went into the kitchen, she asked, "Would you like beer or something else?"

"Beer, thanks." He grunted as he lifted one hip to get onto the barstool. "Hey, Sheriff."

"Ted. What's the new gossip in town?"

As the men chatted about what was happening in the county, Kinsley set another place. Lincoln's questions seemed innocent, but the answers could lead to information about her grandfather's death. She admired his doggedness.

When they finished eating, Ted leaned back and patted his jutting belly. "Hey, Kinsley, I heard from the corporation I farm for. They want to donate all the diesel and anything else we need to harvest Henry's crops. I guess they heard he was a good guy or somethin'. Strange they even knew about Henry because I think they are someplace in Minnesota." Ted tapped his fingers on the counter like he was trying to remember something then gave up with a shrug. "Anywho, my son can drive the grain cart, but we need a semi. What about pay?"

"I can pull the truck out of the barn and drive the

grain to town." The thought of driving the semi-truck again gave Kinsley a thrill. "I'll pay you and TJ for your labor. I appreciate you doing this for me, Ted. While we're on the subject, I wondered if you would still be interested in renting Grandpa's land and farming it for me?"

"Sure, I would. I can show you the contract I have with the corporation I farm for. If that works for you, we can do the same."

To check one more thing off the list was satisfying. "That would be fine."

Ted hem-hawed around before he presented what was on his mind. "If you ever want to sell that land of Henry's, I'd be interested. It's close to mine and it would be easy to farm along with what I have."

Kinsley thought about the increasingly bizarre situation. That section was not particularly desirable, but at least Ted's offer made more sense than Skelly's. "Thanks," she said, "but I'm hanging on to it."

Ted nodded. "Understandable. Dinner was good. Don't get much home cookin' since Marla left us."

"I was sorry to hear she left." Kinsley could imagine how hard life was for him alone.

His pained look dropped to the beer in his hand. "Being the wife of a poor farmer and livin' out in the country wasn't ever gonna work for her. It was hard on TJ. He was close to his mom. Now that she moved to Omaha, he don't see her much."

Kinsley knew how hard it was to grow up without parents, but TJ had a good man in his life, as she'd had. "Farming is a tough life and living in the country can be isolating." She changed the subject. "I have a cherry pie.

Ice cream?" Ted and Lincoln both brightened up like kids at the offer.

Lincoln sighed appreciatively when he'd finished dessert. "Dinner was fantastic. Thank you." He reached over, squeezed her fingers, and turned to Ted. "Kinsley got Leon Boss to come perform Saturday night."

"Really? That oughta be a good time. You have friends in high places, girl."

She laughed; Leon was as regular as they came.

Ted moved the crumbs around on his plate. "You plannin' on staying here, then?"

"It wasn't my original plan, but a lot has happened. I'll be around for a while."

He cleared his throat as he rose. "Hey, I better get out of your hair. Thanks for feedin' me. It was great. I'll talk to you when we're ready to harvest. Probably a couple of weeks, but I'll see you Friday for Henry's service."

Kinsley escorted him to the door then returned to the kitchen. "That was a little odd, right?"

"There are a bunch of odd things goin' on around here lately," Lincoln said thoughtfully. "I want to thank you for everythin' you're doin' for Saturday."

"You're welcome. I hope you can hire help after."

"Me, Butch, Danny, and Charlene are about run ragged. I think we're all hangin' on in hopes the commissioner will lose this next go around, and we can get someone fair in that spot."

"I can see how you'd be exhausted." Kinsley took Lincoln's hand and stroked his fingers. "And, yeah, Skelly needs to go."

Lincoln nodded. "That is a fact. But you work as

much as I do, plus all the other stuff you're doin' for me."

Kinsley leaned forward and kissed his cheek. "No worries. I hired a couple of people to help me."

Lincoln's eyes widened. "When did you do that?"

"This week. We signed the contracts today." A pleased smile settled on her lips.

"It's amazing what you can do without ever leavin' your house. You know my son thinks you are a computer goddess." Lincoln gave her a quick peck. "He's right."

Kinsley turned the color of a ripe strawberry. "Hardly, but Thomas is a good kid. I like having him around. He challenges me. He made the changes to the website today, and I just watched. He's going to be excellent."

Lincoln's mood took a more somber turn. "I should probably share some information about Thomas and my history with his mother. I don't want to keep things from you."

She tensed but gave him her full attention. "I'm listening."

"I married Thomas's mother right after high school. I had joined the Navy, and I left the day after our ceremony. While I was overseas, she got pregnant by another man. We were only married a couple of years, most of that while I was out of the country, and we couldn't get divorced."

Kinsley grasped his hand, realizing the hurt he had lived with. Like her, he was a little broken.

"Thomas isn't biologically mine, and he knows I adopted him, but he's my son, blood or not. Early on, I tried to get his father to come around, but it did no good."

She'd never imagined Thomas wasn't Lincoln's

biological son. To have his wife cheat on him, and then for Lincoln to take care of a child who came from that deception was incredible. "You are a rare human being. You took responsibility when the person who should have stepped up failed."

"It was the right thing to do—and I ended up with a great kid." He leaned in to kiss her but pulled back when they heard Thomas announce his arrival from the front of the house.

He regaled them with tales of the world of pizza, excited to try out the Italian Mario had been teaching him. His enthusiasm sent them all into fits of laughter. Then Lincoln's phone rang.

"Linc, there are cows out on the highway near Henderson's place," Charlene sighed. "Butch is tied up."

Lincoln thanked her and hung up. "Come on, you two, let's go round up cows in the dark." As they piled into his pickup he squawked "Ten-eight" into the radio mic to let Charlene know they were on their way.

The stars sparkled in an inky sky as they drove through the hot summer night—rhinestones scattered across midnight silk. Out here, a person could almost see forever across the flat expanse of farmland. Wide-open spaces revealed little towns miles away, their lights glinting like rubies and pearls. Kansas held a subtle beauty that only a quiet eye could see.

They arrived at their destination, and the men put flares on both ends of the area to warn motorists while they waited for the owner to show. Most of the herd had wandered back toward a hole in the fence, and the three non-cowpokes urged the rest along.

Kinsley heard her phone ringing and sprinted to Lincoln's truck to get it. Charlene spoke rapidly. "I'm sending Danny to your house. The alarm is going off."

An eerie feeling crept over her. "Thanks, Charlene. Let me know if we need to come back to town right away or if that crazy neighbor cat has set it off again."

"Will do, girl."

Lincoln leaned against the bed of his truck next to her. "That fencin' was cut, not torn down."

She frowned. "Charlene just called because my house alarm is going off. She's sending Danny. Set up, you think?"

He pressed his lips into a thin line. "Awful coincidental."

"What would someone want in the house? I've searched it from top to bottom. There's got to be something in there, right? Something we haven't found."

"Maybe they thought you'd be gone by now. As of dinner tonight, Ted knows you aren't leavin'. He might have told someone who wants to scare you off. Could be they didn't know you have an alarm."

An old pickup approached. Lincoln pushed off from his truck and spoke quietly. "Leroy Smalls. A good buddy of Rich Skelly." His eyes slid to Kinsley. "Skelly is lookin' very suspicious right about now."

They left the farmer to his work after prying Thomas away from a calf he had befriended. Danny stopped by when they got home and reported that he hadn't found anyone around Kinsley's house. She called the alarm company to set up an appointment for them to come out and adjust the monitors since the local tomcat had set it off three times now.

Despite her protests that she believed it to be an animal and nothing more, Lincoln and Thomas checked her entire house, but they found nothing that would indicate an attempted break-in. After a night of strange coincidences, Lincoln didn't want to leave Kinsley alone. "Maybe you should come stay with us."

"I'll be fine, Lincoln. Besides, you don't have any room at your house." She brushed her hand soothingly over his upper arm.

Thomas issued a fake cough. "Dad has a huge bed." Lincoln and Kinsley both hooted at his suggestion.

After Thomas and he went home, Lincoln sat on his porch. The cop in him didn't truly believe that a cat had set off the alarm. Could Henry's violent end have been a scare tactic to dissuade Kinsley from keeping the land? But what was the endgame?

He had one more promising lead to follow: Leon Boss. According to Kinsley, Boss had known her grandfather all of his life. While Henry would have most likely protected his granddaughter from any unsavory facts about his past, he might have shared them with a close friend.

Lincoln watched Kinsley's shadow through the curtained window as she sat at her dining room table. Her house was secure, and he had the city patrol doing a round once an hour. Someone would have to be insane to try to hurt her with him so close.

He opened the screen door. Thomas was watching television. "I'm going over to Kinsley's. Lock the door. I have a key." His son nodded but didn't look his way.

Lincoln crossed the short distance and rapped on her door. Kinsley let him in with a quizzical look. "Can I sleep on your couch?" he asked. "I'm worried, and I'll never get to sleep at home."

She gave him a mischievous smile. "No funny business, huh?"

Lincoln put up three fingers. "Scout's honor."

"How could I resist a scout? Let's have a drink, and we can discuss sleeping arrangements."

They talked late into the night, going over all the possible reasons someone might want to break into her house, but none of them held water other than wanting to scare her away. Finally, Lincoln lay back on the couch, and Kinsley snuggled in next to him as they both gave in to exhaustion.

CHAPTER NINETEEN

Goodbye Is The Hardest Word

Kinsley carried a stone in her chest where her heart belonged as she dressed for her grandfather's memorial service. By keeping busy, and even pretending Henry was at the farm and would be back, she'd been able to push away the fact that his absence was permanent. But this final goodbye brought home that he was never again going to walk in the door and hug her or make homemade ice cream. They would never sit on the bank of the tail-water pit to fish and talk, all because someone had ripped him away.

The townspeople packed the Methodist church. Kinsley delivered a eulogy while a video she'd made of Henry Rhodes' life played in the background. There wasn't a dry eye by the time she'd finished talking about the greatest man she had ever known.

The church ladies had put on a lunch. Lincoln and Thomas stayed close to Kinsley, and her heart overflowed at their kindness. Even the bullies kept it in check out of respect for Grandpa.

A large group stayed to share tales about her grandfather's capers. Some were stories she had never heard. Apparently, he'd been quite the ladies' man and somewhat wild in his younger years. Kinsley enjoyed learning about a side of him of which she'd never been aware. To her, he was always just "Grandpa."

Afterward, Lincoln and Kinsley took his ashes out to the farm together. She held the urn tightly against her chest as she looked out over Henry's land.

"I'm sorry he's gone, Kinsley." Lincoln put his arm around her shoulders. "I miss him, too."

"Thanks. I wish Grandpa were around to see us together. He always hoped I'd find someone—I think he'd be pleased it was you." Sadness thickened her words.

Lincoln smiled. "I know, he told me. Henry worried about you being lonely."

Her insecurity immediately roared to life. "Grandpa talked to you about me?"

"Nothing specific about your life now, mostly about when you were little and how proud he was of you."

Cold washed through her. "So, you knew things about me before I got here?"

"General information. Henry loved you. He was concerned about your happiness and safety," Lincoln replied warily.

Anger prickled over Kinsley's skin, and she stepped away from him. "Is that why you're with me? Some deal you made with Grandpa?"

"He did ask me to help you if something were to happen to him—"

She narrowed her eyes.

"Kins—"

She shook him off, stomped into the field, opened the jar, and threw the ashes high into the air. The wind carried them out across the fields Henry had loved so much. Her grandpa was now a part of this land for eternity. She whispered, "I love you, you sweet old man." Then she went back to the pickup and got in without a word.

Lincoln slid in behind the wheel. "Kinsley, it's not like you think."

She focused her attention straight ahead. Her heart already hurt from the funeral; to think that Lincoln was with her because of some agreement, and not because he wanted a relationship, made it infinitely worse. "You can't be with someone because of some deal you made with their grandfather. That's taking the good guy thing way too far. I don't need some pity relationship, or whatever this is."

Exasperated, Lincoln ran his fingers through his hair. "Dammit! I'm not hangin' out with you because I made a deal with Henry! And it certainly isn't out of charity. Yeah, he wanted to set us up the next time you came home because he thought I'd like you, but he died before you came back. You know full well you and I didn't hit it off when you first arrived. All claws and spittin' fire at me." He nudged her arm, but she didn't cave. "Ah, come on, you know that was a little funny, Kins."

Kinsley stared out the passenger-side window, wishing he would start the truck so she could get back to town.

He pushed her hair behind her ear. "I like you. You're witty, smart, and a lovely pain in the rear."

Kinsley expelled the breath she was holding. "So you didn't like me when I first got here?" It was time to ease up; the day had been taxing, and she knew she'd let her mood turn sour when it shouldn't have.

Acting on her lead, he feigned surprise. "Did it show?"

"No, not at all. Making me chase you all over town and ditching me in the diner seemed super friendly."

"In my defense, I didn't know who you were. But I am sorry for that."

Kinsley's anger drained away. "Well, I thought you were a pompous ass, and I wanted to throat punch you real bad, so we're probably even."

Lincoln put his hand around his throat. "Damn, but you are vicious." They both smiled as he urged her across the bench seat and into his arms. "I like you, Kinsley Rhodes. It's as simple as that. No other reason."

"Sorry, I'm such a disaster." Kinsley regretted letting her insecurity come between them. This slow crawl out of the dark was proving much more difficult than she'd imagined.

"It's okay. It kinda' turns me on."

A contented sigh escaped as she relaxed against him. "Really?"

"Uh-huh. I could show you later, if you'd like." His kisses scorched a trail down her neck. "But right now, we have to go pick up party supplies in Guymon, or Charlene is gonna end us both."

"Well, let's get on that, Cap'n." Kinsley landed a peck on his lips.

The radio crackled to life. "Linc, you there?" Charlene asked.

"Yep, out at the Rhodes' farm."

"You need to come to town now." Her voice conveyed uncharacteristic urgency.

"On my way." Lincoln hung up the microphone and swung his eyes to Kinsley. "I'm sorry, Kins."

"You have an important job to do, Sheriff. No need to be sorry." Kinsley fastened her seatbelt. "Drop me at home, and I'll go to Guymon by myself."

"Thomas would love to go with you."

"That's a great idea. I'll send him a text." She smiled reassuringly.

Lincoln raced to town and let her off at home, hollering, "Call me!" before he took off. His pickup tires squealed as he rocketed out of sight.

Kinsley was arming the alarm as Thomas jogged across the lawn. He whipped open the passenger door of her SUV and climbed in. "Hey, Kins. Thanks for taking me with you. Damn! This is one sweet ride. I've never been in a Range Rover." He pushed every button he could get his fingers on as Kinsley tried not to laugh at his curiosity. "I'm going to get myself a nice car after I go to work for you and make the big bucks."

His statement was a revelation. "You know my company doesn't handle game development."

Thomas continued his exploration of her vehicle. "I know, but I can do other work while I talk you into expanding your business plan to include gaming." He grinned impishly. "We'll start with my game first."

"I'll have to watch out for you, or you'll take over my company and kick me out." They were both beaming as she hit the road.

Guymon was situated just across the Kansas/ Oklahoma state line, a short forty-five-minute drive from Harlow. Grandpa had called the road between the two towns 'Smuggler's Run' because it was favored by bootleggers when he was a young man. He told thrilling stories of the illegal whiskey runs in which he'd been a willing participant.

As she drove, Kinsley kept an eye on her rearview mirror; she had become hyper-aware of her surroundings since the night of the cow call.

Thomas surveyed the passing landscape that consisted of prairie grass and yucca plants. "No wonder they call this a flyover state. Sure isn't much to see out here," he observed.

Kinsley smiled and pulled off the road onto a two-lane dirt path.

"Where are we going?"

"I have a surprise for you." She stopped next to the only grove of trees in the wide-open expanse, got out, and went to the back door of her vehicle. She pulled out empty bushel baskets from the back seat. "Watch out for rattlesnakes," she cautioned.

Thomas stopped dead in his tracks and gave her a horrified look. "We'll be fine. Just be aware. They are around," she laughed.

Thomas followed her reluctantly, his eyes trained on the ground. "Why are we messin' round with snakes in the middle of nowhere?"

"I want some cherries for pies, and Sandhill plums for jelly. You can help me." Kinsley had planned to do this with Lincoln, but teasing Thomas was more fun.

"It's called a grocery store. They don't have snakes there." He scanned the area around him as he tiptoed in her wake.

"This is more entertaining. Also, the fruit tastes better." Kinsley started picking plums from the bushes.

"We should hurry. Technically, we're trespassing on someone's land so we could get shot." It was a total fabrication: she had called Scott Weathers yesterday to gain permission to pick fruit.

"Shit, Kins," Thomas protested. "You're dangerous to hang out with."

"If you'll get a move on, we won't have to worry." She waved him toward the cherry tree. "Only the dark red ones, okay?"

Thomas gave her a cock-eyed smile and began to pick fruit from the tree, eating about every third cherry. "Wow, they are good. This is kind of exciting, as far as fruit picking goes."

"Country living has its moments. We can go out to the farm and fish some evening."

"I'd like that. Thanks for this." Thomas smiled at her and returned to picking fruit.

"You're welcome. We weren't going to get shot. I was only kidding you."

"I knew that," Thomas said indignantly, although Kinsley suspected that was a fib.

Once they'd loaded up, they made their way to their destination. The party store had everything boxed and ready for them. With her SUV packed to the roof, they were about to leave when banging on the car window sent adrenaline coursing through them.

Jerking her head toward the sound, Kinsley swiftly assessed the enraged woman who stood next to her vehicle. Out of caution, she rested her hand on the butt of the holstered gun that was concealed between the seat and the console. Thomas glanced down at the weapon, then leaned over her shoulder in a show of solidarity as she rolled down the window a crack.

"Yes?" Kinsley questioned, thinking she should have driven away instead.

"The least you can do is get out and talk to me!" the stranger shouted through the glass.

Thomas grasped Kinsley's wrist in a silent gesture that begged her not to get out.

"I don't know who you are." She searched the woman's features, trying to place her.

"I'm Billy's mom."

Kinsley gasped, every molecule of air rushing out of her. "Billy Long?"

The woman's voice was shrill. "Yes, Billy Long. The same Billy who your grandfather threatened until he joined the army and left. For what? F-For roughing you up a little at a party? If you didn't want to get with my boy, you shoulda stayed home. My son said you fucked every kid there, and he only did it because everyone else did. You dirty whore! You're fine, sittin' here in a damn expensive car, and my Billy is dead because of you!"

The lump in Kinsley's throat threatened to choke her as the rant continued.

"You are evil! I hope you die! You'll get what's comin' to ya, just like your grandfather did!" The infuriated woman kicked the car door with her booted foot.

Thomas leaned further across the console. "Hey, ya old hag, you better watch yourself."

Kinsley slammed the car into gear and stomped on the gas, causing the woman to jump back as they sped off. A few miles further on, she pulled into a gas station and parked. Snapping the holster thumb release back into place, she apologized to Thomas as a stray tear escaped and streaked down her cheek.

He laid his hand on her shoulder. "Are you okay? That was awful. No one should talk to anyone that way. Is that why you carry a gun, because of her son?"

She nodded but didn't look up.

"Kins, that guy was a monster. It's not your fault." Thomas waited for a minute before continuing. "My dad is a good man. He would never hurt you."

"I know he wouldn't. Thank you." Kinsley patted his hand. "I'm not what that woman said."

"Don't worry about what she said. She's obviously unhinged."

To her astonishment, Kinsley found herself hugging him. "Thank you, Thomas. I'm glad you're with me." She sat back and gathered herself. "I'd better make a call before we get on the road." Her fingers trembled as she dialed. "Hey, Charlene, I just had a run-in with Billy Long's mom in the parking lot of the party store. Thomas and I are leaving Guymon now."

"Gawd, be careful. What did Becky Long want with you?"

"Mrs. Long said she would like me to be dead." The words tasted harsh against Kinsley's tongue.

"Oh shit! Is she following you? I can call Dusty and send him your way, if you want. All the guys are tied up."

Kinsley's eyes flicked to the rearview mirror. "I don't see anyone behind me. This is a pretty solid vehicle. We'll be home in no time—but thanks, Charlene." Then she drove as if the devil himself were chasing her down the rural two-lane blacktop.

It was dark by the time they reached Harlow. She dropped Thomas off at the pizza parlor and headed to the sheriff's office. Charlene buzzed her in. "You okay?"

Kinsley pushed past the hurt that roared behind her smile. There was no reason to involve Charlene in her messy history. "Yep, no more problems. How are things here?"

"We have a standoff going on. Some nutcase has taken his ex-wife and kids hostage in her house," Charlene relayed wearily.

Kinsley sighed. "Is there anything I can do? Do the guys need coffee or food?"

The dispatcher picked up a piece of notebook paper and handed it to her. "Here is their order. I was waitin' for someone to show up."

"No problem, I'll go get it." Kinsley worried about how much more of this town's craziness the small police force could take before it shattered.

***

Lincoln pulled the Chevy into his driveway and killed the engine. The day's events were weighing heavily on his mind. A man was dead, and a family was destroyed. *For what?*

A blue glow flickered in the living-room window, indicating that Thomas must still be watching television. Lincoln looked toward Kinsley's house, which was devoid of light.

A broken heart could drive a person completely insane. Garrett Lamar had proved that when he'd held his ex-wife and children hostage, then taken his own life before Lincoln could stop him. Now the Lamar's two small boys would grow up without a father. Their mother, Lavonne, who currently held the position of county treasurer, was likely involved in some shady dealings with Commissioner Skelly that could land her in prison.

Garrett's death was yet another wound that Lincoln would carry with him. Maybe it was time to find a new line of work.

***

Kinsley woke when she heard Lincoln call her name. "Mmm, this is unexpected."

"Can I come in, Kins?"

She flipped back the covers. Lincoln turned on the lamp and removed his shirt and socks before he got in bed. He pulled her against him a little tighter than usual. Kinsley now welcomed his touch, but she still struggled with being held too closely. "Everything work out?"

"It's over," he replied.

Kinsley put her arms around him. Lincoln needed her, so she could endure him holding her tightly for a while.

He stroked her arm with his thumb. "I—"

Kinsley raised her head and tried to read what was going on with him, but his feelings were veiled. "What is it?"

He gave a heavy sigh. "Nothin'. Sometimes my job is hard." He rested his chin on the top of her head. "I'm glad you came to Harlow."

Kinsley didn't let go; she knew something genuinely

awful must have happened for him to act this way. "You better take care of yourself, mister."

Lincoln gave her a half-hearted smile as she looked up at him. "I'll do my best. Let's get a few hours of sleep. We're going to have a long day tomorrow."

CHAPTER TWENTY

Hot Cross Buns

The buzzing of the alarm clock made Kinsley groan. She untangled herself from Lincoln's embrace to reach over and tap the snooze button. When she settled back beside him, he was awake. "Good morning, Sheriff."

"Good-mornin', gorgeous girl. Thank you for lettin' me stay with you last night."

Kinsley propped herself up on one arm and admired his tattooed chest. "You're welcome. I like these." She bent to kiss the inked parts of his skin.

Lincoln released a ragged breath. "Your lips are as soft as a rose petal. Even before we got along, I dreamed about what they would feel like."

She placed her fingertips over her mouth in mock surprise. "Oh my! You had naughty thoughts about me when you didn't like me?"

He gave her his best panty-melting smile. "From the day I saw you walk into the diner in that snug skirt and those high heels."

Kinsley grinned as she pressed against his thigh. "What did you think of doing to me in my skirt and heels?"

Lincoln's voice lowered, "I'd best keep that information to myself. It's not for the ears of such a lovely young lady as yourself." He held her face and kissed her closed eyes, savoring this moment of serenity. Finally, he reluctantly threw back the covers. "It's time I got home and roused Thomas. We'll be late if we don't move."

The dew on the grass soaked the hem of his jeans as, barefooted, he crossed to his own house. Staying in bed with Kinsley would have been a dream, but he didn't want to push her too hard. She needed to know that she could trust him.

After showering, Lincoln made coffee and called to his son who wandered sleepily into the kitchen, poured himself a cup, and took a seat at the island.

"I need to ask you somethin'," Lincoln said. Thomas met his gaze. "How do you feel about Kinsley?"

The boy's eyes lit up. "Are you serious? Kins is the best. I don't know what you're waiting for. I've been angling for you and her to get together since I got here. Talk about two hard-headed people."

Lincoln thought about how to put the next bit delicately. "I like her too—I mean, I *really* like her. But I'm kinda nervous. Relationships have never been my strong point, and her experience with men hasn't been good."

He could almost see cogs turning as Thomas sipped his coffee. "You mean Billy Long?"

Lincoln was shocked that his son knew the name. "What do you know about that?"

"His mother attacked Kinsley's car when we were in Guymon and yelled the most obscene things at her. It was awful. Do you know Kins carries a gun because of whatever that asshole did to her? Someone should kick him square in the nuts."

Lincoln filed away this new information before continuing. "I don't want to make her life worse."

Thomas watched his dad over the rim of the cup. "Mom hurt you so badly that you've been alone ever since. Kinsley needs you, and you need her. Maybe you can fix each other."

Lincoln drank the last of his coffee and set his cup in the sink. He was proud of the man his son was becoming. "When did you get so grown up?"

"I just know you and Kins belong together. So quit messin' around." He got up and wandered toward his room. "I'm showering, then I'll meet you over at your girlfriend's place."

With a wide smile, Lincoln crossed the lawn. When he rounded the corner into Kinsley's kitchen, he gave a low whistle at the sight of her. "Damn."

She spun around to show off her new cream-colored lace dress. "You like?"

He bent and kissed her softly. "You look like an angel."

She slid her hands over his chest, then down to his heavy leather gun belt. "You're hunky. Love the gun."

Lincoln pulled her close. "Will you be my girl, Kinsley?"

She leaned back and searched his eyes. "You want me to be your girlfriend?"

"I do, very much."

"How will Thomas take it?"

"He's all for it. Said we're hard-headed and need to get with the program."

"I guess we better listen, Sheriff."

Lincoln cupped her head and kissed her to seal the deal.

"Lincoln James, you are a wicked tease."

He breathed in Kinsley's intoxicating scent before answering. "I'm completely serious."

Over breakfast, they discussed the day's upcoming events. "I have to take my SUV down to the park," Kinsley remarked as she ticked off her list.

"Why?"

She picked up a piece of bacon and waved it at him. "Because the entire back of it is filled with pies."

He took a bite of the bacon she was holding. "Pies?"

"Yes, I've been baking pies for days. You see, there's this sheriff who needs help, so I said I'd bake pies for his cause."

A look of surprise crossed Lincoln's face. "When did you have time?"

"While you were at work." She arched an eyebrow at his disbelief. "Do you doubt my ability to multitask?"

"Woman, I don't doubt you could do anything you put your mind to. I just thought you were workin'."

"I was, *and* baking pies." Kinsley winked at him.

He scooted her stool closer to him and nuzzled her neck as he ran his hand up her leg.

"Careful there, cowboy. You are about to hit something you aren't expecting," she cautioned him.

When his fingers touched cold metal, he pushed up her skirt to investigate. "Kins, you're carrying?"

"I always carry, Lincoln."

He pressed his lips together as the cop in him took over. "You need a license for that."

Kinsley leaned over and retrieved her purse from the end of the bar, removed her wallet, and handed him a concealed carry card.

"Of course." Lincoln couldn't help but smile. The woman was always prepared.

She put a hand to her chest and gave him her most sincere face. "I'm all about doing *whatever* the law tells me to do. I am committed to pleasing the sheriff." She blew him a kiss.

"You're sexy."

"So are you," she said. His slight blush delighted her.

"Oh hey, they'll be auctioning the deputies and me off. Well, deputy..."

"No worries, you are mine." Kinsley paused. "Unless you go for too much money..."

He hugged her, then leaned back and asked, "You carry when you run?"

"I've carried a gun with me at all times since that night they hurt me. I won't be a victim again." The sadness that crept into her eyes pained him.

"I'm so sorry," he said. "But even when you're under attack, it's harder to shoot someone than you may think. Takin' a person's life is a heavy burden to carry."

"I've taken every gun-safety class available. Many of the police officers and military personnel I've talked with have given me that same warning." Kinsley looked down as she played with her napkin. "I hope I never have to find out."

Lincoln pressed his lips to her forehead. "I won't let anyone hurt you, Kins."

"You can't always be with me. I have to be able to take care of myself."

He uncovered her firearm and pulled it from the holster. "Nice Beretta. Light." Ejecting the clip, the sheriff inspected it then snapped it back into place.

"It looks tiny in your hands," Kinsley said.

"It's a small gun, but it would get the job done," he asserted.

"I have my eye on a Sig Sauer since you talked up the brand. I've been shopping, but I've yet to find one that strikes my fancy." She reached out and stroked the grip on his gun. "Maybe you'll let me shoot yours so I can see what I think?"

"Damn, that was hot, Kins." Lincoln brushed his fingers over her bare shoulder as he exhaled. "How many guns do you have?"

"I kinda' have a gun-buying problem." A big grin split her face.

He chuckled. "You don't look like the type." His eyes roamed over her bare legs. He reached down, pulled a knife out of her boot, and held it up. "Kinsley!" He couldn't help but be proud of the strength of this woman. "My little bobcat."

His phone rang, and she took back her knife. "That would be Charlene chewing us out because we aren't there," Kinsley guessed aloud. She stuck the blade in her boot and holstered her gun.

"Yep," the sheriff said into his phone.

"You, Kinsley, and Thomas get your silly butts down here," his dispatcher admonished.

"On our way, ma'am."

Kinsley put the dishes in the sink and turned toward Lincoln as he approached.

"One last thing before we go." He issued a slow-burning kiss.

Kinsley smiled as she slowly opened her eyes. "Let's

get this show on the road, Sheriff."

As they walked out together, he squeezed her hand. "See you down there, gorgeous."

"Yep."

Her reply pleased him to no end. Miss Rhodes wasn't the same woman who had blown into town with a chip on her shoulder.

***

Kinsley parked her vehicle and walked around to raise the hatch as Charlene sidled up to survey the haul. "Wow, that's a ton of pies. Good job!"

"Thanks. Sorry we were late." Kinsley grimaced.

"You aren't late. I just started harassing early." A hearty cackle rolled out from between Charlene's glossy red lips. "Let's get these beauties to the food stand."

Lincoln parked his pickup, and he and Thomas piled out to help move pies. "Thomas told me what happened to your car." His eyes dropped to the dent in the door of her Range Rover. "We'll call the Longs in for questioning. That's not a normal way to act."

"Billy's mom was irrational—but thank you, Lincoln."

Charlene sent Kinsley to help with the hot-rod check-in. Butch and the officers of the car club were lining up vehicles; they'd had to block off part of Main Street and a few side streets to accommodate the hundreds of custom automobiles for the show. It promised to be an amazing fundraiser.

Kinsley smiled and complimented people until her face felt like it would crack. Lincoln appeared just in time with refreshment. "You, sir, are worth your weight in gold. Thank you," she said as she took the cardboard coffee cup he offered.

He smiled and kissed her swiftly. "How are you doin', my beautiful girl?"

"I'm grand."

Commissioner Skelly stopped at the sign-in table and scrutinized the couple. "Sheriff," he nodded. Lincoln nodded in return.

Kinsley retrieved a judge's nametag and handed it to the commissioner. Skelly looked her over like she was a cockroach that had just crawled across the Christmas dinner table, then he ignored her completely.

She placed a hand on her hip, revving for a showdown, but Lincoln caught her tension and gave her a meaningful wink as he laid his arm across her shoulders.

The commissioner pressed his lips into a thin line. "Sheriff, you and Miss Rhodes are overly friendly."

"Kinsley's my girlfriend," Lincoln stated proudly.

The commissioner raised an eyebrow, grunted, and walked away.

Kinsley pretended to be shocked. "Are you overly friendly with me, Sheriff?"

He kissed her, just as Charlene came by. "Let her go, Linc, and get to work or I swear..."

They both stifled a laugh as she walked on.

***

People were starting to show up in droves. The sheriff joined the men at the grills who were preparing for the crowd. The sweet and savory smell of burning hickory wood wafted through the park, whispering a promise of fabulous food.

Lincoln, Thomas, and Butch were cooking, along with Ted Smith and his son TJ. Ted's son was a few years older than her and a reticent man. Kinsley could see none of his father in him; she decided he must look like his mother's family.

Once most of the classic cars were in place, she checked with vendors to ensure no one needed help or supplies. A guy she knew from high school, Jack, one of the few kids who didn't shun her, had agreed to be DJ for the day. Her eyes drifted to the sheriff, who was joking with his son. When one of her favorite songs came over the speakers, she stole up behind him and sang softly. Turning around, Lincoln took her in his arms, and they danced around tables filled with condiments and buns.

His eyes caressed her face, "I'm crazy 'bout ya, Miss Rhodes."

A heady dose of elation churned inside Kinsley, but the realization that she'd fallen in love caused her to pull away. "I, uh, better skedaddle before Charlene catches us again."

Lincoln graced her with a smoky smile as he let her go and sent a wolf whistle her way. Kinsley blew him a kiss over her shoulder. Despite her pleasure, she was consumed with thoughts of being in love and the trouble that could cause. Thankfully, her cell phone rang and ended the growing squall. "Hello?"

"Princess, we're here but we can't get close."

"Leon! Drive down two blocks east from Main and come up Canal Street to the back of the hall. I'll meet you there."

"Got ya. I'll see you in a bit."

Kinsley texted Lincoln and Charlene to let them know that she was going to the VFW hall, then crossed the park to the DJ booth to get Dusty. "Leon's here. We need to go let them in."

Dusty wrung his hands. "It's freakin' Leon Boss, Kins. He has played the Grand Ole Opry. I'm nervous about meetin' him."

Kinsley patted his arm reassuringly. "Leon's just an ordinary guy. He's super nice. There's no reason to be scared." To everyone else Leon Boss was a country superstar, but she had grown up around Leon and his band. The singer had been like a second dad to her until his record hit big, and he'd left town for Nashville nearly fifteen years ago.

Kinsley and Dusty crossed the park, avoiding Rich Skelly and his brother. "Rich is such a jerk," Dusty whispered.

"Yes, he is."

Dusty smiled big as they made their way around groups of people. "I wanted to tell you that it's been great spending time with you again."

"It has been fantastic." Kinsley sensed there was more her friend wanted to say, but he held back. "Things are going well for you, right?"

"I'd like to go to work for Sheriff James. I wish I was built like him, then it would be no problem, but I look like Barney Fife." They chuckled at his apt comparison.

"What about in the office? You're good with radios— you could be a dispatcher. Do you think you might like that?"

Dusty stopped short as his mouth dropped open. "They have an opening? That would be perfect. And then at least I could be one of the guys."

She loved that Dusty was excited about working with Lincoln, but she had to be cautious not to make any promises. "I don't know what's coming up, but maybe I can help."

He slapped her on the back, causing a surge of fear to rush through her. She tried to hide her adverse reaction and cleared her throat. "Since that night, I..." She took a shaky breath. "I'm not much for unexpected contact."

"I'm sorry, Kins. I won't touch you."

"Don't worry. You didn't know," she said.

"It's because of what those guys did to you?" Dusty knew enough of what had happened that a nod from her was sufficient. "I've wished so many times I could've helped you," he confessed. He hung his head and brushed his hands on his jeans.

Kinsley stopped and turned to him. "You and Gabby saved me that night. I will be eternally grateful for what you did for me. You've always been excellent friends. I've lived under that dark cloud for long enough. I'm starting a new chapter."

He raised his eyes. "Some things people do to you never go away."

Surprised by his statement, she nodded. Kinsley looped her arm through his, and they fell into step as they let the past go for now.

Leon's tour bus rolled to a stop just as they removed the padlock and chain from the door of the meeting hall. Dusty stared at Boss's coach as if it were made of solid gold. "Come on," Kinsley urged, heading toward it as the band disembarked.

"Kinsley!" Leon Boss had a million-dollar smile, and he gave her every cent of it. He took her hand, spun her around like a ballerina and into his arms for a quick hug.

"Leon, I want to introduce you to Dusty Reynolds, a big fan and sound guy for tonight. You're a sweetheart for doing this for the sheriff's office." Kinsley threaded her arm through Leon's and laid her head against him for a moment.

The older man covered her hand with his. "I'm doing it for you, but it's also for a great cause."

Dusty could hardly stand still. "The sheriff is the best guy there is."

His testimony amused Leon. "I see you're a big fan of his."

Dusty grinned and went to help unload equipment.

Kinsley's phone buzzed, and she stepped away to take the call. "Hey, Gabby."

"I need you."

The desperation in her friend's plea sent panic pinging through Kinsley. "Are you hurt?"

"No. I was hoping you could make me look like … like not me. I tried, and I look like a nightmare. Please, Kins."

Taken aback by Gabby's request, Kinsley stumbled to recover. "O-okay. Meet me at my house. I'll be there in fifteen." She turned to the band. "I'm going to leave you in Dusty's capable hands. I'll be back in a little while."

***

Gabby was waiting for her when she pulled into the driveway, and it became apparent instantly that her friend wasn't kidding about the mess. She had on enough charcoal eyeshadow to make Kinsley wonder if there was any left in the compact. Paired with a severe bun, and a white John Deer T-shirt with emerald green around the collar and sleeves, it was a perfect combination of awful.

As they went into the house, Kinsley asked, "Was there a reason for this sudden change?"

Gabby blushed. "I've wanted to go out with Dusty for, I don't know, ten years. Do you think he could ever consider me as anything more than a friend?"

"I think he has a huge crush on you." A smile lit Kinsley's face. "It's easy to see."

Gabby didn't say anything for a few seconds. "Then what's been the holdup?"

"You know Dusty as well as I do. He is the shyest guy I've ever known when it comes to women. If you want to date him, you'll probably have to do the asking. I don't think he's ever dated anyone, has he?"

"There was a girl a few years ago. Pretty, sexy, aggressive. They hooked up for a while, and then she was gone. But I probably don't have anything he would be attracted to. I don't know what I was thinking."

"Gabriella Chambers, you are beautiful inside and out. As if that weren't enough, you're a genius. I've heard about your work at the county office. What's not to like?"

"Kins, you're my friend. You're just being kind."

"I *am* your friend, but that doesn't make what I said

untrue." As Kinsley considered her friend's predicament, an inspired idea struck. She extended her hand. "Come on. We're going to do a little enhancing, and then you'll see."

A short time and many brush strokes later, Kinsley stepped back and evaluated her work. A subtle shade of cream-colored shadow and a darker olive along the crease made Gabby's jade eyes even more dramatic. One last coat of mascara on her long lashes, and the masterpiece was complete. Kinsley smiled and nodded. "Take a look, gorgeous woman."

Gabby turned toward the oval mirror on Kinsley's dressing table. She breathed out as she leaned closer to her reflection. "It doesn't even look like me," she gasped.

"It looks exactly like you, and you are beautiful. Now, what do we have under this bun?"

Kinsley moved around behind her friend and began to pull out bobby pins. "Holy cats, Gabby, did you buy the store out?" Finally, the last clip was removed, and she unwound the mass of hair. Gabby's golden waves came to rest against her back, ending just past her waist. "That is the prettiest long hair I have ever seen," she said. "Why don't you ever let it out of jail?"

Gabby wiggled her fingers as she rubbed her scalp. "I don't know what to do with it."

"The color is amazing. It reminds me of the silk on an ear of corn," Kinsley observed.

With makeup and hair sorted, they moved to Kinsley's closet. Gabby picked out a top and shoes, donned the new outfit, and went to admire herself in the full-length mirror.

As Kinsley watched, tears welled up in her eyes. She had missed so much since that one unfortunate night. Having people back in her life was better than she'd ever imagined. "Come on, beauty. Let's go knock that man's socks off."

CHAPTER TWENTY-ONE

A Gift Horse

Kinsley and Gabby entered the VFW hall as the band was winding down their soundcheck. All eyes were on the willowy blonde as she made a beeline toward Dusty. Just as she reached her dumbstruck target, the band's drummer thrummed out a ba-dum-bum-ching that had everyone chuckling.

Kinsley approached the pair, who had somehow achieved a new level of awkwardness. "Doesn't Gabby look magnificent, Dusty?" He nodded, transfixed. "Did you tell her?" She popped him on the arm, which knocked him out of his stupor.

"Wow, Gabs. I mean, you're beautiful. But you're always beautiful, just different beautiful..."

Gabby flushed as she moved closer, brushing her shoulder against his. "Thanks, Dusty."

Kinsley smiled. Her gal pal knew how to play the game, so she left them to it and went to spread tablecloths on the picnic tables that lined the edges of the room. Her thoughts drifted back to the day after that fateful party eight years ago. Leon had shown up unexpectedly and flown into a murderous rage when he'd seen her battered face and bruised body. Grandpa had kept him in the house until he'd calmed down enough to be reasonable.

Leon had stayed for a week and brought Kinsley ice

cream and chocolate. He sat on her bed and read her those old Louis L'Amour westerns her grandpa loved. Once the swelling around her eyes had abated and she could open them again, they watched movies and played cards together. Leon had always been her hero.

Lincoln sauntered in and slipped his arm around her, just as the singer came off the stage. Kinsley introduced them. "Sheriff Lincoln James, this is Leon Boss." The men shook hands as they sized each other up.

"I see you have your arm around my girl. What are your intentions, Sheriff?" Boss tried to maintain a stern look, but he was a better singer than he was an actor.

"Only honorable, I assure you. She is special to me." Lincoln hugged Kinsley gently.

"You better be good to her. Because even though you are a very large man, I'll crawl up there and kick your ass if you hurt her."

"I promise you, I will take good care of her."

Leon smiled at Kinsley. "Princess, take me for a beer before we rock this joint. You will sing one with us tonight, right?"

"Leon, people want to hear you, not me."

The singer rubbed her arm. "You'll sing one with me because you can't resist my charms." He flashed her a smile full of sunshine.

Kinsley laughed. "You're right about that."

They locked the doors and sauntered to the beer garden. Lincoln squeezed Kinsley's hand. "I need to make my rounds, gorgeous. Keep the talent beered up."

"Will do." Kinsley looked toward Gabby, who was fluttering around Dusty like a butterfly just emerged from her cocoon. He couldn't take his eyes off her.

Lincoln bent and kissed Kinsley softly, then put his mouth to her ear. "You're the kindest person there is, and I'm glad you're my girl."

"I am too." He made her heart explode like fireworks on the fourth of July. Kinsley's gaze followed Lincoln's progress across the park.

Leon smiled. "The sheriff seems like a great guy."

"He is one of the good ones," she replied.

"I'm glad you're happy. It's been so long, I was afraid you might never heal."

"You and me both." She turned her attention to the band before the mist in her eyes turned into something more. "Let's get you guys some good barbeque."

They drifted toward the food tents on the other side of the park. People pointed at Leon and the band as they passed, and the group stopped to catch up with old acquaintances. Kinsley found a place out of the way to people-watch while she waited.

Suddenly a searing pain raced over her scalp as Rich Skelly grabbed a handful of her hair and forced her to face him. The fog of his drunken breath stole her air. Instantly rage placed her firmly in the middle of madness. "You picked on the wrong woman!" she shouted.

Kinsley rammed the heel of her hand up under Rich's chin and snapped his head back before executing a throat punch with destructive force. A barely audible sound gurgled out as he released her hair to clutch his windpipe. While he was wide-eyed and unsteady, Kinsley chambered her leg and slammed a solid side kick deep into his solar plexus. The air whooshed from him like the wake of a freight train as he toppled back and crashed into his brother. Together, they tumbled onto the grass in a whiskey-soaked pile.

Lonnie, his palms held up in a mollifying gesture, stepped between his brothers and Kinsley. "I'm sorry about them. I couldn't get here in time."

Her eyes swept up to his, and everything became crystal clear. She opened her mouth to speak, but Lonnie shook his head slightly. Kinsley studied his features as a familiar crooked grin broke across his countenance. Grandpa's smile. How could that be possible?

Lincoln, Leon, and the band members formed a semi-circle around Kinsley. The city officer, Danny, converged on the group and was first to speak. "I saw the whole thing. Are you hurt?"

"I'm fine." Kinsley tipped her head toward the men who were rocking like upended turtles, trying to right themselves. "Them? Maybe not so much."

Lonnie watched his siblings being loaded into a police cruiser before he turned to Kinsley. "My mother will expect me to take care of this. Would it be okay if I came by to talk before I go back to Dallas on Monday?"

She nodded, still stunned by the possibility that this stranger was most likely her uncle.

Lonnie addressed Lincoln. "I apologize for my brothers, Sheriff." Then he nodded toward the rest of the group. "Leon, good to see you again."

"Lonnie, take care." Leon clapped him on the back.

Lincoln pulled Kinsley close. "You okay?"

"I'm fine. Rich just pulled my hair and triggered my big red crazy button."

Leon's eyes sparkled as a hearty laugh rolled out. "You kicked his ass, princess."

"Years of kickboxing." Kinsley executed a perfect karate bow.

"They made a bad choice picking on you." He smiled at her with wonder. "Lincoln, you have got your hand's full, sir."

"I've never been so happy to have a problem like that," Lincoln replied. "Let's feed you guys so you can burn this place down."

Charlene trotted over to the group and tapped Kinsley's arm. "You're fine?"

"Yep."

"You should teach a self-defense class for women."

Kinsley nodded. "Self-defense is important. I'd be glad to show you some of the basic moves."

Charlene clapped excitedly. "Watching you in action was amazing! Like a martial arts film."

Kinsley doubted that she moved like Bruce Lee, but she took the compliment with grace. "Thank you kindly."

Charlene's attention had shifted to the star of the event. She tugged on Kinsley's skirt.

"This is Leon Boss." Kinsley stepped aside as she made introductions. "Leon, Charlene Grainger. She takes care of the office and keeps everything running for the sheriff."

When Leon took her hand and pressed his lips firmly to the back of it, Charlene giggled like a schoolgirl. "I'm a huge fan."

He turned his charm up to a level no woman could resist and folded her hand over his arm. "Thank you, lovely lady. How about you and I get some food?"

Charlene could manage little more than an awed stare and a nod.

Lincoln brushed Kinsley's shoulder to get her attention. His gaze followed the contours of her face as he pulled her close. "Seriously, you aren't hurt, are you? It happened so fast, they were all down by the time I got here."

She wrapped her arms around his waist. "I promise Rich did no lasting damage."

Lincoln smiled. "You certainly took him out." He swept her into a dance, his eyes devouring her.

The speakers overhead crackled as the DJ's voice drifted out across the revelry. "Time to announce the winners of the car show. Would Sheriff James please go to the stage?"

"Go get 'em, Sheriff," Kinsley encouraged.

***

Lincoln had just reached the risers when Max Skelly stopped him. "Your relationship with that Rhodes woman is inappropriate, Sheriff."

Lincoln narrowed his eyes. "It's none of your business. Back off."

He hated these public events, but he managed to look pleased, shake hands, and congratulate those who'd won. As he presented the last trophy, a tap on his shoulder drew his focus to a brown-uniformed courier. "Sheriff Lincoln James?" the messenger queried.

"You got him."

The courier handed him a shipping envelope and

held out an iPad. "Sign here, please."

Lincoln complied. Without another word, the messenger turned and left the way he'd come. Lincoln tucked the parcel under his arm and finished his ceremonial duties. When he rejoined the ladies, Charlene nodded at the packet. "What's that, Linc?"

Anxious to know himself, he pulled the zip tab and opened the flap. Inside was a letter. He passed it to Charlene, who said, "It seems we've been chosen to receive a donation from a company in Texas that supports law enforcement. How much is it?"

Lincoln peered inside the envelope and pulled out a check. A heady mix of elation and disbelief zigzagged through him. What the hell? Surely he couldn't be seeing the amount correctly. He handed it to Charlene. When she looked at it, a little squeak popped out. "Oh, my good Lord in heaven, no."

Stunned, she passed the bank draft to Kinsley, who whistled. "Now that is a chunk of change."

Charlene snatched it back and held it against her chest. "Half a million dollars," she whispered. "This can't be real. Who do you know in Texas?" she asked Lincoln.

"I don't know anyone but my sister, and it sure ain't her. It must be our guardian angel—the same one who paid for meat for the barbeque. Shit, that is a lot of money." He couldn't imagine where it could have come from.

Charlene giggled and hugged them both tightly, making Kinsley grimace. "Sorry, Kins, I forgot."

"It's okay. I'm getting used to it," she reassured her.

Charlene went to the office to lock up the donation

and check on Danny, who was on duty watching the jail. When she returned, she reported that the Skelly brothers were passed out drunk.

The band had finished eating. Leon made his way back to Kinsley. "It's time for us to give these people a show."

"Men, let's get this party rockin'!" On her cue, the DJ announced that the dance would start shortly. They opened all the doors of the hall, and Leon's band cut loose. After the first set, they called Lincoln up to the stage and presented their donation of twenty-thousand dollars.

It was as if the heavens had opened and carried Lincoln's worries away. The budget problems were gone, and his son was with him after years of wishing Thomas could be close. He raised his eyes from the payment in his hands to the woman in a strapless summer dress who had his heart, and wondered if it was all just a dream.

When Leon's band took a break, the car-club president announced the bachelors' auction. Everyone started with tiny bids, like a dime for Butch, who was thoroughly embarrassed, then they bid higher to help the sheriff's office. Butch seemed pleased to be sold to Diana Locke for three hundred dollars. A bidding war broke out for the sheriff, with Kinsley the ultimate victor. She would tease him later that a thousand dollars was more than he was worth.

Finally, Leon took the stage again. A hush fell over the crowd as he spoke. "Recently, I lost my best friend and the kindest man I've ever known. This next one is for Henry Rhodes. Kinsley, come on up here and sing with me."

She joined him reluctantly, and he hugged her close. "From all of us who thought you walked on water, this one is for you, Henry." A reverent silence fell over the crowd as the music began.

The words to this song were so Grandpa; to her, he *had* walked on water. Kinsley had to shut off her feelings to keep from crying. When she and Leon finished singing, the crowd nearly brought down the roof.

Kinsley escaped to the safety of Lincoln's arms, and they danced the night away until it was time to get things cleaned and shut down. Afterwards they met at their vehicles. It was nearly 2 a.m. Not a breath of air stirred around them as they stood together, thinking about all that had happened in the past twenty-four hours.

Gabby and Dusty waved as they got in his car together. Thomas cruised up and put his arms around his dad and Kinsley. "I'm going with my pals. They'll bring me home in the morning. You two go have some fun."

"Be good," Lincoln called out as his son hurried to catch up with a group of guys. He met Kinsley's look and smiled. "Let's go home."

CHAPTER TWENTY-TWO

Heaven On Earth

Kinsley pulled into her driveway as Lincoln came across the lawn. "Hey, cowboy, wanna play rodeo?"

Lincoln grinned as he took her hand and they went into the house together. He got them both a beer then leaned against the kitchen counter, contemplating the unexpected events of the day. "I can't believe someone would give our office half a million dollars. Who even has that kind of money to give away?"

Kinsley shrugged. "Drink your beer, Sheriff, and get yourself prepared to hire some help. Oh, by the way, Dusty would love to work for you. In case you couldn't tell, he thinks you're awesome."

"Dusty, huh?"

"A person doesn't have to be a huge, hunky cowboy to be a dispatcher or something like that, right?"

"You're sweet to the core." Lincoln leaned in for an unhurried kiss.

Kinsley nipped his bottom lip. "I want you."

The sheriff sat his beer on the counter and laid a string of kisses along her décolletage until he reached the delicate skin under her ear. His rough voice skittered across her goose-pimpled flesh. "And what do you want me to do with you, baby?"

Kinsley pressed her palm against his erection. His

jeans kept them apart as she rubbed his rigid length, leaving no doubt what was on her mind.

Lincoln's hands encircled her waist, and he sat Kinsley on the counter, kissing her as he stroked her thigh. His progress halted at her gun. He unstrapped the holster and laid it on the counter. "It's like tryin' to make love to an assassin."

She chuckled and moved his hand higher, whimpering when he reached the apex of her thighs. Her silk underwear only served to intensify his feather-light strokes. Her voice was a breathy whisper. "I'm burning up."

He stopped and raised his head to watch her.

"Tease," she sighed.

Lincoln pressed his lips against her sensitive flesh. "I won't make you beg me."

Shallow breaths shuddered out of her as his caresses resumed. "I ache. Please, Lincoln, I need you."

He unbuckled his gun belt and dropped it on the counter with a heavy thud. "Let's go to bed."

As he picked her up, Kinsley wrapped her legs around him, nuzzling his neck. He stumbled into the barstools. "Don't drop me, Sheriff," she giggled.

Once they reached her bedroom, she released her legs and slid down his body to stand in front of him. "What do we have under here?" she smirked as she unsnapped his shirt. Her fingertips skimmed over his stomach, enjoying the way his muscles quivered at her touch. Lincoln's half-lidded smolder made her melt. She stepped closer to him and glided her hands over the hard plane of his chest, pushing the shirt off his shoulders, and letting it pool on the floor. Her eyes drank in his bronze skin, following a tattoo that snaked over his shoulder and down his upper arm. Her fingers shadowed her stare.

She moved around him, trailing her fingers over his side, memorizing his form. His back was broad at the shoulder and cut to his waist. Another tattoo disappeared around his rib cage, playing hide-and-go-seek with her hungry eyes. She leaned forward and pressed her lips against the ink where it vanished around his side. His deep spicy scent saturated her senses. She ducked under his raised arm and stood facing him. "You are a beautiful man," she whispered.

"Beautiful." Lincoln's eyes twinkled like sapphire stars. "No one ever called me that." He didn't move for a moment, then he bent and captured her lips with his own.

"I can't wait anymore." Kinsley quickly stripped, threw back the covers and crawled to the far side of the bed.

Lincoln pulled the top button on his jeans, and the rest came undone in quick succession. He left the remainder of his clothes in a heap and joined her, pulling her back against him and nestling his erection between Kinsley's buttocks. A slow exploration of her willing flesh ensued.

"Lincoln, please. You're going to kill me," she begged him.

"Be patient, my love," he said as he kissed her shoulder.

She turned to face him, curling her leg over his hip. They fit together like puzzle pieces. Lincoln's normally gravelly tone took on a whole new level of smoky as he spoke. "You feel amazing against me."

Kinsley's past reared its demonic head, and she consciously fought back the impulse to stop him. Tonight, she would exorcise it once and for all.

Lincoln smoothed her hair back from her face. "I love you, Kinsley."

She searched his eyes and saw nothing but the truth. Kinsley urged him over her.

His muscles were strung taught as he pressed forward cautiously in case it was too much for her, but Kinsley took the lead. She pulled against him and thrust her hips upward. Her sharp exhale made Lincoln freeze. He framed her with his forearms. "Did I hurt you?"

With her palms against his back, Kinsley shook her head. "I've never done this before. And you're..." A blush crept over her cheeks. "You're a lot to take."

He ran his thumb over her full bottom lip. "Should I stop?"

"Please, don't stop," she whispered.

He moved slowly. "You feel like a dream."

Paradise descended, and Kinsley's desire became so urgent that she began to grind against him. Lincoln put a hand on her hip as they moved together. "Kins, you're perfect." His breath on her skin made electricity radiate out from where they were joined.

She grasped his buttocks, encouraging him to move faster. "Don't stop." As a mind-bending explosion roared through her, Kinsley arched against him and his name tumbled from her lips. "Oh God, Lincoln..."

Lincoln was buried in the best place on earth when ecstasy wound around him. Any sanity he'd held on to was gone as he drove into her. Her name was little more than a groan ripped from his chest as he found his release.

Kinsley held onto his neck, lying under him perfectly still, and then Lincoln felt her shake. "Baby, what's wrong?"

"Nothing." Her choked whisper belied the truth.

He rose to his elbows so that he could see her face. "What is it?"

She laid her arm across her eyes and sobbed. "I love you."

"You're cryin' because you love me?"

"It hurts. I never expected loving someone to hurt," she confessed.

Lincoln couldn't hold back a smile. "You're the only one my heart wanted from the first moment I saw you."

He rolled onto his back and snuggled her up against him as she eased into sleep. There was not one thing about this woman that wasn't glorious to him. He put his face to her hair and inhaled her honey scent.

Suddenly the memory of a story from Greek mythology that his mother recounted when he was a boy flashed through his mind. She'd told him all people have another half of them out in the world. Lincoln hugged Kinsley tight, knowing that he'd found his split-apart.

CHAPTER TWENTY-THREE

The Past Comes Home

Kinsley slipped out of the house for a pre-dawn run, but it wasn't long before a replay of the previous night's activities had her turning back. The years that she'd been held captive by her fear of intimacy were only partly due to trauma. All along, she'd been waiting for someone patient enough to gain her trust.

Quietly re-entering the house, she peeked into the bedroom. Lincoln was lying in bed with his arms behind his head, looking like the cat that got the cream. "Good morning, handsome," she greeted him from the doorway.

"Good-mornin', baby. Have a good run?" He glanced at her through half-closed eyes.

Kinsley placed her hand on her hip, working up her most serious look. "Yep. I have something to show you in the shower. I think there is a wetness. Do you want to check it out?"

Lincoln's grin said he was on board. "I definitely wanna check it out. I believe I have the tool to fix it." Kinsley sprinted to the bathroom, leaving a trail of laughter in her wake as he sprang out of bed and chased her.

An hour later, showered and dressed, Kinsley placed pans of cinnamon rolls in the oven, and put plates and silverware on the counter. As Lincoln picked up the stack, she couldn't resist teasing him. "You are seriously going to get in trouble with the man club."

"We just won't tell 'em, will we?"

Kinsley raised her hands in surrender. "They won't hear it from me."

Lincoln put the dishes aside and took her in his arms. He pressed kisses down the side of her neck as she wrapped her arms around his shoulders and ran her nails over his back. They swayed to music only they could hear.

"Thank you for fixing me, Lincoln."

He raised his head. "I can't take credit. You fixed you."

The stubble on his jaw tickled her fingers as she touched his face. "No other man would have been as patient. Also, there is the whole thing of me being a huge pain in the rear."

"Nothin' worth havin' is easy," he declared.

Kinsley smiled. "Lincoln James, you are a big ol' angel."

"I've been called a devil." He winked.

Thomas loudly announced his arrival as he came in the front door. "We're in the kitchen," his father yelled back.

Between the three of them, they had everything ready just as the doorbell chimed.

Leon was still on a high about the fun they'd had playing the dance. "Princess, we should plan to come back every year for this bash," he said as they all sat down at the table.

"That would be fantastic. We brought in people from all over the state because you guys were playing." Kinsley imagined how much interest she could generate if she had time to advertise, which she hadn't this year.

Leon took a swig of his coffee, and surveyed Henry's

dining room. "I'm shocked you decided to stay here for as long as you have."

Kinsley nodded at Lincoln. "All his fault. Had you talked to Grandpa recently?" she asked while refilling Leon's coffee cup. He frowned. "What is it?" she asked.

"There are things you might uncover that would be upsetting. Henry tried to protect you. He loved you more than anything in the world."

This warning only served to heighten her curiosity. "What are you talking about?"

"Your mom and dad—"

Kinsley leaned forward, listening intently. She had never been given much information about her parents.

"They were real messed up, sweetheart. Henry did what he thought best by keeping them away from you."

"They signed me over to Grandpa and split, right?"

Leon took another swallow of coffee before he continued. "They did give you to Henry, but they came back a couple of years later and wanted to take you with them."

"What?" His statement conflicted with everything Kinsley thought she knew about her life.

He shook his head, his brow furrowed. "We should let the past stay there."

"Please tell me."

Meeting Kinsley's look, he acquiesced. "Your mom and dad had serious drug issues. They stayed together after they left you here with Henry. They had another baby." Leon paused, shifting uncomfortably in the chair. "Your mom took drugs during the pregnancy. The baby was ... bad off."

Kinsley held her breath.

"The little girl died. The police suspected your parents might have killed her, but they couldn't prove it. Your parents came to get you right after that, and Henry wouldn't give you up. I was here the day they came. He was livid, and told them he'd see them both dead before they would take you." Leon hesitated momentarily. "They wanted money for you."

Kinsley turned deathly pale.

Leon continued cautiously. "When they left that day, Henry made me promise never to let them near you if anything happened to him. He was afraid their drug habit could make them capable of anything. We signed papers making me your legal guardian in the event of Henry's death."

Kinsley was overcome by his kindness. "Thank you, Leon."

"I love you as if you were my own, and I gladly signed the papers. Henry gave them money here and there over the years to keep them away. I tried to help him, but you know how stubborn he was. At least the old coot let me help with money for your schooling and such. He refused to turn them into the police—Henry loved his son, despite how troubled Darrell turned out to be. After your dad was killed, Henry found out that they'd had another child."

Leon's eyes moved between Kinsley and Lincoln before he went on. "The story we heard is that they sold the baby for drug money. Henry was sick at what might have happened to the child. He tried to find him but he never got anywhere."

Revulsion at Leon's revelations boiled inside her. "How old would the child be now?"

"Around thirteen. I know that they were down in Oklahoma City. I hired an attorney for Henry, to help find the boy, but it did no good. Then your mom showed up out of the blue a couple of years ago. Darla had been coming around every so often, trying to get Henry to tell her where you were living. He said she had some new boyfriend who was bad news."

"Do you know what happened to my biological dad?"

"Darrell went to prison for child trafficking and drugs. He took the whole wrap and kept your mom out of it. He was killed in prison," Leon relayed.

Kinsley lowered her head. She'd imagined that was probably the case, although Grandpa never would tell her anything about her father.

Leon took her hands. "The best of both of those people is sittin' right here."

"Thanks." She swallowed hard. "You and Grandpa were the best dads a girl could have."

Lincoln couldn't let this opportunity pass. "Did Henry ever have any enemies that you know of? Someone who had a serious problem with him?"

Leon shook his head. "None, Sheriff. Henry Rhodes was a kind man. If someone hated him, it was over some fabricated notion—except for Max Skelly. After last night, I think it's pretty obvious what's going on there, right?"

Lincoln and Kinsley both nodded.

Leon finished his coffee and stood. "I hate to go, but we must. Got another show tomorrow in Dallas." He held open his arms. Kinsley stepped against him and hugged him tightly. He kissed the top of her head before he let her go. "I love you, princess. Call me."

"I love you back. I will. Thanks again for what you did last night. It was wonderful seeing you. Let's not wait so long between visits."

Leon shook hands with Lincoln. "I don't know what you're doing, but keep it up. I've not seen Kinsley this happy in a very long time."

"I'll take care of her. Thanks again. Tell that bus driver of yours to keep it between the lines."

Leon chuckled. "Will do."

***

The fact that Kinsley had been unusually quiet since breakfast told Lincoln a great deal. He guessed she'd had her suspicions about her parents, but to hear it laid out bare had to be hard to take.

He thought about his own family; for all their flaws, he'd had nothing nearly as hard to deal with. How was she supposed to process a father who'd died in prison, a druggie mother, and now a little brother who might be in danger? All on top of Henry being murdered. Lincoln intended to investigate her mother and the woman's bad-news boyfriend. It was a lead he couldn't ignore, though he hoped to hell her mother hadn't done this to Henry.

He stepped up behind her and wrapped her in his arms. "Can I do anything for you?"

"You're already doing it." Kinsley leaned back against him, then turned and looked up at him. The weight of all she carried shone clearly in her eyes. "I need to send an email to my lawyer to make sure that boy is okay."

"You think you can find him?"

"I'm going to try," she said. "I don't want to interrupt the child's life if he is fine, but if he's not…" Kinsley laid her cheek against his chest. "…If he's not, I will take care of him."

"You are the sweetest woman." Lincoln squeezed her. "I'm sorry, but I need to go to work for a while."

"I need to do the same."

Lincoln called goodbye to Thomas on his way to the door. Consumed by game coding, his son merely waved over his shoulder.

The sheriff crossed the lawn to his pickup. As he drove to the office, thoughts about a new future began to form.

***

Lincoln settled into his desk chair and started a thorough review of every interview they had conducted thus far. When that yielded nothing new, he walked to the whiteboard and went over the information to ensure all connections were in place, adding Darla Rhodes' name to the lineup of possible suspects.

Poring over the list of those under suspicion, he focused on the Skelly family. Lonnie was the only one with a solid alibi and, after Lincoln's recent interactions with the man, he didn't seem to fit the profile. However, Lonnie's illegitimacy might still be a factor. Lincoln moved closer to the whiteboard, as if doing so might cause it to yield some of its secrets. What was he overlooking?

He ran his fingers through his hair, took a seat, and considered motives. The land kept coming up. Did someone beat Henry Rhodes to death for a piece of property? If the farm was the objective, that meant the killer hadn't factored in Kinsley, or had assumed she would be willing to sell.

The letter from a survey company Kinsley had found in Henry's papers came to mind. When she'd called them, they'd referred her to another outfit named FORTRANK in Dallas. That firm had blamed budget constraints for their phase-out of test wells in the area, which seemed plausible. They wouldn't have backed off if there were something valuable to be had.

Henry was a bit of a ladies' man, but Lincoln had interviewed the woman he had dated in Guymon and she'd insisted that there was no other man in her life. Lincoln had found no evidence to the contrary, and he was sure it couldn't have been a love triangle.

His thoughts were building steam when the buzzer on the security door sounded. He looked up as Brice Clements stopped in the doorway of his office.

When the commissioners had cut budgets for local law enforcement, they had also dismissed the Chief of Police, leaving Lincoln as head of both city and county forces, such as they were. Brice was a part-time officer working a few days a month to help out.

"Hey, Brice. What's goin' on?"

"Hi, Sheriff. Saw you were working. I heard you're going to be hiring for the county."

"Yep, we had a good fundraiser." The mystery money flitted through his mind.

Brice came into the room and considered the whiteboard for a minute before taking a seat. "I have a good friend—we were in the army together. He's a cop in

Abilene, but he's looking for something new."

"Sure. Kinsley put an application form on our new website. Have him fill that out and give us a call. What's his name?"

"Ben Adams. Thanks, Sheriff, I'll tell him. Any luck with Henry's case?"

Lincoln shook his head.

"I've been keeping my ears open. There's nothin', which is unusual because this town talks about everything. Whoever did this is playing it cool. Hard to believe they could keep something this big quiet for so long." Brice got up and studied the investigation board.

"I agree." Lincoln joined him. "Everythin' else goin' okay for you?"

"Yeah. Don't know if you heard yet or not, but I knocked up the wife again." The young man radiated pride.

"Congratulations!"

"Thanks, Sheriff. I'll tell Ben about the job." Brice headed out the door.

"Talk to ya later." In need of a break, Lincoln went to the kitchenette. As he waited for a fresh cup of coffee to brew, he called his mother.

Connie answered on the first ring. "Hi, sweetheart."

"Hey, Mom. How's things?" He fiddled with coffee stirrers next to the pot.

"Nothing new here. How about there?" she asked.

"Thomas is doin' fine, and I have a girlfriend."

"Oh, honey. I'm so happy for you. Kinsley? That's her name? Thomas told us. When are you bringing her down here?"

Lincoln warmed at her response. "I hope to come

down soon. I need to hire help before we can get away."
He listened as she excitedly gave his dad an update.

"We're just delighted and can't wait to meet her."

"Thanks, Mom. Tell Dad I said hi." Kinsley would love
his family, and they would love her. Of that, he had no
doubt.

"I will, son. We'll talk to you soon."

As he clicked off, Lincoln heard the familiar creak of
the entry door being opened. This place was bustling for
a Sunday. He walked to the front to see who had come
by. A man he didn't recognize stood in the lobby. Lincoln
pushed past the security barrier. "How can I help you?"

The stranger swept James with a cautious look. "I'm
here to talk to the sheriff."

"You got him." He held out his hand to shake while
noting the man's expensive suit. "Sheriff Lincoln James."

"I'm Colby Tanner. I went to the Guymon Police
Department first, but they told me my grandparents'
farm is in Stevens County and directed me here."

"What can I do for you, Colby?"

"My grandparents passed away a few years ago, and I
inherited the farm. It's out on the Oklahoma state line.
I live in Houston, so I don't come back very often. The
man who rents our land, Ted Smith, keeps an eye on
the place." Mr. Tanner paused for a moment as if lost in
thought. "Anyway, my grandfather's pickup is missing. I
was here a couple of months ago and it was in the garage
then, so I'm not sure exactly when it was taken."

Lincoln retrieved the appropriate forms and they sat
at the table in the outer office to work through them
together. Before Colby left, the sheriff assured him that

he would keep a close eye on his farmstead.

As he paced back to his office, Lincoln studied the papers they'd filled out. The soothing hum of his computer starting up and flash of the county logo when the machine came to life barely registered as he began questioning what he knew about Ted Smith.

Ted and Henry had been friends all their lives, and there was no animosity between them. Smith wasn't a big guy like Diana had seen leaving Henry's house that night, and he didn't fit anywhere with the facts they had. But there was Ted's offer to buy Henry's land—and someone had tried to break into Kinsley's house the night the farmer had learned that she wasn't leaving.

Lincoln scrutinized the suspects. Ted had no affiliation with the Skelly family, and it felt like Rich Skelly was somehow connected to Henry Rhodes' murder. Nevertheless, Lincoln added Ted's name to the list with a question mark, even though his possible involvement in the tragedy made no sense.

CHAPTER TWENTY-FOUR

Secret Relations

As she laid out plates and silverware on the table, a sense of foreboding stalked Kinsley. Hearing the truth of Lonnie Skelly's paternity and why it had been such a big secret might change her idealistic memory of Grandpa. Maybe Leon was right: sometimes the past should stay there. Unfortunately, that train had already left the station. Lonnie would be arriving at any moment.

She went back into the kitchen and opened the box of pastries she'd picked up earlier, just as Lincoln walked in. "You doin' all right, Kins?"

"I'm nervous. Thanks for staying with me. Life is strange. Since Grandpa died, I've learned more about him than I ever knew when he was alive. He had to know about Lonnie. Why didn't he ever say anything?"

Lincoln slipped his arms around her waist. "I don't know. Maybe Henry thought it was better for Lonnie to live here without the stigma of being illegitimate. Secrets that are kept for a lifetime generally come out once the keeper is no longer there to suppress them."

She nodded just as the doorbell rang. "Here we go."

When she let in their guest, she noted how he fidgeted nervously with the ball cap in his hands. It was some consolation that the anxiety about this meeting wasn't hers alone. "Thank you for coming by," she said,

"I thought it might be easier for us to talk here instead of at the diner."

Lonnie grinned, and Kinsley's breath caught. It was like looking at grandpa.

"Yes, the ever-listening ears of this town." He gave her a commiserating look. "I'm sure many have their opinions about me."

"Lincoln is here." Kinsley tried to cover her discomfort with a forced smile. "I hope that's okay."

"I understand. You don't know me, and your time with the Skellys hasn't been the smoothest."

Lincoln entered the dining room carrying the plate of pastries and a pot of coffee. The two men exchanged pleasantries before all three of them sat at the table. Her newly discovered relative looked around before his eyes came to rest on Kinsley. "I suppose you've figured out that I'm your uncle?"

"It would be difficult not to see Grandpa in you. When did you know?"

"I guess I always knew there was something different about me. Max kind of ignored me, like I was an irritant. Mom was good to me, but Harry and Rich look alike, and I look exactly like Henry." Lonnie paused. "When I hit puberty, all those hormones kicked in and I flew off the handle at Max. He told me my mom was pregnant before they were married, but he didn't know I wasn't his at the time. As I grew up, my paternity became obvious." A sadness passed over his face that made Kinsley's heart ache.

"I came to talk to Henry when I was sixteen. I was angry that he'd let me grow up with *them*..." Lonnie shook his head then smiled. "Henry was great. He said that by the time the truth came out, I was already six or seven. Skelly had raised me and given me his name, so they decided to leave things as they were. I can see now that he and my mother were trying to shield me from ridicule." He shrugged. "They did what they thought was best in a bad situation. I can't judge one way or another."

"Did you have any contact with Grandpa?" Kinsley asked.

"I spent some time with Henry out at his farm after our first uncomfortable meeting. Being able to get to know him was nice. I had to get over my mad first, but yeah, we kept in touch. He was a good man, and he loved you more than anything. I'm sorry he's gone. I know our family is screwed up, but I hope you and I can get to know one another."

"I would like to know you better, Lonnie."

"Look, I know Rich is a dick, but I'm not associated with any of his mess, or with Max. I don't want any part of anything they are involved in. I only come home to see my mother."

Lincoln had been listening intently. "And what *are* they involved in?"

Lonnie looked down at the table for a moment before raising his gaze. "I couldn't say for certain, but you know as well as I do that Max is all about power. He'll stop at nothing to have influence and money. I don't talk to them about their business. I speak with my mother, but she would never tell me anything. Max has her right where he wants her, needy and scared, and there's nothing I can do to pull her out of it. Lord knows, I've tried. The best advice I can give you about the lot of them is never let your guard down."

"I agree with you wholeheartedly," Lincoln replied.

Kinsley and Lonnie exchanged information before she walked him out. This new knowledge weighed heavy on her. The years between the incident in high school and Henry's death had had a singular focus for her: work. Her life had been solitary, ordered, and without drama. Now she hardly had time to work as the craziness kept coming.

"How can I help you, sweetheart?" Lincoln asked as she returned to the dining room.

She met his fretful look. "Just keep loving me."

He kissed her forehead. "That I can do." They wrapped their arms around each other and soaked in the quiet while they had the chance.

"I have interviews this mornin'. I'm sorry, I have to go." Lincoln said as he cupped her cheek.

"It's okay. I have to get back to the grind, too."

***

At the station, Lincoln dropped doughnuts off on Charlene's desk. Not in the mood for company, he went to his office while he reflected on Lonnie Skelly. Lincoln had a gut feeling that man hadn't killed Henry, but after the revelations of the morning, a bit of digging into the other Skellys' 'activities' was about to commence. Lincoln had focused so intently on who murdered Henry that he hadn't considered there could be a back door to the truth.

"You seem to be deep in thought today," Charlene said, as she crossed the room and handed him a folder. "Here's the information for Ben Adams and Dusty

Reynolds. I've put in background requests. They usually take a couple of days."

"Thanks, Charlene. Hey, do you know Lonnie Skelly?"

His interest was piqued when the woman reddened until she was the color of her hair. Charlene rarely blushed about anything. "Yes, I know him. Why?"

"Just wonderin' about him. What can you tell me?"

"He's not one of them. Lonnie is a good man. Did he do something?"

"No. Just curious."

"I dated Lonnie a long time ago … a long, long time ago. He's been in Dallas ten years, if not more. I saw he was at the barbeque. He doesn't come back often." She waited impatiently for the sheriff to clue her in. He said nothing, but he couldn't keep a sly grin from tugging at his lips.

"Damn it, Linc. Just tell me. I was Lonnie's girlfriend for a time. I know he's Henry's son."

Lincoln raised a brow. "Fascinatin'," he teased.

Charlene gave him her best I-am-not-amused look. "I've had boyfriends. What did you think, I'm a nun?" With that, she turned on her heels and stormed out of the room.

He moved to the whiteboard. Scanned the names and picked up the eraser. Butch came in just as he was erasing Lonnie's name. "A Skelly off the list, huh?"

"Yep."

Butch whistled low. "Ted Smith? How did that happen?"

Lincoln shared the information about the missing pickup and his trail from there. "I can't imagine Ted was in on this, but it's churning all around him somehow." His deputy nodded and chewed his lip.

The buzz of the intercom ended their contemplation. "Linc, Ben Adams is here."

"Send him back, Charlene." Lincoln put the cover back over the board and stepped into the hall to introduce himself. Together, he and Butch conducted interviews for the positions of deputy and dispatcher. They let both Ben and Dusty know they'd be in touch by the end of the week.

Lincoln closed the door, sat down, and picked up his coffee cup. "Well, what do you think?"

"I think Dusty might be in love."

Butch's joking caused Lincoln to choke on the sip of coffee he'd just taken. He wiped liquid from his chin and tried not to smile.

"I'm sorry I said that." The deputy backtracked. "He's a good kid, and you're a man to be admired. I like Dusty. He's an enthusiastic, solid guy. I wouldn't be opposed."

"Good. I want to bring Charlene in on his second interview. She should have a say. What about Ben?"

The deputy nodded thoughtfully before answering, "He has the experience. Ex-military, that's a plus. Even temper—I could work with him."

Lincoln cleared his throat. "Butch, you've been a godsend to me and the county for years. I haven't been able to do much for you in the way of money, even though you deserved it."

Butch colored at the praise. "Aw, Linc. You've done all you could, and I appreciate the way you treat me. I know my Christmas bonus has come out of your own pocket for the past several years. We're good."

Lincoln reached into his desk drawer and removed a box. "You're a dependable man. We had a great fundraiser this year, and now I can do for you what I couldn't before. I would like to appoint you undersheriff." He raised his hand to silence his deputy, who was about to protest. "Now, before you decide, you should know that the promotion comes with a raise and a new unit."

Flabbergasted, Butch stood up. His smile was wide as he shook Lincoln's hand like he was pumping a water well. "Thank you. I'm… Well, I'm without words."

"You earned it, my friend. Thank you for stickin' with me through tough times." Lincoln tapped the box on his desk. "Your new badge."

Butch flipped open the lid and removed the shiny gold star.

"We'll schedule second interviews with Ben and Dusty," Lincoln confirmed. "I'll let you know when. I hope to hire one more deputy and another dispatcher." The men chatted as they moved toward the front of the office.

After Butch headed out with a spring in his step, Lincoln asked Charlene to set up second interviews with both candidates. "I want you in on the dispatcher interviews. After all, they will be working for the head dispatcher."

Charlene's head snapped up. "Really, Linc?"

"Of course. And it comes with a big fat raise. I couldn't do this job without you."

Overwhelmed, Charlene ran around her desk and grabbed him in a bear hug. "Thank you so much!"

"Hey now, don't get all mushy on me," he chuckled.

She swatted his arm. "You are a softie, Lincoln James. Thank you again." She was smiling ear-to-ear as she went back to her chair. "Oh, we had another application come in from a police officer in Houston." She held out papers.

"We might not have to advertise for help at this rate," Lincoln said, scanning the application. "He knows Ben and Brice. Go ahead and run the background. I'll talk to Brice about him."

As he headed back to his office, his cell phone rang. He looked at it with a smile. "Hey, son."

"Dad, I have the best news. I got a scholarship for college in Liberal. A full ride, books, and everything. They called this morning, said the person who won it backed out so I was next in line."

Relief washed over Lincoln; he'd been worried about how he was going to come up with money for college. "That's great news, Thomas. It looks like you'll be a college man come fall."

"Yep. Hey, I have to go. We're painting Kinsley's living room. We'll see you at lunch."

"Okay. Tell Kins I said hi, and be good."

"Always." Thomas hung up.

Lincoln felt years of struggle start to melt away. Everything seemed to be falling into place.

CHAPTER TWENTY-FIVE

Move Over

They had broached the subject of living together on several occasions, but this time Kinsley wouldn't let it go. "Lincoln, you're sneaking back home just about every night. I know you're concerned about what kind of example we'd be setting for Thomas. It's just—"

Before she could finish, Thomas stepped into the kitchen and joined in. "Come on, Dad, you shouldn't have to be away from Kins because of me. We're here every day. We eat here, and I work with her. I already know you come back when you think I'm asleep. Just pretend like you're married, if it makes you feel better."

"Did you just say the 'M' word, son?" Lincoln asked with mock horror. His statement made all three of them break into laughter.

As the merriment died down, Thomas continued. "I'm nearly nineteen. I'm not a kid anymore. I know you love Kins. We're kinda' like a family already."

Lincoln considered his son's words. The sheriff wanted to be near Kinsley, not only because he loved her, but also because he had a powerful sense of dread that a tempest was building around her. "You make a convincin' argument. Okay, you and I will move over."

"Come with me, you two," Kinsley led them to one of the spare bedrooms. As they moved around the space, she made suggestions. "We can get you a bigger bed, paint, whatever you want."

"I have some paint in the garage," Lincoln chimed in.

As they stepped into the hallway, Thomas pointed to a closed door. "Where does that go?"

Kinsley hesitated. "Well, that's my old room. All of my things from high school are still in there. I should have cleaned it out already."

"Can we take a look?" Thomas asked.

"If you want." She put her hand on the knob, but didn't move to open the room to them.

"Are you all right, baby?" Lincoln placed his hand on her back.

"Yes, I'm fine. A lot of memories in here." She pushed open the door.

"This is cool!" Thomas hurried past her, heading directly to the band posters hanging on the wall. "You saw Clear Blue?" He ran his fingers reverently over scrawled signatures. "The posters are signed."

Fond memories of those shows warmed Kinsley as she joined him. "I did, and the concerts were amazing. They played at a small local venue because they were new back then. Easier to get in and cheaper tickets. They're huge now."

Thomas swung his eyes from the posters to her. "I know, I love them. Can I have your room? You don't have to change it."

"Sure, if you want. The charcoal grey walls are a bit gloomy. I had a touch of 'goth girl' back in the day, but we can paint. I need to clean out the dresser and closet for you."

Thomas flopped down on the bed. "It's perfect just like it is." He threaded his fingers behind his head like Lincoln often did, a big smile on his face. "Thanks, Kins. I promise I won't let you down. Not after all you're doing to help me with school and such."

"You're welcome, Thomas."

"Liberal is less than thirty miles away, you know. I can commute from here," he added.

Lincoln meandered around the area, looking at artifacts of Kinsley's past. "I like that idea."

Kinsley surveyed her old room. It felt better; new life had chased away the darkness. Thomas was right. They were a family now. Kinsley struggled to voice it, fearing that the universe would snatch away her happiness out of spite.

"Oh, I forgot to tell you, I need to register by tomorrow," Thomas said, ignoring his father's eye roll.

"Thanks for the notice." Lincoln shook his head as he retrieved his phone from his shirt pocket. "I'll call Butch and see if he can cover my shift so we can go get you registered now."

***

When they returned from Liberal, Lincoln sat on Kinsley's porch to make some calls while she and Thomas went into the house. He'd begun investigating her mother, and he didn't want her to overhear him talking about the case.

"Hey, Butch, I'm callin' to catch up on what's been happenin' today. Thanks for coverin' for me."

"No problem. Ben and I worked out coverage. Are you planning to interview that friend of Ben's again? Dixon Carlisle."

"We can give him a second look. The first interview went well. Did Dixon say when he can come up from Houston?" Lincoln thought Dixon was a little intense for their small town, but he was built like a brick house, which might make people think twice about crossing him.

"He's ready for a move. Said he could be here tomorrow."

"Sounds good. Please set it up for both of us to be there in the afternoon. How is Dusty working out on the desk?"

"Charlene said he's picking it up real fast. He's a good addition," Butch replied. "I found some info on Kinsley's mom, Darla. Her last name is still Rhodes. Six months ago, she was arrested for possession in Dallas. Her boyfriend's name is Gus. His last name changes often, but legally it's Renfron. He's got a sheet as long as your arm—narcotics charges, theft—but no murder. He was in jail in Fort Worth when Henry was killed, so it couldn't have been him."

"Thanks for lookin' into that." Lincoln breathed a sigh of relief that Kinsley's remaining parent didn't seem to be involved in Henry's murder. "Nothin' else has come in, right?"

"Nope. I interviewed the Longs. They have some sore feelings surrounding their son and Henry, but they both have airtight alibis for the night he died. It is possible that Henry's murder was random, and whoever killed him was someone just blowing through town."

"It could be a stranger, but it still doesn't feel like it."

"No, it doesn't, but how is the killer keeping it quiet?" Butch posed.

"I have the same question."

Silence stretched out as they thought about this seemingly unsolvable case. Finally Butch said, "Tell Kinsley hi. And don't worry, we've got things covered."

"Thanks. I appreciate that. I'll see you tomorrow afternoon." Lincoln got up and went into the house. Not seeing anyone in the main rooms, he called out, "Where is everybody?"

"In Thomas's room," they both replied.

He found Kinsley and Thomas sitting on the floor, flipping through a photo album. "Kins has pictures from the concerts. We should see where Clear Blue is playing and go to a show together," Thomas enthused.

Kinsley pulled open a dresser drawer, took out a threadbare shirt from the initial concert, and held it up. "I'm ready. I still have the gear."

Lincoln recognized the top as the one she'd worn the first night he'd met with her. A deep grin formed as he remembered the see-through material and her sexy, black-lace bra. Kinsley blushed as if she could read his mind.

Lincoln held out his hand to her. "Goin' to bed, son. See you in the mornin'."

CHAPTER TWENTY-SIX

Run

Kinsley slipped quietly out of bed, trying not to wake Lincoln. As she dressed in the dark, a feeling that she could conquer anything took hold—but world domination would have to wait until after coffee.

She was raising a freshly brewed cup of java to her lips as Thomas stumbled into the kitchen. His usually perfect hair stuck up in every direction as he rubbed his face and yawned. "Why are you up in the middle of the night?" he asked.

"I run before work."

Thomas groaned. "You run? By yourself? At this ungodly hour?"

"I'm certainly not gonna join her." Lincoln came into the kitchen and ruffled his son's hair.

Kinsley poured coffee into his favorite mug. "Okay, men, back in a bit," she said and took off.

As she jogged toward the business district, a dense fog created an eerie, boxed-in feeling. Even the birds were silent. The level of humidity that would cause such weather was unusual for this part of Kansas, given its arid climate. Her shoes hit the pavement steadily as she tried to remember if she had ever seen murkiness like this before in Harlow.

Donna Davies stood outside her doughnut shop

puffing on a cigarette as Kinsley passed. A plume of smoke haloed the baker's head in the calm of the pre-dawn hour. Ahead, a pair of headlights sliced through the darkness. The police cruiser slowed, and Danny hollered, "Good morning!" as he passed.

Kinsley crossed Main Street and jogged around the perimeter of the park. She noticed a pickup parked along the barely lit back of the city sanctuary. A wary side glance revealed a dark shape inside the vehicle. Suddenly, a screech of metal on metal splintered the calm and sent a chill down her spine. Unnerved, she took a sharp left, cut through the park, and sprinted toward home. The grounds were only a city block wide, but it felt like a forest ten miles deep.

Don't look back. Kinsley's heart was beating wildly as she silently chanted, *Don't look back.*

Her frantic pace didn't slow until she leapt onto her porch, her breath coming in short gasps. When she scanned the dark street behind her, no one was there.

"Kinsley?" She jumped before seeing that it was Lincoln who was sitting in the rocker. "What happened?" The concern in his voice was evident, even though his features were hidden by the gloom.

She inhaled deeply and stretched to get the stitch out of her side. "I scared myself."

"How exactly did that happen?"

Her eyes adjusted enough to make out the scowl that marred Lincoln's handsome features. "There was a pickup at the park. I thought I heard the door open as I ran by, and I freaked. Nothing happened. I don't know why it scared me. There isn't usually anyone around there when I run." She stood up straight. "I burned a bunch of calories this morning. Damn."

"Was it a man or woman in the pickup?" Lincoln prodded.

"I couldn't see very well because it's dark on the backside of the park. It wasn't a small person—they took up quite a bit of the cab."

"What kind of pickup?" The cop in him was taking over.

"Lincoln, I swear it was all me."

"Just humor me, please."

She knew he wouldn't give in. "Old, maybe late seventies. Could have been burgundy. It had a broken tail lens on the driver's side."

Lincoln pulled out his phone and put it on speaker. "Danny, can you make a swing around the park? See if there is an old pickup, red or burgundy, parked at the back."

"Sure thing, Sheriff."

"Thanks." Lincoln hung up and held open his arms. "That was unusual. You run every mornin', and you've never been scared."

Kinsley crossed the porch to him. "I don't know. Maybe it was a combination of the fog and a stranger so early in the morning. The driver could have been sleeping." She curled up on Lincoln's lap, and they rocked together before their day started.

***

Kinsley was making breakfast, Lincoln was in the shower, and Thomas was still in bed when a call came in from her lawyer. She talked to him nearly every day, but Schneider wasn't usually an early riser. "I didn't know you woke before nine o'clock," she said.

"Good morning. I sent you an email from the private investigator you had me hire. You need to read it."

"That sounds ominous," Kinsley joked, noting his tone was more abrupt than usual.

"It is, and I'm worried. I want to send security for you. Some bad things are going on out there, Kinsley."

"I appreciate your concern, Bill, but I'm not going to have some stranger following me everywhere," she protested.

"Promise me you'll be careful?" His tone softened slightly.

"I promise. Thank you for taking care of everything. All will be well."

"Sure thing. Talk soon." Bill ended the call.

After Lincoln left, Thomas and Kinsley turned the dining room back into an office and went to work. Anxious to see what was concerning her lawyer, she opened her email. Bill's report made it clear that Commissioner Skelly was deep into some corrupt ventures. This situation would turn into a shit storm when it all came out.

"Kins." Her focus cut to Thomas. "Won't it be cool when I'm done with school? It will be just like this, you and me working on important programs together."

His excitement was contagious, and it pleased Kinsley to see him happy. "You might not want to live with us forever."

"Oh no, I already have that figured out. I'm going to live in Dad's house and come over here to work. It'll be great."

"It would be wonderful if you stayed near him—us."

She meant every word. Lincoln's son had become an essential part of her world, and she hated to think of him being too far away.

"I'm glad you and Dad are together. I like it here," Thomas murmured as he typed.

"Thank you, Thomas. I am delighted that Lincoln has such a wonderful boy."

"Hey now! I'm not a kid. We adults are starting a new journey, and it's pretty sweet."

Kinsley saluted, but couldn't stave off her amusement. "Yes, sir."

The day flew by and, before she knew it, Thomas had left for work at Mario's. While she waited for Lincoln to come home, she worried how he would react to the news that she had secretly hired a private investigator.

***

When Lincoln walked in, he found Kinsley sitting at the dining table with her head resting against her hands. He pulled up a chair next to her. "Is everything okay, baby?"

"I need to talk to you." Kinsley glanced up and caught the worried look on his face. She ran her fingers lightly over his cheek to reassure him. "It's not about us. Don't..." She stalled. "Don't be mad at me, okay?"

"Kinsley, what is it? You're scarin' me."

"When I came to town, I didn't know you, or what your skills were as a police officer. Then when Skelly started bothering me, I..." she paused "...I hired a PI to snoop around and watch the Skellys."

"Okay. And?"

Kinsley handed him a stack of printed emails. "This

is what he's found so far. I haven't told anyone else."

Lincoln read the reports while Kinsley paced. When he'd finished, he looked up at her. "Holy shit. These crimes are bigger than county business—they involve state, federal, DEA, immigration. The whole damn government is gonna come down on Skelly. Would you please get me everything the investigator has?"

Kinsley picked up her phone and placed a call. "Hey, Bill, the sheriff needs what your PI has on Max Skelly. Photos, recordings—everything."

The lawyer was quick to respond. "Sure. I'll email all I've received."

"Thanks. I'll call you tomorrow." As Kinsley placed her phone on the tabletop, she started to worry. Had she put Lincoln in danger by revealing what the private investigator had uncovered?

"This is the biggest thing I've ever been involved in," Lincoln said. "There are so many levels of corruption here. I'm gonna do a little investigating of my own before I call down the lightnin' on the commissioner. I did see your PI around town a while back and had him checked out. He's the real deal. I figured he was here watchin' someone's cheatin' husband. This is an interesting turn of events. I'm proud of you for takin' charge."

"I'm relieved you're not angry with me." She approached his chair and ran her fingers through his hair.

His tongue slid over his bottom lip as he positioned her astride him.

Kinsley laid soft kisses along his jawline. "Mmm, you didn't shave this morning." She rubbed her cheek against his stubble, enjoying the tingle, before pressing her lips to his ear and neck.

Lincoln wrapped his hands around her hips and moved her against him, making Kinsley groan. "That feels good. Do you like me a little, Sheriff?"

"More than a little. You make me as hard as steel, woman. I can feel your heat through our clothes." Lincoln dispensed with her shirt and slipped the cups of her bra under her breasts, framing them in electric-blue lace. "Damn, you're sexy."

"You're going to make me explode," she whispered in his ear.

A low rumble pulsed from his chest and raced across her skin—then the sound of footsteps on the porch brought their interlude to a sudden halt. "Oh, shit," Kinsley exclaimed as she jumped off Lincoln's lap and ran for their bedroom. His laughter followed her hurried departure.

Thomas hollered, "Kins, you left your clothes all over the floor. I get in trouble for that."

Thoroughly embarrassed, she emerged in shorts and a T-shirt. "I thought you were meeting your girl?" Kinsley raised an eyebrow at him.

"Um, I did, and we ate, and I sent you that text two hours ago." Thomas teasingly shook his head. "How 'bout we play cards and listen to those old records? I brought leftover pizza."

As Kinsley moved to the stereo, turned on the power, and placed the needle on the smooth vinyl surface, she thought about the cataclysm that was most likely headed straight for Harlow.

CHAPTER TWENTY-SEVEN

Hidden Agendas

Mondays were always busy, and this one was no exception. Tackling small jobs first, Kinsley knocked out a few new additions to programs that were already in place before attending a series of meetings online with clients.

As her last call ended, an email from her lawyer arrived. Bill had found her brother and reported that he appeared to be well-adjusted and living with a good family. When her parents had tried to sell him, a concerned citizen had called the authorities. They had placed the boy with the state for a short time, then arranged for him to be adopted legally.

Kinsley sent Bill a reply stating that she didn't wish to disturb the teenager. He'd been through enough hell; there was no need to add the chaos of new relatives to the mix.

Her phone vibrated against the wooden table, and she pressed the speaker button to answer. "Hey, Sheriff."

"Hi, baby. I'm not gonna make it in for lunch. Sorry."

"Okay, thanks for calling."

"See you tonight," he replied as his pickup engine roared to life in the background.

Thomas came out of his room and stopped in the doorway. "Hey, Kins. I'm gonna shower, then go to work."

"Sounds good. Would you throw all your dirty clothes in the laundry room for me, please?" With a nod, he left. She gazed after him, thankful that he had run from Tulsa and ended up here with his father.

***

With the house to herself, it felt strange to be alone, a distinct change from the solitary life she'd led before. Kinsley turned on some music and sank into her project. The debugging was nearly finished when a knock halted her progress. She saved her work and then hurried to the front door.

The visitor was a shock. "Hi, TJ, what a surprise to see you. Please come in. Can I get you something to drink?" Kinsley hadn't spent much time with Ted Smith's son. The man was always so quiet when she was around.

"Sure, I'll have a beer if ya have one. Dad sent me by with some bills." TJ's voice barely had any modulation, which prompted a silvery ping of unease as they moved toward the kitchen. She admonished herself for letting her past color her reaction; the guy had been an honorary pallbearer for Grandpa, for heaven's sake.

Kinsley handed him a beer before picking up her phone from the counter, hoping that holding it might be a source of comfort until she could move past this unfounded fear.

"Dad said you'd be stayin' here." His expression never varied from a deadpan stare as Kinsley scanned his eyes for any spark of personality.

"I don't plan to leave now that Lincoln and I are together."

"Are ya plannin' ta keep Henry's land and farm it? Because my dad would like ta buy it." TJ peeled the label from the bottle and stuck it to the counter with a loud smack. "It's close to ours, ya know."

His action annoyed her more than it should have. "I'm not looking to sell, though I did ask your dad to farm it for me. Are you going to be farming too, or are you going into another line of work?" Kinsley did her best to remain conversational.

"I'll farm. Don't know how ta do nothin' else." TJ fidgeted with his beer cap then took a drink. His eyes slid over her before he looked down again. "Rich tried ta buy the land from Henry."

His voice changed to a less even tone, prompting Kinsley to put a bit more distance between them. "It was Grandpa's livelihood. He wouldn't have sold it."

Being alone with this guy gave her a terrible sense of dread. She swiped her thumb across her phone to unlock it. "Is that what you came by for? To see if I'd sell my land to your father?"

When he narrowed his eyes, Kinsley pressed the send button to call the emergency line, but TJ was on her too fast. His fist glanced off her jaw as she tried to dodge the oncoming blow, and she stumbled backward over a case of soda Thomas had left by the stove. The floor rushed up to meet her as Dusty answered her call, but the impact sent her phone skittering across the linoleum out of reach.

Then TJ unleashed hell.

***

Lincoln pulled into Ted Smith's driveway. He'd been trying to catch Smith to talk about Tanner's stolen pickup, but somehow kept missing him.

Ted came out the front door as Lincoln exited his pickup. "Hey, Sheriff. What's goin' on?"

"I came to see if you knew anything about a vehicle out at Tanner's farm. Colby Tanner came in and reported that his grandfather's pickup had been stolen. Do you have any idea when it might have been taken?"

Unease twisted Ted's expression. "Shit. I asked Tanner's secretary for permission. I can show you the email. My son TJ has the pickup."

Icy panic seized Lincoln as the last piece of the mystery clicked into place. "Where is TJ now?"

Ted's eyes widened. "He went to town. I gave him bills to drop off at Kinsley's. I don't rightly know where he is, but I could call him."

TJ—it all fit. Why hadn't he seen it sooner? Lincoln was already running toward his pickup. He slammed his vehicle into gear and hit the gas as Dusty's tense communication came over the radio. "Lincoln, get to Kinsley's now!"

The sheriff whipped the mic off its holder, fumbling it before recovering to issue an order. "Send everyone! I'm out in the country, but I'm comin'!"

Dusty's next transmission could not have been more devastating. "They're too far away."

Lincoln's heart was in his throat as he prayed for the first time in years: *Please don't let TJ kill her.*

***

TJ raged like a madman. "You shoulda' sold the land, Rhodes!" Blow after blow rained down on her. Kinsley rolled away from his punches as much as she could, which kept TJ from landing a solid hit, but the coppery taste that filled her mouth told her he was doing damage.

"You're just like Henry. It coulda been easy. Sell the fuckin' land! Skelly said there's oil under it. Now you have ta die, too. Stupid! Stupid! Stupid!" He shrieked the word over and over like a cadence for his fists to follow.

Kinsley reached up to gouge at his eyes but missed. Instead, she raked her fingernails down his face, and the skin curled where her nails left furrows on his cheek. The injury only served to infuriate him.

Most of TJ's punches were body shots, so she rolled into a ball to protect herself. Terrified, she pulled her knife from her boot and lashed out wildly, going for his throat, but he moved at the last second, and she cut a deep gash across his upper chest. Blood gushed out, covering them both.

TJ's fingers dug into Kinsley's flesh as he slammed her arm across his knee repeatedly to force her to drop her knife. When her bones snapped, the weapon slipped to the floor.

Fight or die! Filled with overpowering fear, Kinsley reached up and jammed her fingers into his eye socket. The soft tissue tore as she cupped her fingers and ripped them back out, bloody and flecked with bits of flesh. A yelp flew from Smith's gaping mouth, and he flattened his hand against his injured eye. Kinsley grasped the dangling skin where she'd cut him and jerked.

Howling, he recoiled as his flesh gave way with a

sickening rip. That gave her enough room to scramble to her feet and run for the dining room. With TJ right behind her, Kinsley grabbed her gun from the table and turned toward her attacker. He gripped her broken arm, and dots swam before her eyes as red-hot pain exploded from her shattered limb.

Then a deafening crack echoed around the room. Kinsley had squeezed the trigger. A wave of nausea washed over her as she realized that she had shot him.

Momentarily stunned, and still holding her by the arm, TJ gripped his abdomen with his free hand and stumbled forward before he went down, pinning her under him. He ripped the gun from her grasp and tossed it aside, then wrapped his large hands around her neck and squeezed.

Frantically, Kinsley felt around for the cast-iron Scottie dog doorstop she knew was nearby. With her functioning hand, she gained a solid hold on the metal and brought it around in an arc that connected with his temple. TJ wailed and let go. She gulped in air, trying not to pass out as she wriggled out from under him and retrieved her gun.

When TJ grasped her ankle, Kinsley leveled the weapon at his chest and pleaded, "Please don't make me kill you."

"Go ahead," he dared her, wiping blood out of his eye with the back of his hand.

Her finger trembled on the trigger. It was the moment of truth.

"Kinsley!" Lincoln shouted as he ran through the door with Butch right on his heels. "I'm here." The sheriff knelt beside her, placed his hand on top of the firearm, and slowly lowered it to the floor.

Tears coursed down Kinsley's bloody cheeks. "He killed Grandpa."

"I know. Have you been shot?" Lincoln began to check her injuries.

"N-No. The b-blood is mostly his."

He slipped his arms around her and held her briefly.

The undersheriff had managed to cuff TJ and was trying to inform him of his rights as they waited for an ambulance—not that TJ was listening.

Kinsley gripped the front of Lincoln's shirt. "I shot him." Her voice quivered. "He was going to kill me."

"I'm here. You're safe. Where are you hurt?"

She swallowed back tears and held out her crooked limb. "He broke my arm. Everything hurts." Kinsley pulled up her shirt, and Lincoln examined the purpling marks where TJ had punched her. Her lip was split, and one eye was beginning to swell shut.

"Where did this blood come from? Is it yours?" Lincoln touched the sticky crimson that covered her.

"I c-cut him." Her eyes moved from the stain on her shirt to Lincoln's face.

"I'm sorry, Kinsley. Dusty heard it all over the phone. It's recorded. TJ won't get away with any of it. Come on, sweetheart, I'm taking you to the hospital." Lincoln picked her up with infinite care and carried her out to his pickup.

The faded red Ford parked across the street caught her eye. "Whose vehicle is that?"

"TJ borrowed the pickup from a house where his

father farms. Is it the same one you saw at the park?"

Kinsley nodded. "He meant to kill me that morning."

"It seems so." Lincoln's face was grim.

The sheriff delivered her to the ER and stayed while they set her broken arm, put it in a cast, and moved her to x-ray. TJ had cracked several of her ribs, which meant her recovery would be slow and painful. The doctor wanted to keep her in overnight, but she insisted on being released. They let her go with Lincoln's promise that he wouldn't let her out of his sight.

With adrenaline pulsating through her, Kinsley insisted that she be taken to the sheriff's office to give her statement to Butch while events were still fresh in her mind. On the way, Lincoln filled her in about TJ's status. The man was in surgery to repair the damage the bullet caused, and he needed stitches for a deep gash across his chest, but he would more than likely survive.

When she was settled in the interview room, Lincoln turned to leave. "I'll be right outside," he assured her. Kinsley had never known him to be so quiet. His demeanor was almost menacing.

The undersheriff closed the door behind him and took a seat across from her. "What is going on with Lincoln?" she asked.

Butch met her stare. "That man is crazy in love with you, Kins. He's tryin' not to end the guy who did this. Lincoln used to be a SEAL. He has some deadly skills."

She concentrated on this new information. "I knew he was in the Navy, but SEALs are special ops."

"Linc isn't someone anyone should mess with." Butch flipped on the recorder and prompted her to begin.

Kinsley recounted what had happened from the moment TJ came into her house until help arrived.

When she'd finished, he turned off the tape. "I'm sorry for all of this. TJ has been on antipsychotic meds for years, and he's had violent tendencies in the past, but none of us knew. Ted had him seeing a doctor in Amarillo, and they kept it under wraps. According to his father, TJ recently quit taking his medication, which leaves him prone to delusions and easily angered."

Butch filled in a few more lines of text on the report in front of him before he continued. "TJ told us before he went into surgery that Rich Skelly had him convinced that his mother had been seeing Henry secretly, and that's why she left his father."

"A supposed affair is why he killed my grandpa?" Kinsley could hardly believe it.

"Not exactly," Butch said. "TJ and Skelly went to see Henry that night to buy his land, and things got out of hand." He let out a long sigh. "That's all the information TJ gave us. We've no proof Rich was involved."

Rich Skelly—still bullying the weak. Kinsley had no doubt Rich had masterminded the whole plan, and now he had put someone with a mental illness in the frame.

"It was TJ who executed the murder and the attack on you. Unless some evidence turns up, more than likely all punishment will fall on him, and nothing will happen to Skelly," Butch added.

Kinsley shook her head. "Rich Skelly should burn for what he's done. What can we do?"

"The law has to be followed. There'll be a trial, but it's TJ's word against Skelly's that Rich was pushing him to commit the crimes."

Kinsley gingerly placed her head in her hands. The day's events were starting to close in. "No one in this town is safe as long as the Skellys are free."

Lincoln stood when Kinsley came out of the interview room, lines of worry etched across his face. She stepped into his arms. "Thank you for saving me."

His chest heaved as he wrapped her in his embrace. He was angry with himself for not realizing sooner that it was TJ. As he kissed the crown of Kinsley's head, the moment was shattered by his ringing cell phone. Lincoln looked at the caller ID and answered.

"Rich Skelly is running, Linc," Ben puffed. "I'm in pursuit, but we're about to cross into Seward County. I need help."

Lincoln looked at Kinsley. "Baby, Rich is on the run and—"

She stopped him. "Go get that sorry prick!"

He ran through the outer office, barking an order to Dusty to call the Seward County sheriff. "Advise them we're pursuin' a suspect into their county."

Kinsley made her way painfully to the front of the office. Thomas was waiting; he jumped up, holding out his hands awkwardly, afraid to touch her. "Are you going to be okay?"

"Broken arm and some cracked ribs. They'll heal." Kinsley plastered on a smile.

The young man reached out and touched her cast. "I was so scared, Kins. Please don't die."

"I'm trying very hard not to. Thank you for caring about me, Thomas. Everything will be just fine."

She went to the dispatcher's desk, where her friend was sitting. "You saved my life. Thank you, Dusty."

"I couldn't do anything but listen to what was going on. It was the most helpless feeling I've ever had."

"You called in help. You were my lifeline. There aren't words to thank you enough."

Gabby and Charlene burst through the exterior door, and Dusty buzzed them in. "Oh, my heavens, Kinsley," Charlene cried.

"Cracked ribs, don't squeeze me!" Kinsley warned.

Gabby shook her head. "TJ Smith. I never saw that coming. He was always quiet, almost invisible."

Charlene touched Kinsley's arm tentatively. "I can't imagine what would possess him to kill poor Henry then try to kill you. It's insane." She turned to Dusty. "You, my fine friend, did an excellent job."

The new dispatcher's chest swelled a little at her compliment. "Thanks, Charlene."

What had happened finally caught up with Kinsley. "Thomas, could you take me home? I'm worn out all of a sudden." She turned to her friends. "Thank you all for being here for me."

Thomas guided her to his pickup, opened the door, and helped her in.

***

As they pulled into her driveway, the little white house where so many awful things had happened lately didn't feel very comforting. "Thomas, what would you think about living out in the country?" Kinsley asked quietly.

"I wouldn't mind. Do you want to move?"

"Maybe it's time we started someplace new."

"Do you want to stay at Dad's house instead?" Thomas proposed. Silent tears slipped down her face, and he rubbed her shoulder clumsily. "What can I do for you?"

Kinsley wiped her eyes with the back of her hand. "Yeah, let's stay at your dad's for tonight. I can't go back in there right now. Thanks, Thomas."

"Sure." He turned his gaze to her house. "What happened in there ... that maniac nearly took you from us. I'm sorry I wasn't here."

"You have nothing to be sorry for. I'm glad you weren't home. I couldn't stand it if something happened to you." Kinsley squeezed his hand.

***

After a restless night, Kinsley felt the bed shift as Lincoln joined her. She turned to face him, and a long groan rattled in her throat when pain sprang to life. "Thank you for getting to me so fast today."

"I wish I'd been there sooner." As the sunrise pushed through the window above the bed, his eyes touched her battered face. "He'll pay for what he's done."

Kinsley curled close to Lincoln, hoping the worst was over.

CHAPTER TWENTY-EIGHT

Secret-Agent Man

Lincoln stood as Butch and Sean Young, the private investigator Kinsley had hired, came into his office. He hoped this meeting would give them something solid to use against Rich Skelly. When they'd finally caught him and brought him in for questioning, Rich had denied any involvement with TJ Smith and lawyered up. Now his team of attorneys was stonewalling.

The men sat at the small conference table. Sean pulled open his bag, removed his laptop, and placed it on the table. "Man, I have rarely seen more crime in such a concentrated space, Sheriff James. William Schneider said you need all I have between Rich Skelly and anyone he's met with."

"Right. But, as you know, anything that wasn't collected when he was in a public place won't be admissible in court," Lincoln advised.

"That little asshole is not very private with his life. He thinks he's king shit. I'm not sure who you've got your eye on, but I'll show you all of the meetings along with my notes and photos, and you can tell me what you need. There's a ton of material." Sean opened several files. "Mr. Schneider assigned me to watch the Skelly family. Max, the dad—holy shit, he kept me busy. You received all the reports, right?"

"Yes, I did. Thank you for your thorough work. It's been turned over to other legal entities, and they will be takin' the lead." Lincoln thought about the children of Garrett and Lavonne Lamar. The ex-treasurer's underhanded dealings with the commissioner were now documented; she would be prosecuted for embezzlement, at the very least, which would mean her children would go into foster care. The sheriff vowed to keep an eye on them and make sure they found a safe place.

"Max Skelly is one bad SOB—redneck mafia, if you ask me." Sean tucked a lock of hair behind his ear.

Lincoln studied the private investigator with interest. He looked to be in his early thirties, medium build, brown hair and eyes, average looks. Nothing about Sean Young stood out, and that was precisely what made him a good PI.

"Okay, here we go. There's this guy who Skelly met with early on. They talked about doing a repeat. I didn't know what that meant, but the guy's name is Brian Johnson. This was collected at the diner. I was sitting in the next booth."

Sean pushed the laptop forward and played the video feed. Lincoln and Butch watched as Rich and Brian discussed a repeat performance of the show he'd put on eight years ago. Brian said he'd had a glimpse at the liquor store, and it made his mouth water.

Lincoln slid back in the chair. Kinsley said Billy had called his friend, Brian, the night he'd hurt her; it was Brian who had held her and taken pictures. Were Rich and Brian planning to rape her? His stomach turned at the thought.

"You can shut it off." The sheriff decided he was going to have a private meeting with Brian. "Please send it to me."

Butch looked on with concern. "Are you all right, Linc?"

"Yep." What had happened to Kinsley needed to stay in the past. Lincoln would take care of this on his own. "Let's keep lookin'."

"Then there are these guys, but they had Texas tags. Again, it's code talk, but it's something sketchy. I set up at that church across from the park. They were out in the wide open."

Sean pushed his laptop forward again. The trio watched Rich talking to two men about securing the asset, 'and then they would be golden.' The suited men assured Skelly that they had their side ready; all he had to do was get his part finished. Rich explained that it wasn't as easy as they had imagined. Roadblocks he hadn't expected were showing up.

"Yep, we need that information. Do you know who these guys are?"

Sean opened a Word document and read through it quickly. "I ran their tag. Some development company out of Fort Worth, the FORTRANK Corporation. I didn't do any facial recognition on them. They were leaning on Skelly, but he's the bad guy, so I didn't worry about it much."

Lincoln nodded. "Please send me that file."

Sean gave them an I-hope-you're-ready-for-this grin. "Then there is a lot of this, with multiple women. That is one horny dude. I tell ya, I look forward to never seeing his dick again. I've seen his more than my own. There are six women he's screwing besides his wife."

Lincoln looked at the names on the list that included Sheila and Debbie from the diner. "I doubt we need that, but his wife might be willing to pay handsomely for the footage."

The PI searched through files and opened a new one. "Oh, you're going to love this next guy. He is one freaky hombre." Sean prepared to play the video. "Ol' Skelly handed over stacks of cash to this one."

The clip was clearly taken at Pearl's. Rich was telling TJ not to take his medication, and promising to help TJ get his life together. The clip ended abruptly.

"Is that all there is?" Lincoln prayed that there was more.

"Oh no, I have hours of those two. The way they fought, I thought it was his younger brother or a relative of some sort. I'll send all I have."

"Thank you, Sean. We'll review everything. What you've collected could help put these guys away for a very long time."

"You're welcome, Sheriff. It's been pretty damned exciting. You got yourself quite a little monster of a town here." The PI closed his computer.

Unfortunately, Lincoln had to agree. "We hope to change that."

Sean shook hands with both officers before he packed his laptop ready to head out of town.

***

After lunching with Gabby, Kinsley pulled into her

driveway. She eyed a black Mercedes parked in front of her house, and instinctively her hand closed around her gun. The car door opened, and her lawyer got out. Shocked to see him, she hopped out of her Range Rover and went to greet him. "This is unexpected."

Bill's face was drawn. "Shit, Kinsley. The PI called me and said you'd been attacked. Are you all right?" He cast a wary eye over his client.

"I'll be fine. Wow, I can't believe you're here."

He rolled his eyes. "Of course, I'm here. I wanted to know how badly you were hurt. The way you make light of everything, I had to see for myself."

"Unwrinkle your face, Bill, or it will stick that way, then you won't be able to use your good looks to charm those twenty-year-olds you like so much." Kinsley smiled, wincing when the action pulled at her split lip.

Schneider started to defend himself, then threw his hands up in defeat.

"Come in. I'm glad you're here because I was going to call you. We have big trouble."

He surveyed the property with a look of distaste. "I guess you do. Is this where you've been staying?"

"This is the house I grew up in," she chirped.

Bill's eyes flicked from the house to Kinsley, and back to the house. "I never imagined. You've come a long way."

"I have beer or beer. Which would you like?" she offered as they entered her living room.

Bill hooted, which caused Kinsley to stumble, astonished by his out-of-character levity. "Careful there." He put his hand out to steady her. "I'll take the first beer. You're funnier than you used to be."

"Yep, that's me, a laugh a minute." Kinsley disappeared into the kitchen and returned a few moments later with refreshments. "Please have a seat."

"What the hell happened?" Bill sank into the well-used couch that was in sharp contrast to his custom-tailored suit.

Kinsley relaxed into a rocker opposite him. "It seems there are some folks here who wanted Grandpa's land because they believe there is oil under it. Rich Skelly, the local rich guy and bully, convinced TJ Smith, who has some mental issues, that my grandfather was to blame for his parents' divorce. If they could get Grandpa's land, the money from the oil would bring his mom back. Then I showed up and decided not to leave, so Skelly sent him to get me too. That's the story TJ told the police—but we need evidence."

"So this Rich Skelly is the one behind it, but only TJ will get punished?"

Kinsley nodded. "I believe the evidence needed to convict Skelly will show up sooner or later, but until that happens we need a lawyer for TJ. Someone who will keep his case going long enough to rope them all in."

The counselor couldn't hide his dismay.

"I'm not trying to help TJ get away with what he's done," she explained. "I've had time to think about this, and I'm mad as hell at the horror TJ has inflicted on my family. But I'm trying to look at this logically. What I want is to bury the Skellys for their involvement."

"Kinsley, this nutcase killed your grandfather and tried to kill you for a piece of land!"

"Yes, he did." Kinsley fiddled with the cap from

her beer. "But I believe Rich used TJ and exploited his weakness to get him to do the dirty work. I can't in good conscience let TJ take all the blame. If we don't do something, Skelly will walk. I'll never be safe in this town, and neither will anyone else. This is our best chance to stop them. We have to take it."

Bill studied her before he spoke. "You *have* changed."

She nodded without looking up.

"This sheriff must be something else." When she met his steady gaze, he smiled and changed gears. "Do you have anything to eat in this Podunk town?"

Kinsley stood and tipped her head toward the kitchen. "Just this way to Rhodes Diner. What are you in the mood for, Mr. Schneider?"

Bill followed her toward the back of the house. "Pasta of some kind?"

"That I can do." Kinsley opened the refrigerator and laid ingredients on the counter. "Pasta is coming right up. Have a seat and tell me what's new with you."

Bill settled on a barstool and rested his chin between his thumb and forefinger. "Kinsley, I've been your lawyer for a very long time. You're more than my boss, you're my friend."

She glanced up and saw a look he usually reserved for someone he was cross-examining. "What are you getting at, Bill? You've never been one to beat around the bush."

"Have you even tried to tell the sheriff?" the attorney questioned.

"No, I haven't. What difference does it make? If I tell him, he'll be upset, and he never has to know unless I die."

"Tell me what?"

Kinsley jumped. She and Bill turned to find Lincoln standing in the kitchen doorway. Knowing he had heard their conversation, fear raced through her.

"Tell me what, Kinsley? And who is our guest?" he demanded.

"Lincoln, this is my lawyer, William… Bill Schneider. He heard I'd been attacked and came to check on me."

Bill stood and shook Lincoln's hand. "A pleasure to meet you, Mr. James. I've heard a lot about you."

"Funny, I've heard nothin' about you. Comin' out here to check on a client is goin' a bit over and above the call of duty." The tension in Lincoln's voice vibrated off the hard surfaces of the room as he repeated his earlier question. "Tell me what?"

Schneider cleared his throat. "I'm Kinsley's lawyer, but also a friend. I was worried about her."

Lincoln acknowledged his words with a curt nod, but didn't move his intense scrutiny from Kinsley as he waited for an answer.

She could sense his anger beginning to boil. "Bill thinks I should tell you what provisions I've made." She sighed and prepared herself for what she feared might come. "I have money, Lincoln. A lot of it. I would have told you eventually, but I didn't think it mattered. I've made sure you and Thomas are taken care of if anything should happen to me."

"How much?" Lincoln held her gaze as his tension eased.

"My company is worth eight million. My personal net worth is six million."

Lincoln stood perfectly still. She wasn't sure he was even breathing until he blinked. "Million...? Six million dollars?" Kinsley nodded and watched him closely. "And you thought that was not worth mentionin' to me? You were gonna leave me some kind of inheritance or somethin'?"

Kinsley nodded again, silently waiting for the fallout.

"Shit. Who even has that much money? That's ludicrous." He brushed his palm over his mouth and down his chin.

"I'm still just me," Kinsley said, trying to smooth the waters.

Lincoln uttered one single word, "Showerin'," and left the room.

"I'm sorry, Kinsley, you were right. It was better that he didn't know," Bill soothed.

She plated pasta for her guest and tried to swallow past the colossal lump that had formed in her throat.

"Go talk to him," her lawyer advised. "He can't be mad at you because you have money."

"I don't know, Bill. Lincoln isn't like any person I've ever known. He might not want to be involved with the mess of it." A dull ache had started in her gut at the thought of losing what they had.

"Kinsley, seriously. You live less like a rich person than anyone I've ever known. Other than the Range Rover, you never buy much of anything. You don't go anywhere. You give endlessly to charities and causes. No one would know you have money by looking at your life. Talk to him. So what if you worked your ass off and made a ton of money?"

***

Lincoln sat on the edge of the tub and listened to Bill and Kinsley talk. *Six million dollars.* He couldn't wrap his mind around the number. He considered all the time she'd spent cleaning Henry's house, cooking meals, and baking pies for the benefit. How could she have that much money and not say a word? Then the truth hit him like a ton of bricks.

He walked back into the kitchen and sat down. "You gave the sheriff's office half a million dollars, didn't you?" Kinsley didn't reply, but he knew that he'd found the source of the mysterious donation. "Kins, you can't do that kind of thing."

"You needed help. I have money." Her eyes misted as she blinked back tears.

Lincoln came around the island and wrapped his arms around her. "Baby, I'm shocked—and yes, a little peeved—that you gave my office half a million dollars. I love you. You bein' a millionaire won't change that."

Kinsley gave a great sigh of relief. "Just pretend you don't know, and everything goes back like before," she suggested.

Lincoln addressed her lawyer. "I don't want her money. I only want her." Calmer now, he went around the bar and took a seat while Kinsley made him a plate. "So, Bill, do you give this kind of personal service to all your clients?"

When he'd spotted the Mercedes parked out front, he'd been intrigued, but then to walk in on some secret conversation between his love and this movie-star-looking stud… Lincoln didn't want to admit it, but the green-eyed monster had him by the throat.

"I work exclusively for KDR Enterprises as lead counsel. Kinsley has varied interests. I do other tasks when she needs them done, in addition to being her corporate lawyer. Our Miss Rhodes is a powerful woman running an extremely profitable corporation. The business side of my job is a large undertaking in itself."

"So what kind of jobs does *our* Miss Rhodes assign?" Lincoln cocked an eyebrow.

Kinsley intervened. "Lincoln, Bill handles whatever I need. For instance, he found my brother in Oklahoma City. He hired the PI to watch the Skellys for me. Ted talks to him as the corporate contact concerning farming. He…"

Lincoln put his hand up. "Wait. What? Ted talks to him about farmin'?"

Kinsley continued cautiously, "I wanted Grandpa to be happy, so when a piece of land came up for sale near his, I bought it so no one could bother him. I own every piece of land around his section. Ted farms them for me—for the corporation—and his contact is Bill."

Lincoln tapped on the Formica counter. "When Ted was here that night talkin' about showin' you a contract from the corporation he farms for, it was a contract he has with you?"

Kinsley nodded.

Lincoln's lips twitched, and then a laugh rolled out of him. "Baby, how did you keep a straight face when he was talkin' about showin' you your own contract?"

The tension was finally broken. "It wasn't easy, but I don't want him to know I own the corporation."

"Wow, you are complicated." Lincoln looked at Bill.

"Okay, so you do pretty much anything she calls and asks you to do? What was your advice about me?"

Schneider looked at his employer, who gave him the go-ahead nod. "Kinsley has a soft heart, and she is one of the kindest women I've ever met. I'd never seen her get anywhere near a man in all the years I've known her. So, when all of a sudden she hooked up with you, naturally I was concerned. I advised her to take time and make sure. It's my job to protect her when she doesn't see a situation clearly."

"Did you run a background on me?"

"Thoroughly. Yes, sir."

Lincoln looked lovingly at Kinsley. "I would never hurt her."

"Sheriff, I don't have designs on her. She is my boss and my friend. I don't have many true friends. I've been her lawyer since she started the company, and I've watched her work herself to the bone building this magnificent corporation. I came out here because Kinsley tends to sugarcoat things, as I'm sure you're aware. When the PI told me she'd been attacked and nearly killed, I knew she wouldn't tell me the whole truth."

"Thank you for carin' about her." Lincoln relaxed to a degree.

"Well, you two," Bill said. "Where is a good place to stay in this hole in the wall? I need the internet so I can start checking on that lawyer for you, Kinsley."

"What do you need another lawyer for?" Lincoln probed.

"It's not for me. It's for TJ."

"Why in the… You can't be serious!"

Kinsley explained that she felt it might be their only chance to make the town safe once and for all by taking down the Skellys. Neither of the men said a word. "I've been bullied all my life, and their abuse nearly destroyed me. Even a stable person can turn into someone they never imagined. I won't let Skelly continue to exploit the weak."

Lincoln's expression softened. "Kinsley, you are something. I never expect what you're gonna do next. Smith is a killer, no matter what Skelly did or said."

"TJ should pay for what he's done, but so should Rich. I'm sure that he instigated my grandfather's death. The legal team the Skellys can afford will be hard to beat, but with good representation, the trial will continue long enough to lasso them all in."

Kinsley circled the island and squeezed Lincoln's shoulder as she passed. "Come on, Mr. Schneider. I'll put you up at Lincoln's house next door."

"Well, that's convenient —you're neighbors," Bill said as he winked at Lincoln.

CHAPTER TWENTY-NINE

Dessert Is Served

Halloween was barely a month away and Lincoln looked forward to the cooler temperatures Autumn would bring. It had taken him and Butch weeks to sift through the private investigator's findings. They'd found enough evidence to arrest and charge Rich Skelly, but the sheriff had feared that it wouldn't be enough to convict him. Their break came from the most unlikely place: Harry Skelly.

When Rich's brother took a deal, he turned over a cell phone with texts between Rich and TJ detailing Henry Rhodes' death. With a signed confession from TJ and the cell phone tying Rich to the crime, Lincoln was confident there would be justice for Henry.

Charlene's voice over the intercom beckoned him out of his office. Two men in suits were waiting in the lobby. Lincoln looked quizzically at his dispatcher. When she mouthed KBI, he had to work hard to control his elation. "Gentleman, I'm Sheriff James. How can I help you?"

After a flurry of brief introductions, one of them explained. "Sheriff, we'd like your assistance with the arrest of Max Skelly since a large number of his crimes were perpetrated in your jurisdiction."

"I'm only too happy to help. Max is headin' up a board meetin' at the bank as we speak."

The men loaded up in an SUV and headed out. While they rolled through town toward their target, Lincoln silently revisited the charges. Max and his sons, Rich and Harry, had spearheaded a multitude of criminal activities that included paying guards to look the other way while people illegally crossed the Mexican border into Texas. Skelly employed these illegal workers for low wages, forcing them to labor, and threatening them with deportation if they complained. Other charges included kidnapping, extortion, embezzling funds from the county and city governments, and laundering drug money through the Skelly businesses. The men would be lucky to see the outside of a prison again.

The imposing triad of officers entered the bank where a gape-mouthed teller pointed the way without a word. Lincoln rapped solidly on the door before swinging it wide, stirring a pricey cloud of Hugo Boss and Channel perfume that hung heavy in the enclosed space.

The opulent boardroom was jam-packed with county high rollers, including the bank's owners who lived out of state. Those seated at the table scanned the new additions with curiosity. This arrest was going to be something of legend.

Max jumped up, burning with righteous indignation. "James, you can't do whatever you wish, no matter what you think. Get out!"

The KBI officers waited at the door as Lincoln ambled into the room. "Max Skelly, you have run this county into the ground. Today is the day that all stops."

"Get out, James. I won't tell you again," Skelly bellowed.

Lincoln reached back and removed his handcuffs from the holder on his belt. Several of the attendees gasped audibly. "You are under arrest. Now, you can come quietly or not. Personally, I'm hopin' for not." Lincoln's grin was so intense that his cheeks ached.

"What am I under arrest for?" Max sputtered. "Someone call my lawyer."

No one moved an eyelash as they watched the drama unfold.

"Embezzlement, human traffickin', money launderin'. Shall I go on?" Lincoln held out the cuffs. "What's it gonna be, Skelly? Easy or hard?"

The commissioner put out his wrists in surrender. "You won't get away with this, James. You're nothing," he hissed.

"Oh, I wouldn't count on that, Max. These two fellas are from the Kansas Bureau of Investigation, and they've come to take you away."

The commissioner's eyes moved from Lincoln to the duo at the door. The knowledge of what was about to go down registered on his face as he was led away.

CHAPTER THIRTY

One Straw Too Many

The scandal was the biggest the area had ever witnessed. Lincoln was so busy with the Skelly chaos and TJ's trial that he hardly had a moment to spare.

Kinsley had been right to hire an attorney for TJ. A less-seasoned counselor could never have waded through the potholes filled with muck that Rich Skelly's high-dollar team of attorneys created as they did their best to get him off with probation by arguing that he was merely an innocent bystander in the murder of Henry Rhodes. Just before the trial started, the Feds swooped in and froze all of the Skelly family assets. Without money to pay their exorbitant fees, the legal dream team quit, and the playing field between Skelly and Smith was suddenly leveled.

On another front, the removal of the commissioner from his various positions of power had the effect of cutting off one head of a Hydra. In its place, two more appeared. Lincoln found himself watching the Dulcans, the Newcombs, and the Bradys, to name but a few. Max Skelly's shady counterparts crawled out of the woodwork as the struggle for power and the fight for his holdings began. Stir in the influx of newshounds, and Harlow had become a three-ring circus, one of which the sheriff was rapidly losing control.

When Lincoln dragged himself into the house at

nearly midnight, Kinsley looked up from her computers. "You look worn out, Linc. Can I get you something to eat?"

"No. Thank you for askin'." He sprawled out in the chair at the head of the table and watched her type. "You can't keep transferrin' money back into my account, Kinsley."

"I can. You need the money. I gave it to the sheriff's office, and I'm not letting you return that or Thomas's tuition," she stated boldly, refusing to look up.

"I'm givin' it back. I don't want to owe you. Why can't you understand how this makes me feel?" He leaned forward and placed his head in his hands.

"Don't be so old-fashioned, Lincoln," Kinsley chided.

He suddenly pushed back his chair. The squawk of wood against wood was unbearably loud in the otherwise quiet room. "Do you have to be so damned stubborn all the time?" Kinsley only managed a slack-jawed stare. "I need some space," he grumbled before he strode through the living room and out the front door.

***

Kinsley reached over, pressed the snooze button on the alarm clock, then rolled on to her back to stare at the ceiling. She was hounded by thoughts about the chain of events that had landed her in this awful situation.

Lincoln hadn't been angry with her until the truth of what she'd secretly done had been revealed. The fact that she'd paid for repairs to Butch's work vehicle and meat for the barbeque was bad enough, but that she'd kept it from him had pushed him over the edge.

A fat tear rolled toward her ear as she curled into a ball. He hadn't spoken to her in two days. Thank heavens Thomas was in Tulsa visiting his grandparents and didn't have to witness their disintegrating relationship.

Her phone rang. Kinsley cleared her throat and tried to sound normal. "Hey, Bill, what's going on?"

"Good morning. I need to know what you want me to do with your personal items from your condo. The new owner is taking possession in a week." She could hear him tapping a pen on his desk while he waited. "I can have someone box up everything and send it to you in Harlow," he added when she didn't answer.

"No. I'm going to come up to Kansas City. I need to get away from here for a while."

"Has something else happened that you need to tell me about?" Her attorney's voice rose an octave.

"I just need some new scenery." She inhaled to cover her heartbreak. "I'll see you tomorrow."

"Sounds good. Be careful." He ended the call abruptly. Bill never pushed her when it came to personal issues; it was one of his best traits.

Kinsley stared at Lincoln's name on her phone screen for a long while before she called him. His voicemail picked up. "Lincoln, I'm going to go back to Kansas City." She paused, then said softly, "I love you."

Thoughts of money, the man she loved, and the crumbling dream she would leave behind made Kinsley's stomach ache. Lincoln wasn't thinking clearly. He'd hired three new people and raised salaries. She couldn't take the money back—that would leave the whole force high and dry.

CHAPTER THIRTY-ONE

Something To Talk About

Lincoln sat in his office, dwelling on the final quarrel that had sent Kinsley running for cover to Kansas City. No matter how many times a day he checked his phone, she still hadn't called.

"Linc, Thomas is here," Charlene squawked over the intercom.

"Please send him in."

Thomas came blasting through the door and flopped down in the chair across from his dad.

"What's goin' on, kiddo?"

"Oh, nothin'. It's lonely at home by myself, so I came to bother you. What are you doing?"

The sheriff knew there was more, but he would let his son come out with it in his own time. "Just work. Nothin' exciting. How was school today?"

Thomas' face lit up like a firefly. "Mr. Johns asked me to help some of the other students. He said my programming is genius. That's what he said—genius."

"That's great. I'm so proud of you."

"Thanks, Dad. Have you heard from Kins?"

A jolt of pain shot through Lincoln at the mention of her name.

"Dad?" Thomas watched him closely. "Kinsley is coming back, isn't she?"

Before Lincoln could answer, Charlene came over the intercom. "Linc, come out here!"

The sharp crack of wood splintering carried through the closed door, prompting him to rush to the outer office. Brian Johnson was in the lobby tearing the hell out of the place.

"I called Dixon. He's on his way." Charlene scrunched her shoulders up to her ears as a chair broke against the bulletproof glass next to her head.

Brian roared, "Get out here, James! I know it's you blackballin' me all over town!" He picked up another chair and shattered it against a cinderblock wall. "I won't let that little Rhodes whore destroy me!"

Thomas stood at Lincoln's shoulder. "He can't talk about Kinsley that way. Kick his ass, Dad, or I'm gonna!"

"Calm down, Thomas. Stay here."

Lincoln watched as Dixon took his stance outside the entry door. With a nod, they converged on the irrational man. The new deputy got there first and took a hard punch to the jaw that momentarily stunned him. Lincoln grabbed Johnson's arm and applied a hammerlock, subduing him until Dixon regained his senses and cuffed the perpetrator. The booking process proved no less challenging as Brian continued to rage, spouting threats of what he would do to Kinsley and the police department.

Lincoln had been beyond furious when he'd found out about Brian and Rich Skelly's plan to assault Kinsley. As he'd poked around town, he'd found that she was only the first of many women this evil man had hurt. The other women were scared, and wouldn't come forward or even make a clear statement as to what Brian had done to them, but from the revulsion the sheriff saw in their eyes, he knew. With no substantiated claims to Brian's abhorrent acts, Lincoln couldn't charge him, so he'd let the gossips do the job. The stories had grown until there wasn't a woman in town who wasn't afraid of Brian, and not a man who wasn't ready to beat him to a pulp.

Johnson had taken himself down today. The creep wouldn't be hurting any more women where he was going; destruction of county property and battery of law enforcement meant he would most likely be doing a stint in the pen. When Brian got out, he'd have a record that would follow him. One misstep with another woman, and he would go away for a very long time.

For once, the rumor mill had done something right.

CHAPTER THIRTY-TWO

Full Circle

"Any idea when Lincoln will be back?" Kinsley addressed Charlene through the speaker in the bulletproof glass while she traced the infinity pattern that had been carved into the worn-out Formica counter.

"Sorry, Kinsley, he didn't say." Charlene's smile couldn't mask the concern in her eyes. "Do you wanna come in and visit for a while? I haven't seen you in forever."

"Thanks, Charlene, but I'd better go home. Would you please tell him I'm in town?" Kinsley could barely keep her feelings in check, and she didn't want to blubber all over her friend.

"Sure, I'll tell him. It's real good to see you," Charlene said.

With a promise to meet soon for dinner, Kinsley was off. She drove unhurriedly, thinking about what to say to the sheriff. It hurt for Lincoln to be angry. Her repeated refusal to take back the remaining funds hadn't helped, but she wasn't changing her mind. His message last night asking her to please come home so that they could talk had nearly been her undoing. There would be no coming back from this wound.

***

Kinsley pulled into her driveway and considered the little

white structure she had thought would be her home but was merely the location for another sad ending.

Exiting her vehicle, she moved across the lawn. She had just stepped onto the porch when her cell phone vibrated. A glance at the caller ID stirred up a mixture of butterflies and nausea. "Hi, Lincoln." Her voice faltered as she flopped onto the porch swing and waited for the axe to fall. "I'm back in town. I'll be home if you want to come over, or we can do this over the phone."

"What exactly will we be doin' over the phone?" Lincoln questioned.

The man was exasperating to the bitter end. "You left me a message about wanting to talk. Everyone knows what that means."

"Kins—" he started, but she interrupted.

"Lincoln, please let me say something first. I understand that I betrayed your trust by secretly doling out money to help you. I also understand that you're a proud man, and you need to take care of the people you love. I'm sorry for the way I went about things, but money is a part of my life, and that isn't going to change. You've made it clear that, if that is the case, you don't want me around."

"Kinsley, just lis—"

"Give me just a few more minutes. I'm almost done." She took a deep breath. "Please keep the money, Lincoln. It will help you, Harlow, and everyone around you. I'm truly sorry things turned out this way. I had the best intentions."

Before she had time to think, Kinsley was startled by the creak of the screen door as Lincoln stepped out onto the veranda. With the phone still pressed to her ear, she heard his response in stereo.

"Woman, am I ever gonna be able to get a word in edgewise?" A sparkle sequined his eyes as he hung up. He came toward the swing and took a seat beside her.

Kinsley watched him cautiously. "Doubtful," she replied.

"Kins, I'm sorry for the way I've been actin'. I let my pride get in the way of what's important. Bein' without you…" Lincoln bowed his head for a moment and then looked at her. "You took the sunshine with you when you left, and it made me realize that I don't give a damn about the money."

Kinsley was taken aback. "So you're not breaking up with me?"

Lincoln grinned. "I have somethin' else in mind." He opened his hand, and Kinsley stared at the gold band that lay on his palm.

She was almost lost for words—but not quite. "Lincoln James, you are the most infuriating man I've ever met."

The sheriff chuckled and pulled her close. "Is that a yes?"

Kinsley relaxed against him. Suddenly it all made sense. Every broken road had led straight to Lincoln.

"I wish you to know that you have been the last dream of my soul."

Charles Dickens

ACKNOWLEDGMENTS

As the proverb says, 'it does take a village' and some of the best people inhabit mine. It took an exceptional group of individuals to get this book across the finish line, and I adore each and every one of them.

My dream of becoming a published author was fostered by my grandparents' love of the written word. I know they are smiling down at me from a fluffy cloud on high; I'd never have made it without their pioneering spirit driving me on. And I owe my husband a debt of gratitude for enduring this long road with me. Gabriel, you are a man of your word and my rock.

Now for those fantastic folks whose hands were on the oars, helping me to row...

My sister from another mister, Jill Corley, whose belief in this book refilled my well of hope. My lifelong buddy, Lisa Riner, who loved Lincoln first and urged me to share him with the world. My gal pal Jenna Martin, whose early reads helped me to carve an angel from the marble. Retired Chief of Police, Steve Lewis, who shared his years of law-enforcement knowledge and had a laugh with me while doing so. And lastly, to my mate Daniel Adam Garwood from across the pond, who swooped in to put a shine on the final tweaks—out of that collaboration, a fabulous friendship was forged.

Just saying thank you seems inadequate. I am fortunate to know you, one and all!

I am equally blessed to have received encouragement and support from my friends, family, fellow writers and readers in real life, and those I know through social media. They are as splendid a bunch of humans as you'd ever meet!

To Catherine, Karen, Charlotte, and the team at 2QT Publishing you made my gratitude cup overfloweth! Thank you for going above and beyond to make my book stand out.

To you, dear reader, I am grateful that, out of a multitude of books, you've chosen mine. I hope your trip to Harlow, Kansas, has been something of an adventure. The scenes of Kinsley as a small girl at the farm were drawn from my own childhood experiences, and it was a privilege to share them with you.

If you liked *Broken Rhodes*, it would be a tremendous help if you could leave a star rating and a few words of review on Amazon or Goodreads.

Thank you for spending time with my crew and me. I hope we meet again soon!

All the best,
Kimber

ABOUT THE AUTHOR

Kimber Silver was born and raised in Kansas and spent most of her childhood at her grandparents' farm. However, her love of travel has taken her on many adventures and broadened her horizons. Kimber lives with her husband and two rescue dogs in central Kansas. *Broken Rhodes* is her debut novel.

www.kimbersilver.com

Twitter: @kimber_silver21

Goodreads: Kimber Silver

Facebook: AuthorKimberSilver